DANCE WITH THE
SWORD

Other Series by Sarah K. L. Wilson

Dragon School

Dragon Chameleon

Dragon Tide

Bridge of Legends

Tangled Fae

Empire of War & Wings

DANCE WITH THE SWORD

BLUEBEARD'S SECRET
BOOK 2

SARAH K. L. WILSON

PUBLISHED BY SARAH K. L. WILSON, 2021

DANCE WITH THE SWORD
First Edition. August 1, 2021

ISBN : 978-1-7772645-9-8
Cover Art byKristen De Palma
Written by Sarah K. L. Wilson
www.sarahklwilson.com

They say you should write with
just one reader in mind.

For this book, that reader was
Melissa Wright.

She says she likes it, so that's
good enough for me.

PENSMOORE
SALAMOORE
ROURANMOORE
AYYADMOORE
QARAMOORE
PTOLEMOORE
ILKANMOORE
MORAVIDMOORE
MORTAL LANDS

BOOK TWO

Fly with the Arrow

Dance with the Sword

Give your Heart to the Barrow

Die with your Lord

CHAPTER ONE

The Law of Greeting bound me to him. The Law of Unraveling stole me away.

No one had told me about that law, either, but something in my bones already knew about the dark law that streaks all our memories with tiger-striped charcoal. It's the law that tells us nothing lasts forever. The law that reminds us that you can't account for everything that might happen before it does. The law that determines that if something bad *could* happen … then it will happen.

And it was *tha*t law which stole me away. That, and my own foolishness. For in this, as in so many things, I was author of my own undoing, crafter of my own sorrow, grand architect of my own destruction. I had betrayed my husband and with him, I had betrayed myself.

And though I tried to pull my way free of my brother's grip, though I tried to wrench the hood from my face, all I received in return was his firm rebukes and gentle shushing.

"Hush, Izolda. You have suffered a great harm and you are mad with it. You are drunk on magic. You will come back to sanity soon enough."

Sanity? I was sane as any other. Saner than him, perhaps, as I had not spent my life hunting a lost sister.

Sane or not, my heart felt like a patchwork quilt torn asunder by giant hands. One half flapped in tatters reminding me of my family and hearth, urging me to think of a brother's love so deep, so protective, that it crossed the walls of the world to come and snatch me from the hand of death.

But the other half fluttered and snapped and forced to my mind the look on my husband's face and the agony in his eyes as he bent to kiss me before I was torn away from him. It forced me to remember his hearth with its living tenant fire and his people with their fates caught in his hands.

And these two halves turned from torn halves to gnashing wolves that chased each other round and round in a vicious circle until I could not tell which was eating the other and which I wanted to survive. But with every bite that one tore from the other, it tore a chunk of flesh from my heart.

Eventually, the hood fell from my head and though Svetgin still held my arms tight at my sides, I could see again.

My breath gusted into the air in little puffs of lamb's wool, hanging so innocently for a bare moment before being snatched away by the wind as we rode.

We rode through the darkness on a well-traveled road, the moon – shockingly large and yellow for all that it was the lesser light of the heavens – coated the snow and trees with vermeil. It gilt each of our compatriots so that their horses looked as if by a snap of the fingers they could be frozen and placed on the mantle of a great room for the entertainment of guests centuries to come.

Each face I saw was human and grim as though they had ridden through death's halls and plundered the depths of hell itself – as I supposed they had.

And I was the trophy they returned with – a plain human girl made less plain by this strange mortal light.

I saw no sign of my husband and heard no echo of him in my mind.

But my brother spoke of him as we rode, his voice stuttering slightly as the horse's trot jarred us. "You'll forget whatever that reprobate did to you, Izolda. In time, you'll heal from it. I'll secure you a good husband. A sound one. One who does not steal you away. And our name will be cleansed of the reek of ill luck."

"I'm already married," I said through frozen lips. My words sounded too soft, too intangible.

"It wasn't real," Svetgin said. "It wasn't to a real person. It was like being married to death. You'll see. You'll understand. You just need time."

But time was what he was taking from Bluebeard because if my husband did not have my days, then he would not be able to play the Great Game of crowns and fates, and if he didn't play, all would be lost for Svetgin and for Pensmoore and for the mortal world.

An owl hooted in the shadows above and I shivered at his aching call. But still, the horses kicked up sprays of gilt snow like showers of cider and the shadows danced to the heavy drums of the hooves beating the ground. The snow was sharp-edged and sugar-slick as it is in late spring when winter tries with all her heart to cling to the world she's lost.

I tried to squirm in my seat to look behind us. Had they taken anyone else? Did they have Bluebeard back there somewhere?

My heart, my heart, what had I done? I'd betrayed him, I'd offered up life for death and full arms for a breast bereft of life.

But Svetgin held me fast, whispering, "Almost there. Almost there," as the hours bled one into another.

My heart beat as hard as the hooves of the horses and my breath raced so fast that I tasted blood in my breath, but it wasn't until we rounded the corner of a cliff that it was truly snatched from my lungs.

Before us, seated next to a river rushing with spring swell, stood a tower capped in a peak like a spiraled onion. I had heard of the peaked towers of Aayadmoore, but never see one before.

"Our allies," Svetgin told me, sounding relieved. "The Towers of Aayadmoore."

Within the tower was a light, and the light glowed through the stripes that spiraled vertically through the onion tower top. They must have been made of panes of glass cut to fit the curve of that tower peak. But who had such mastery at their disposal and why would they use it for that? The spiraled windows threw light across the ground around us, and shadows, too, and because of how the onion was curved, the light looked like claws trying to shred us to pieces.

"Why are we not in Pensmoore?" I asked, trying to keep my voice steady. If I objected too strongly – if I seemed anything other than grateful to have been wrenched from the arms of my husband – he would think I had gone mad. Something inside me prickled, warning me that no good could come of that. They locked mad women away in towers, didn't they?

I watched the tower and tried to clamp down on the voice whispering in my head that it was already too late, that my ruddy-cheeked brother had brought me here to live and die out my days in that tower top above.

I could taste the lack of magic in this world as one tastes burnt garlic on the back of the tongue. The colors of the indigo forest were less vibrant, the scents of pine and spring-melting snow less pungent, the timbre of voices less shivery. It was as if I had sucked the juice from a piece of summer melon but left the flesh unbitten. It was a pale miserable thing where once it had been bright and full and I itched with the loss of it – a ghost limb no longer mine.

Hooves pounded on the road, turning from the dull thudding of iron shoe on ground to the harsh clop of iron shoe on cobble. We were among the houses like a dog among grouse – sudden and predatory. I half expected them to scatter – but no. Only the houses of the Wittenhame flew. These buildings were nothing more than false teeth in a craven man's jaw – lifeless, ill-fitting, a shade of what could be.

Men in uniform let us pass through iron-wrought gates, saluting as if to superiors, and then we were in among closer, darker buildings seeming to crawl with military uniformed men like a hive of bees arranging itself for conquest.

And of course, this was so. I tried to remember who had pulled Aayadmoore's name for the Great Game. Was it not the Sword? Was this not his pawn in that game of kings and fates?

The sound of forges working into the night rang out, but there was too much bustle and hurry, too many moving bodies and animals for me to count or keep a tally of what we would face if ever we were again free.

We reached the dread doors of the palace far sooner than was reasonable. Far sooner than I would have liked. And Svetgin – finally – released my wrists as he drew me from the back of his mount. She huffed, shaking her matted grey mane, and rolling her horsey eye at me as if in reprimand for the scent of magic that clung to me still.

I shied back from her and found myself suddenly surrounded by the men who had kidnapped me and brought me to this foreign place. They formed up around me like an honor guard, leaving Svetgin in the middle with me as we were greeted by a man with a snowy white beard and the air of a chamberlain.

He bowed deeply. "We honor you, Brotherhood of Stolen Sisters. We honor your bravery. We honor your success."

There was a murmur from those around me that sounded like agreement.

"Please," the man said, "follow me. Refreshments have been prepared for you. The Lord Saberac has sent word that he is on his way and will offer you audience as soon as he arrives."

We were led into the tower and to my surprise, it was richly decorated – so richly that it seemed like too much. No one needed so many silken hangings, so many gilt doorways, so many small curiosities on tables and shelves, in corners, and lining the walls. They combined with the cloying smell of rose water to make my stomach clench within me.

But it was not long until we found the small dining room set aside for our use – and, I noted – guarded by soldiers whose uniforms did not match my brother's, nor any of the other men in our escort. Svetgin followed my eyes and whispered, "The hospitality of Aayadmoore is generous, is it not, sister?"

I offered a close-lipped smile. If ever there was a time to keep my lips closed, it was now.

"Is our mother well?" I asked him cautiously, but his face fell.

"Dead these ten years past," he said quietly, grief painting his face. Something lurched in my chest – something wild and painful that hurt and caught and tore at me.

I had been very fond of my mother. She was everything I was not in all the best ways.

"Father?" I gasped.

"Last winter the cough took him."

He wouldn't look at me now, wouldn't meet my eyes. I felt my lip trembling.

"Rolgrin?" I asked, barely able to choke out his name.

Svetgin coughed, trying to disguise his emotion. "The same cough a week later."

"Then you are Lord Savataz," I said and it felt like I had swallowed a lump of porridge too quickly and it was lodged in my throat.

"You are the last of my family," he said helplessly, and he seemed glad for the chance to turn away from me to other things.

The men sat without delay, feasting on the roasted meats and vegetables and toasting one another with wine for their great success – all but a spare few whose wounds were being treated in the room beside ours. And though my worried brother offered me a plate and then tried to ply me with morsels of his own, I did not eat or drink as if it were this world rather than the world of the Wittenbrand that might trap me within if I tasted their food or drank their wine. Already I felt trapped by it, caught in a nightmare I would not wish on my worst enemy. My family gone except Svetgin, and he so changed I did not recognize his heart.

The thought of eating made me ill, but the speculative looks of the men around the table when they eyed me made me more ill.

"You'll find a groom for her then, Savataz? A lordling of your nation?" one of them asked in an accent I did not know. He was not much older than I was. Far too young to be the brother of any bride my husband had taken.

I looked around the table. With the exception of one older man who stared at his lamb with hollow eyes and my brother, none of these men could be truly a brother or father of those he had taken. Was it a mantle passed from father to son, then? Carried through the years like a prized axe or a medallion of note?

"Indeed," Svetgin said firmly but when the man opened his mouth again my brother gave him the slightest shake of the head as if to silence him, and his mouth closed with a click. They deferred to him. Good. That meant we wouldn't see trouble from them.

But I froze when four men came in an hour into the feast, their hands shaking and eyes haunted.

"Is it done then?" the one who had inquired about my future asked, but he was waved off irritably by the newcomers who did not eat but buried themselves deep into their cups.

What were they waiting for? Could it have something to do with Bluebeard?

I watched them all with great care until the little chamberlain returned, his eyes bright as lingonberries and his smile more oily than the lamb dish.

"The Lord Saberac has sent a gift for the rescued lady," he said, bowing to my brother. "He will gather you forthwith to the top of the tower but bid me present this, first."

There was a gasp from around the table as the chamberlain held out a gold dress trimmed in olive green. It looked like the overly decorated room we were situated in. It looked like something a princess might wear to a fancy ball – but not a Pensmoore ball with that low V cut so deep into both the front and the back that it would brush my waist at either side and a pair of ribbons that ran to a heavy gem collar from the sleeves and across the shoulders to keep it up.

"A grand gesture," my brother said, looking at the garment warily.

"And yet I find I am clothed well enough and far too simple a woman to wear such finery," I said, sparing him the need to turn down the dress. My heart seized in my chest at the sight of that dress. Whoever wore it would be collared like an animal and no amount of gems could make up for that.

"You'll wear it all the same, fair lady," the chamberlain said smoothly, "and it will suit you well, for today is your wedding day."

A gasp went up around me and two of the men whooped, clinking their glasses.

"I'm already married," I said calmly. Surely, they'd realize this was a mistake.

"Her wedding day?" Svetgin asked, looking between the shock on my face and the excitement of his fellows.

"The Lord Saberac has declared he will marry your sister himself, Svetgin Lord Savataz, honoring you and erasing forever the shame of your house."

My heart sank at the look of relief on my brother's face. There would be no help from him. He was as relieved as if he had been told a death sentence had been lifted from his neck.

"And my living husband?" I pressed, needing to know the answer, and dreading it all the same.

"The Lord Saberac wanted you to be well assured that he would take care of that complication."

CHAPTER TWO

When I had been caged within the dress and in the confines of its heavy collar, the chamberlain led us up spiraling stairs to the top of the tower. Two of the older men led the procession, bearded chins tilted upward in pride. They took time to brush their coats and give their sword hilts a quick polish while I was dressing. Such care inspired me to wonder who this Lord Saberac was that he had inspired such devotion in his men.

Curiosity pressed upon me, a leaden weight on a stack of papers, until I finally bent to its demand.

"Who is Lord Saberac?" I ask my brother as we mounted the stairs.

Even here, the iconry was heavy and rich. Such alcoves were set into the wall beside the staircase as could rival any collector's. Each alcove housed a sword of a different design, their designations and the battle they were known for displayed on plaques beneath.

In the center of the staircase where one could peek over the banister to the floor far below, there was a hanging display of more swords held at fanciful angles so that it could almost be imagined that they battled one another without any need for a man to direct their blows. I held my breath for the barest moment, daring one to move, to scrape metal upon metal, but no. They were locked in eternal struggle in this high column of blade brothers, entangled forever in enmity but they were mortal wrought and mortal displayed and would not spring to life and skewer us as they might in the Wittenhame.

I swallowed down worry. My practical eyes told me that so many swords spared for decoration means there were many more already in the hands of deadly men. It was that I ought to focus on and not the whims of the master of this tower who used perfectly good tools as fanciful decoration.

I forced myself to think past my fear. What did it say about this man that he hoarded gold to line his walls and swords his towers? Surely such a one would feel entitled. Those with much often felt they were due much more.

He had certainly helped himself to a bride thinking that was his due.

I gritted my teeth against a knot of fear in my throat. I had already been forced once into a marriage not of my choosing and though I had betrayed Blubebeard, he had not betrayed me. He had not laid a finger on me in any way that would cause me pain or grief. Something about this sword-lover made me think I would not be so lucky twice.

"The honored Lord Saberac saved this city two decades ago from a terrible flood," Svetgin said in an undertone, finally answering my question. "He arrived hours before it came with a dire warning to flee, but the people had not enough boats or carts to take their things with them, and so in his generosity, he provided ships and carts to load their precious things and keep them safe throughout the flooding. This city is wealthy because of his help."

"He had ships and carts waiting?" I asked, trying to keep the thorn from my words. Surely, I was not the first to notice how convenient that was for him. A flood was easy enough to cause if you had large horses and men to craft a dam and then burst it.

"He had been on a mission to bring sacred icons to the Seer of Tides and was returning, his fleet and carts emptied of their wealth."

I gave my brother a long look and trembled at what I saw because his face glowed with admiration and devotion. He did not see the obvious – that anyone can cloak their intentions with claims of reverence or that it was easy to be the savior of a city if you were the one who set it up for disaster.

I bit my lip and phrased my next question with care. "Surely they paid him for such a service? When they owed everything to him?"

"He would not hear of taking the riches they wished to lavish upon him," Svetgin said and for the first time since I had seen him as a man, he had some of his boyish energy back, some of the spark back in his step and gleam in his eye as if this story brought back memories of his youth. "We heard the tales even from where I was stationed with the army in Pensmoore. How he took only a tenth for all his trouble and expense. How the people were so grateful at such humility that they turned over to his use this tower and the keep below. There was little else on our tongues that spring."

"Indeed," I said noncommittally but to me this sounds like a Wittenbrand trick, and a simple one at that, for with a single swindle this man has bought for himself a reputation, a palace, and enough wealth to fund an army.

And now he had selected me as a bride. Why?

"It is a great honor to be his bride," Svetgin assured me. "An honor so deep we will never be able to repay him."

"Perhaps we could offer a tenth," I suggested and tried very hard to keep the bite from my tone.

Ahead of us, the chamberlain opened tall, gilded doors and proclaimed, "The Brotherhood of Stolen Sisters, the Pensmoore Lord Savataz, and his sister who is to be bride to the Lord Sabarac, Izolda of Savataz."

The Brotherhood swept into the room, carrying Svetgin and me in with them. The room was large and wide and the dawn outside the narrow windows broke in a red line across the horizon as if someone was gutting the dying sky like a brook trout.

I was wrong about the windows. No glass filled their empty settings. The wind, taking advantage of this, swept in – an uninvited and cold-fingered guest. The Brotherhood positioned themselves carefully as they spread out, keeping real metal behind their backs and not empty sky or tumultuous breezes. In this horrendous dress, the cold air kissed my skin with toothy bites, leaving me prickled and wary.

And as the Brotherhood opened up and out like an untimely flower caught blooming, I stole my first look at the man standing at the heart of all of this theatre.

I reeled back a step, gasping, prevented only from collapsing completely by my brother's firm hand on my arm.

"Well now, little darlin', I knew my collar would fit that pretty throat, but I wondered if you'd set it there yourself or have to be fitted for it," the Sword drawled. He stood where the bloodred dawn could highlight the edges of his golden hair and cheeks, making it appear as if he had dusted himself with dried blood.

He wore scarlet brocade as another might wear ermine, the

jacket lined with sealskin and unbuttoned to the waist like he thought he was Bluebeard – or perhaps was imitating him. His thread-of-gold lace-cuffed shirt was equally unbuttoned, showing a pale swath of hairless chest and chiseled midsection. I thought perhaps it was meant to look attractive. Instead, I found my tongue-twisting back in my mouth as if I'd eaten something rotten.

In one hand, he held the pole on which Grosbeak swung. He gestured to it with a smirk. "I brought to you your trinket – a pretty for my pretty."

"Run, Izolda," Grosbeak warned me – the words running out in a single breath before the Sword flicked his wrist and Grosbeak's severed head swung on its chain and struck the wall so hard there was a meaty *thunk.*

I swallowed down bile.

Svetgin cleared his throat awkwardly.

"Ah, my brotherhood, my knights, my crusaders in this cold dark world," the Sword said, sounding both sincere and mocking at the same time. He pulled a mother-of-pearl comb from his pocket – a cleverly designed little item, and combed back an errant lock before continuing. "You've succeeded where all else have failed and you have brought back behind this mortal veil one of your stolen sisters."

There was a ragged cheer as the Sword played to his audience, posing so that he was leaning on the post that held Grosbeak's severed head like a conquering king looking over his kingdom.

"And from it," he drawled, "you have snatched this artifact of devilry – this evidence of the evil of the man you begged me to help you conquer."

Another cheer.

"And I … I will honor that boldness. I will honor that bravery. I will honor the men with the intestinal fortitude of *bulls* who tore into their enemies and snatched back from them this prized lady. And I will honor you by marrying your stolen sister, sealing her honor, and removing from her the stain of her unholy marriage. And she and I will dance at our wedding before all my friends. What say you?"

His blue eyes twinkled, and I realized that by some magic he has made them look mortal.

The Brotherhood around me cheered, and my brother cheered loudest of all – almost as if they were under a geas, but I knew no magic was at work upon my companions except the magic of hope and ambition that sometimes make fools of otherwise moral men. I was deep in thought because I realized that what I said next would determine not just my own fate, but possibly the fate of Pensmoore, because the Sword wasn't playing for Pensmoore. I knew that. He was playing for Aayadmoore, and with it, the fate of our entire world.

I was so caught up in weighing my words that it was a moment before I noticed the chairs placed behind the Sword. They looked like upholstered thrones. One faced toward us, but the other was facing away, and chains were strung across the lowest point of its high back and those chains were very minutely moving. They appeared to be iron.

"But before I fulfill that promise," the Sword said, eyes glinting. "There is the matter of a fiend who needs to be dealt with."

He set Grosbeak's head down and with one wrenching movement, turned the backward chair around so that we could all see the occupant of it. And if I was not afraid before – and oh, but I was – now, fear took up a home in me, hollowing me to the core.

In the chair, chained with heavy iron, sat my husband, his beard blue and his bright eyes flashing. The red sunrise edged his chair in ghost flames so that it looked as if he were lit on the pyre, set ablaze with holy judgment.

His gaze was only for me. It found me from across the room and clung to me.

"And now I win the game, Arrow," the Sword whispered.

"Speak to my riddle, Sword," Bluebeard said with a twist to his mouth – his lip was split and bloody and a tiny trail of red rolled down and dripped from his chin. "What has blunted points and a blunted mind? What gold without to hide rot behind?"

"I'm done with your riddling," the Sword said, and I thought that maybe he'd forgotten his audience now that he was looking only at his enemy.

Quick as the tongue of a snake, he flicked a knife out and sliced through my husband's jacket and shirt, ripping them away from his body so that his silvery-scarred skin glowed lightly in the red dawn.

He spun, remembering us again.

"Long have your courts and kingdoms respected the strength of leaders who can vanquish their enemies completely. Today, you will help me vanquish yours."

"No," I said, clear as a bell. I hadn't come up with a speech. I didn't know what to say. And I had no weapon or clever idea, and yet the idea of standing here silent while Bluebeard was at this Wittenbrand's mercy wrenched something in me. I could not do it.

The Sword prowled over to me, a cat waiting for his moment to pounce, and just as I knew he would, he waited until he was only inches away before his hand shot out and gripped my throat. He did not squeeze. He merely held it.

"Your sister is bold, Savataz. Is she not my willing bride?" Dangerous, was the gleam in his eye.

"Of course she is," my brother said, looking shakenly between him and me, and I wondered if he remembered the day that was years ago for him but only a short week for me, when I had been stolen from him the first time. It had been a lot like this. Only that time an innocent man had died for me, and this time it would be my Wittenbrand groom. "There is no need to threaten her."

But I would not be spoken for any longer.

"There *is* a need for threats," I said smoothly. "The Sword has the right of it. For if he marries me against my will, I will do everything I can to turn all things against him. I will poison every dish and turn every blade. I will not rest until he is forever resting."

It was not a practical thing to say. The sensible thing to do would be to wait while he did as he willed to Bluebeard and then quietly allow him to marry me and keep myself still and composed until he inevitably grew bored and moved on to other things while I escaped his notice. And yet, I found that with my husband behind him, beaten and chained, practicality was slipping through my fingers.

The Sword patted my cheek and Svetgin tensed beside me. "Ah Izolda, your mind is twisted by all you have suffered. Is that not so, Lord Savataz?"

"It is," my brother said vehemently. "Blood and bone, but it is."

"And here, I wish only to spend her days as her ruthless rogue of a husband did – only for better, purer things."

My stomach flip-flopped.

"Hold her fast against her madness, Savataz. Hold her fast or I will not be responsible for what comes to pass."

My brother grabbed my arms firmly, standing behind me. "Is this necessary, Lord Sabarac? Can she not retire to some calm place while this necessity takes place?"

The Sword smiled lightly. "I think not. She must witness this death if she is to be my bride. I am told she says she is already married. Well. So she is. It is said in the long story of the founding of humanity that a man was born of dust and breath and from him was plucked a single rib – formed to be a woman. 'Why a rib?' it is asked. So that she may be close to his heart, closely tucked under his arm."

My brother sounded fervent when he said, "And so Izolda will be to you, only do not make her watch you slay her captor. She is already shaken, and women are gentle creatures."

Obviously, my brother had not married.

The Sword leaned in close and whispered to Svetgin, "Hold her, or she will pay with him, as will you." I felt the shock in Svetgin – in how he held me in wooden hands as the Sword whispered then in *my* ear. "And if you so much as flinch I will have you wear a rope of your brother's intestines as a garter at our wedding."

He drew back enough to meet my eye and then kissed me chastely on the cheek.

His kiss burned. Like a living thing I could not dislodge. Like a leech latched upon my face.

I quivered with fury.

Behind the Sword, someone cut our dialogue by yawning very loudly.

"If you're about done, Sword, I grow weary of theatrics," Bluebeard announced. "Dramatic talkers so rarely do dramatic deeds."

CHAPTER THREE

The Sword whirled and his blade leapt from his scabbard as if it were alive. He tossed it in the air, let it spin three times, and then snatched it from the air, holding the hilt in a backhand. I barely had time to catch my breath before he had it spinning again, but this time, I ignored his trick. I didn't need to watch men show off. I'd seen enough of that to last my entire life – short as it may be.

"Stand him up," the Sword barked, gesturing to the Brotherhood men closest to Bluebeard. "Mind his chains. The ones on his wrists must remain."

The Brotherhood scrambled to obey and there was an edge of anticipation to their actions that I did not like – the brightness of raven eyes and crow beaks just before they fall upon the fallen.

Why was Bluebeard doing nothing? I knew he was powerful. I'd watched him take the head from a man like another might pluck an apple. I'd watched his magic heal grievous injuries. I knew he didn't need to let himself be manhandled, and yet, he did. And all the while, his light cat's eyes were locked on mine, never wavering. As if he were speaking some wordless ballad to me in his every stillness.

"Hold your sister, Savataz," the Sword said, his voice again both sincere and mocking. Perhaps he was insane. It would explain so much. "Remind her not to flinch."

But I was not a swoony girl. I would not faint or flinch. Not even for this.

It took all my willpower not to grimace when the Brotherhood men stepped back, leaving Bluebeard standing on his own, hands trussed before him. Where the iron chains had touched his skin, the skin was red and puffy as if he'd been burned. His lip and one of his eyes were swollen and darkened.

Even so, he watched me, his eyes never wavering, that single line of blood down his cheek looking forever as if he had shed a single crimson tear.

The Sword leaned in toward Bluebeard and whispered something to him, and I knew what it would be – it would be an identical threat to the one he'd made to me. I knew it like I knew my own name. He was that predictable.

And then he danced back a step, the lightness in his feet holding a strange joy incongruous with the moment, before his blade flicked, *swish, swish, swish,* and my husband's clothing fell to the ground, leaving him in nothing but his iron chains.

I felt my cheeks flame, but I held his gaze as he held mine.

"You're not my type, Sword," he drawled. "And that was my favorite pair of buckskins. You owe me five gold pieces for those, though I'll forgive you the shirt. It was last season's fashion."

"When I'm done here, I'll owe you so much more than five gold pieces," the Sword hissed and to my horror, I felt anticipation growing in the air around me. I risked a glance to the side and saw the Brotherhood men were tense – but not with the tension of those about to fight but with the tension of those about to savor. They wanted my husband's pain. They wanted it very badly.

"How comes it, Lord Riverbarrow, that you are the same as any mortal man when stripped of your finery? Shall we toss a coin for his fate, men?" the Sword asked, rolling his sword handle around his forearm in a neat trick that made it appear almost as flexible as leather instead of pure steel. "You can call the toss, Arrow."

"Heads," my husband said, smirking at Grosbeak whose eyes flicked back and forth between him and the Sword as if he was watching a game of shuttles. "I collect them, you know."

"Not anymore you don't," the Sword said with a laugh but as he produced a gold coin, Bluebeard's eyes locked on mine again.

I swallowed at the intensity there and then gasped when his mind met mine with speech.

Speak to my riddle, wife of mine.

I thought we'd lost that when we left the Wittenhame.

My mouth was suddenly very dry.

What must the think of me, he who had been stripped bare by his enemies and paraded before them in chains because of me. Because I took a single day of my life and allowed it to be stolen by his enemies. Tenson danced down every nerve.

Who cuts out my heart and wears it as her crown? Who holds its shattered fragments in her palms?

Anguish wrung my heart like a rag.

I gasped. His eyes – blood of gods and men – those eyes. They gutted me. And yet, I could not lie to him. I could not betray him in that, too.

I do, I said.

And before I could say anything else, the Sword's blade spun through the air again, and this time when he caught it backhanded, he spun with it and plunged it directly into Bluebeard's side with a slow flourish.

A scream tore from my throat, but Svetgin held me fast, not letting me so much as move an inch.

My husband's gaze was still locked on mine. It glazed over for a moment as pain washed over him. He coughed, blood spattering from his lips in tiny droplets.

Through gritted teeth he spoke, enunciating each word with care.

"It's a good sword, Towerrock, but I do so hate it when they stick."

A foul expletive tore from the Sword and then he twisted the blade and a moan twisted from Bluebeard's mouth with his movement. The Sword leaned over my husband trying to free his blade, and I bit hard on my lip until blood wetted it as I tried with all my power not to move, not to flinch.

Husband of mine, I reached for him with my mind, but found only pain. *Master of my fate.*

But why was I holding myself back from flinching when the Sword had already done his worst? For what could be worse than this?

"No," I gasped, wrenching against Svetgin's powerful grip. "Leave him. Take my life instead."

The Sword turned to look at me and nausea rippled through me at the look of sheer delight on his face, but more than that, at what was in his hand. He sheathed his sword, cupping his prize in his palm.

"How do you sever the wife from the husband? A puzzle for the ages. And one I have solved, friends," he said.

Behind him, Bluebeard fell to his knees, chained hands moving so that his bare arms could cup the ragged hole in his body. His eyes caught mine once more. In them, violence and certainty, fury and agony all mixed up in a poison so potent I could feel it from here.

I'm sorry. I'm so sorry. Tears streaked down my face, but my mental voice could not call back my betrayal. It could not bring back his life.

His eyes glassed over, and his head slumped forward.

A sob choked in my chest.

"Hand me the gold item you see beside you, Knight Wheavon," the Sword ordered and one of the Brotherhood passed him an item that looked very much like a crown. But it was fitted with a locking bracket and into that bracket, the Sword slotted his trophy. It fit perfectly into the swirling metalwork meant to hold it – a ghastly, white rib, streaked in the blood of my husband and wrenched from his breast by this mad Wittenbrand. "Death may not be enough to sever the tie between man and wife. This I know. But what if I take back what is hers by right? And what if I take it for myself? The ancient rib from which woman was formed. Poetic, don't you think?"

Triumphantly, the Sword crowned himself with the bloody crown.

"I need no marriage vows to own you, Izolda Savataz. You are already mine."

But I didn't care what he did – he and his bloody trophies. I didn't care what claims he made on me. There was only one man I cared about. And as I watched him, my eyes burning with unshed tears, he looked up one more time and I could tell the effort cost him, naked, ruined, and murdered as he was. His mental voice was still clear even though it was faint as a whisper.

One bone of mine he has taken, and yet in the marrow of each of the rest is the song of your name.

And before I could say anything in return, he lurched to his feet, slipping in the pool of his own blood, and without a word, he leapt like a dog into a lake – full-bodied and joyful – out one of the gaping spiral holes in the side of the tower.

I wanted to scream. I did. But it was like the scream was stuck inside me, like it was screaming me and not the other way around.

The Sword cursed loudly. And I could not understand why, because my Bluebeard was gone – fallen to his death. No, *leaping* to his death.

A monstrous choice.

The room swam with my tears. I dashed them angrily aside and now – now! – Svetgin released me so that I could wipe them, and I bolted to the gaping hole in the tower, not caring that my skirts trailed through my husband's blood, searching for his pale body on the rocks below.

What I saw instead, was the wings of a great raven – greater than I'd ever seen before – glowing with the gold of the bright dawn. My breath hitched in my throat at the sight of him. On his back, he carried the Arrow, Lord Riverbarrow, Prince of the Wittenbrand, and the one man who I had just realized owned my heart.

CHAPTER FOUR

I watched the Sword fighting to compose himself and for just a single moment his eyes flickered like he couldn't control whatever illusion made them appear human and then he turned to the Brotherhood. His calm smile didn't even appear forced. He was very, very good at hiding his emotions. I made note of that. I might need to remember he could do that.

My mouth was dry as dust. I ran a thick, dull tongue over my dusty lips.

"Well, we had a little of our own back before the end, did we not brothers?" There were murmurs around us and the Sword half-bowed his head. "You all know why I came to you – how I had a sister stolen from me. How I was determined to stand with you – to finally lay hand on the inhuman creature who was stealing our sisters. Our revenge has been met and now I will honor Svetgin's sister with the marriage promised her. One that is blessed, chosen by her family, and a haven to her and her children."

I did not believe a word he said. I watched him from the side of my eye – the gore-flecked bone in his crown drying as he spoke. A scrap of flesh hung off it, fluttering when he turned his head too fast. He'd need that mother-of-pearl comb again to tidy his hair when this was done.

One thing, I knew. I had not lied. If he forced me to marry him, I *would* find some way to kill him. I had not thought myself a murderer before I was stolen away to the Wittenhame, but the death of such a one would not burden me with guilt. And I had seen better men slain before me.

My hands flexed and unflexed as I thought about the open swirl of window I stood beside. I could feel the breeze stirring over the waking city below, sucking at me as if calling me into its embrace. The hot white of full-blown dawn washed warm over me as if the sun wished to offer succor, as if the sky itself wished to bless me, or maybe to welcome me.

If I tried to push him over the edge, would I go over, too?

Could I do that?

My thoughts raced, mounting to a conclusion. My parents were dead. My only living brother caught in the fist of a mad Wittenbrand. My husband named me betrayer.

I swallowed and now the dryness of my mouth was tickling my throat.

I was not done living. Not yet ready to end my life intentionally. No, I would be sensible about this. I would bide my time and find a more subtle means of murder – a means that would achieve my ends without taking my own life with it.

They'd been speaking behind me as I weighed the worth of my life, but now someone cleared his throat gently and I turned to see my brother. There was a look of compassion in his eye as he offered me a hand and also – was that an edge of terror. Did he begin to realize what he had dragged us both into?

"Come, Izolda, the priest is here."

"You know your Lord Saberac is no good man, do you not,

Svetgin," I asked gravely.

He did not look me in the eye. "You have been promised to him. I cannot change it now."

I tipped his chin toward me with a single finger, and he met my eyes reluctantly.

"The moment you leave this room," I breathed, "Run as far and as fast as you can go, brother, and do not look back to this place. Not to save me. Not to come to the aid of a friend. Not to carve out your revenge. Or you will be caught into this spider's web with the rest of us and you have seen now for yourself that the only way free is with the price of much blood."

He swallowed, but I did not want to hear his response. I wanted to leave my words to sit heavy on him – a mantle he could not dislodge.

I turned. And when I did, I was surprised to see that already Bluebeard's blood had been scrubbed from the floor and his chair removed. A priest in full raiment stood with holy chalice in hand and beside him, the Sword had posed himself, one hand behind his back like a lord at a ball.

I could see no reason why the Sword would want to marry me. Was it only to spite Bluebeard? Or did he really think that he could spend my days, too?

My brow was furrowed as I lifted my blood-soaked hem and stepped to where the priest and the Sword waited.

"I do not wish to remarry," I told the priest.

"It matters not, lady," he said seeming unconcerned. "We care not for your whimsical Pensmoore ways here in Aayadmoore. Your guardian has sworn you as bride. Your bridegroom accepts you as such. You have no will nor wiles here." Well, then. It seemed there were madder lands than even the Wittenhame. The priest turned to the Sword. "Have you paid the price to the guardian?"

"I have," he gave a confident smile as if he was a true bridegroom sure of his suit and not a monster wearing the rib of my husband for a crown. "By the rescue of Izolda Savataz – led by me – I have obtained the right of marriage."

"And do you confirm he has paid in full?" the priest asked my brother.

"I do," my brother's voice was shaky.

I had no allies in this room.

Except one.

I stole a look at Grosbeak. His head had been all but forgotten by everyone assembled. A strange and horrible curiosity to the mortals and a traitor to the Sword. He frowned at me and then winked. I thought that must mean he was still with me – still my creature, or guide, or whatever he was to me.

It gave me the courage to keep my head high.

"And do you assembled here declare that you are witnesses to this agreement and covenant between these two houses?" the priest asked.

There was a murmur of approval amongst the Brotherhood. I turned to look in every eye. They had lived their lives and possibly given their fortunes in pursuit of sisters lost long ago to them. And yet now they blithely gave a woman away unwillingly to a husband not of her choosing. My tongue curled on the bitterness of irony – thick as the scent of blood still lingering in the air.

"Then by the authority of crown and kingdom, you are husband and wife," the priest said.

A shiver of fear rushed through me as the Sword's calm façade cracked and a look of predatory anticipation filled him. He hunched forward slightly, as if he wanted to reach for me and was only just stopping himself, and then the predatory look shifted to one of concentration and then confusion.

"They're not there," he whispered. "Not there. But they must be." He shook himself and looked at the priest. "Fully married? Man and wife?"

"Yes, indeed," the priest said, beginning to move toward the door. "And may you have many years of prosperity together and heirs of your body to maintain your line."

My second husband's hand shot out and caught the priest by the collar. "You're certain, priest?"

The priest raised an eyebrow, and the Sword removed his and with a slight nod of his head that was almost an apology.

"You're as married as any other man in Aayadmoore. As much as priest and ceremony can make you, at any rate."

There was an edge to the Sword that almost looked like panic and for a moment I was confused and then my lips parted as I understood. My days. He thought to secure them by marrying me. He must not be able to access them as Bluebeard had.

He crossed to me in a single step and grabbed me by my hair yanking me close to him. "Where are they? Why can I not feel them?"

I gasped in pain, but I said nothing. I would not help him. Not even to understand what was so very plain to me – that he could not steal my days from Bluebeard and that if it were in my power, I certainly would not give them up.

His brow furrowed and then cleared, and his bright eyes shot up to me in sudden revelation. Ice ran cold through me. That look in his eyes was too close to the one I'd seen there right before he took my true husband's rib.

"Out," he said, his voice like a sword cutting through the air. "All of you, out."

"Out, my lord?" Svetgin asked nervously. "Will we not toast the happy couple?"

"But we are not a couple yet, are we, Savataz?" the Sword growled. "We are only half married. Married by ceremony but not by deed."

My brother's face paled as understanding dawned and I felt myself go suddenly lightheaded, too. I'd been spared the cruelty of an unwanted wedding night once before. It seemed I would not be spared again.

CHAPTER FIVE

"You dishonor my sister with such boldness, sir," Svetgin said and something like hope sprang into my breast.

"I said, *out*," the Sword roared, backhanding Svetgin when he took a step forward. The movement pulled my hair and I blinked back tears, grabbing the Sword's fist in both of mine as I tried to keep my head close enough that he wouldn't yank out all my hair by the roots. "A deal was made, Savataz, and a bride given. Would you claim now that you have been cheated?"

"I thought you were a good man," Svetgin said thickly, cupping his cheek with one hand. "A man of honor."

He reached for his sword, but one of his fellows slammed the hilt back into the scabbard, giving my brother a silent shake of the head in warning.

"Come, Svetgin," another said. "Leave him to his wedding night."

"That is my sister. And he speaks of her like she is property," Svetgin said, chin trembling.

"You sold her to me as property," the Sword said, dragging me with him as he stalked forward. "You offered her up to me as mine – her inheritance and her body to be used by me as I will. What did you think you were doing when you made our bargain?"

My brother's face went deathly pale – as if he had just realized what he'd done. As if he'd just realized that this day is a mirror to the last day that he was held back by others and I was sold away. Only this time, a whole nation wasn't saved with my innocence. This time it was only a ragged patch on his reputation. It must be a terrible thing to realize you are a fool and have been a fool all your life.

I tried not to judge too harshly knowing how painful that must be, but it was hard not to condemn with the Sword making threats against my person.

I swallowed down a burst of fear. I must not let myself imagine what would come next or it would paralyze me. My husband lost a rib for my betrayal. I would lose my dignity and my agency and the last shreds of my innocence.

No, I must not think of it.

I wanted to be ill.

I wanted to be dead.

I closed my eyes for too long and it was only the yank of the Sword tugging me again by the hair that snapped them back open. Blood and spittle flew across my face. He had hit my brother again. Stark red blood on a shining floor. Harsh bruises blooming on a swollen lip.

"Take your treacherous brother away," he said to the Brotherhood. "And leave me to my wedding night."

What is it in a man that leads him to do what he says he will never do? What is it that makes him go against what he has proclaimed to be his virtue? Is it shame? I thought it might be, for there was shame in every face as they dragged my brother away, ignoring his cries and pleas.

I shook so hard my teeth rattled as the men left – every one of them refusing to look at me, refusing to let their eyes stray on what they were about to allow.

It was shame that filled me from brim to bottom the same as it did to them. Deep, terrible shame. For I could not blame anyone for what had happened but myself. If I had not taken that gem from the hourglass, I would not be in the mortal world now. If I had told Bluebeard what his enemies were planning, I would be with him still, he would be uninjured, and he would have the head of any man who so much as touched me.

The door shut with a snick and the Sword did not wait before flinging me against the remaining chair. The world reeled as I hit it, striking so hard that the chair toppled, taking me with it. I blinked back pain and tears as pain blossomed in my back and head and one of my shoulders from where I had struck the ground.

I was sprawled across the chair, the room spinning around me in a whirl of gilded metal and bright sunlight.

I needed to find my feet.

I needed to get a weapon.

I scrambled to my feet, tripping on my dress. I was like a newborn kitten. None of my limbs was obeying me.

"I'll have those days, mortal," the Sword said, looming over me. "I'll have them if I must take your tainted mortal flesh to mine every night from now until the end of the Game."

He worked at the remaining buttons on his jacket and then flung it to the side, turning to his shirt and with each item he removed I felt fear coil deeper in me, swelling up within me until thought was squeezed out entirely and only terror remained to gibber at the back of my mind.

I felt something like a prick of surprise – or possibly rage – in the back of my mind but there was no room for any thoughts of that. I had seen a chance.

I sprang, leaping as far and fast as I could go, and snatching up Grossbeak's pole in both my hands. I held him out in front of me like a talisman.

"I don't like this! I don't like it at all!" Grossbeak shrieked.

The Sword dropped his shirt to the ground and looked up, surprise and then delight flooding his features. He drew his sword silently from the scabbard, stalking forward.

"A little dance before we couple, mortal girl? A little game to get the blood flowing? I'll play your games, but know, I will not hold back. I will take you to wife bloody and broken if I must, or if you surrender, I will relent and leave your skin in one pretty piece."

"We both know I'm not very pretty," I said, trying to space my feet out well to give me room to maneuver.

"And yet, your value lies elsewhere. How many mortals have I tried to take days from? And none has given up a single one. And yet my rival has married sixteen women and taken their days, taunting me with his added power." Here it was. The reason his teeth were clenched. The reason he stalked me and made me prey. "I will have what is his. If he can take them from you, then so can I. And I will wring them from you by whatever means I must."

"I don't stand up well to sword slashes," Grosbeak interrupted as I held him higher, his voice trembling. "I really think I should warn you about that. I won't last very long as a weapon."

I ignored his panic, waiting. I knew the Sword was not a patient man. He would not hesitate in striking first.

I had judged the Sword accurately. He whipped out a single thrust and I batted it away with the pole from which Grosbeak hung. The chain rang against the blade and Grosbeak screamed. "Gourds of the Netherworld!"

I spun backward, keeping the lantern pole high.

"You'll not have me," I told the Sword firmly when Grosbeak's echoes had faded. "Not as wife or as anything else."

"I have had many things that uttered the same," the Sword said languidly.

I was not skilled with the sword. I was not large enough to make this a fair fight even if I was. And on top of that, it was clear he was very skilled – and toying with me. He stretched out the showy musculature of his arms and shoulders as he moved, glancing at himself from time to time in the small stand mirror to one side of the room as if he enjoyed the sight of himself playing with me as much as he enjoyed the game.

I fought determinedly, using every scrap of energy I had to parry his thrusts and turn his blade. I was light on my feet and had good balance, but that wouldn't have been enough even if my newly healed back had not made me stiffer in movement than I would have preferred.

"I have enjoyed this game, mortal girl," the Sword said, "but now I run low on patience. Let's have this marriage completed that I may spend your days as I must."

And this time when he thrust his blade it narrowly missed my head. It was all I could do to dodge away but his quick second strike knocked Grosbeak's pole from my hands, ringing the metal so hard my fingers buzzed with the strike.

His sword hilt crashed against my cheek before I could gasp, sending me spinning. I hit the ground hard, not even sure which parts of me had struck, only that I must find my feet again or all was lost. I scrambled upward, my heart racing, too filled with the urgency of the moment to feel the pain of my injuries.

The world reeled and spun as if I were in a small boat instead of on land.

I'd just made it to my feet when his hand shot out and seized my throat. He took two steps forward, driving me backward. I tried to squirm from his grip, but my feet slipped, tangled in my too-full skirts. No wonder he put his women in these dresses. They were as immobilizing as chains. The thought felt foreign in my pounding head.

He pinned me against one of the winding wall sections, his grip around my throat like iron. I grabbed his wrist in both hands, fighting against it. I couldn't catch a full breath. My throat ached from his grip.

And now panic flared in my belly. I had thought to fight – and if it had looked as if I might fail, then to fling myself from the tower. I had not thought he could so easily overpower me, and a sense of furious futility wrenched through me.

His eyes were bright and mad. He would have no pity on me until he'd claimed what he came for.

"Enough with this dance, let's see it done with," he snarled.

A knock came – sharp and urgent – again and again.

"What?" the Sword roared.

"Lord Saberac! Lord Saberac, it's urgent!"

His face flushed crimson. "Not urgent enough to disturb me. Leave!"

Again, the wild knocking, and the Sword spun, though his hand kept my neck pinned to the wall.

"If you interrupt me at my sport a second time, I will take your head!" he roared.

"Lord Saberac, they are at the tower gates and will soon overwhelm us!"

"Viscera of the seas!" he cursed and his hand dropped its grip leaving me to slump to the ground.

I heaved, all my suppressed terror suddenly spilling out.

He flung himself away from me and toward a window so that he had a hand on either side of one of the openings while his whole body leaned out and over to survey the land below. A stream of curses turned the air a vibrant blue.

Curious – too curious, since it was curiosity that led me here – I crawled to the edge and looked down below.

The ground crawled with figures in the stark black uniforms of Pensmoore. Their banner flew over them, snapping in the morning wind. As I watched, the air over one part of the city shimmered, and then a tear – as if in a piece of cloth – opened and men poured from it like water from a hole in a bucket. As fast as they arrived, they made war upon the city, tearing guards from their posts, skewering horses on their spears, and kindling angry flames. Watching them aged me a year in the blink of an eye.

"Psst, lady," Grosbeak whispered.

His pole was right beside me. With trembling hands, I reached for it, barely catching it in my grip.

A blow sent me sprawling backward, head ringing.

"Do you see what you've done?" the Sword asked, his words deadly quiet compared to how he'd roared at the messenger – but I was much more terrified of this quiet Sword. "You've distracted me as my enemies close in."

I tried to reply but nothing came from my crushed throat except a croak. I clutched at it, panic flaring. I had no voice to even scream.

He took a stalking step toward me and froze, a look of utter terror painting his face as he looked up at the window. A shadow blocked the bright morning sun, and a voice rang out.

"Sword!"

I pushed up to my elbows just in time to see a cloud of colorful songbirds – birds of every size and color and kind – fly in through the open window in a rainbow burst. They bore a great burden on their many tiny bodies – my cat-like husband. A cacophony of fluttering filled the air, a thousand lacy wings caressing the strands of the winds as he arrived in their flurry, prince of wings, sovereign of wind.

A single blue feather drifted to land right in front of me as my mouth fell open in awe.

In one hand, he gripped his sword. With the other hand, he tossed a severed head at the Sword.

"Yours. I believe."

My eyes were full with the sight of him, my heart racing.

He was arrayed in fine clothing and finer weaponry. Which

alone was stunning when he'd left here only perhaps an hour ago and then he was both naked and mortally wounded. But though he was dressed, there was a bloody red stain across his side, soaking shirt and jacket and trousers in bright crimson.

My eyes flicked from that to the head as the Sword caught it. It was – or at least had been – Knight Wheavon, the member of the Brotherhood who had handed the Sword his crown. Bluebeard's eyes never took it in at all. They were all for me.

"This," Bluebeard said, striding toward me, "is mine."

He offered me a hand with a questioning quirk to his eyes, but I did not hesitate at all. I grasped it firmly and let him pull me to my feet. I snatched up Grosbeak from the ground while I could. He was my only weapon.

"I thought you collected these," the Sword said, staring at the head. His voice tried for nonchalant, but only managed hollow.

"Heads or wives?" Bluebeard asked flippantly. "I collect both. But while I'm happy to give you that head as a gift – a tip of the hat from one competitor to the other – if you harm my wife again, I shall not suffer you to live, rules of the great Game aside."

The Sword looked up, and for a moment his eyes sparkled like he meant to attack Bluebeard, and yet, there was fear in his movements. Perhaps Bluebeard unchained was an entirely different thing.

"My city is being ransacked. My bride stolen. If you think this is over, Lord Riverbarrow, you have not thought at all," he said, instead. "I will make war on you. And it will not matter that killing you would lose me the game because I will revel in your suffering for the rest of your shortened life. I will take from you every slice of life you wish to taste and sour it with the life's blood of everyone you love."

“Then I suppose it’s a good thing that I love so few,” Bluebeard said, spinning me suddenly and lifting me in his arms like a bridegroom carrying a bride. “Next time you try to steal a man’s wife, you should confirm that she wants to be stolen. A woman taken against her will is never truly yours.”

The Sword sneered. “You would know, Arrow.”

“You’re a tasteless unworthy thing, Sword. I spit you from my mouth.”

He lifted me into the air so suddenly that I barely had a chance to gasp, and then we were carried out the window on the backs of hundreds of colorful songbirds, their songs and cries below us punctuating every movement, leaving the Sword behind with a dead man’s head in his hands, a look of shock on his perfect features, and my husband’s rib in his crown.

CHAPTER SIX

Bird song can be ephemeral and uplifting or insistent and obnoxious. Here in the sigh of the wind and the gasp of the air, it carried the melody of relief. Having never been a bird, I had never flown, and yet it was not the curiously unsteady sensation of flying that gripped me now but the warring fears within me. Somehow, though they opposed one another, that only increased the power of each one over me.

I was terrified of the conflict unrolling underneath me, the tiny bloody figures rolling across the ground or lying slain in final repose were like the denizens of a particularly gruesome tapestry. But I was just as afraid of flying up so high above them even though that meant avoiding the conflict. Could these little birds truly hold us? What if they perished in the attempt and we – also – fell to our deaths. My face hurt from where I'd been hit – aching so much I feared one eye might swell. If a single blow could do that to me, what might bearing so much weight do to these small birds?

And this was not my only fear. I was utterly terrified of what the Sword had planned to do to me – both in ravaging my physical body and my spirit. But I was nearly as afraid of what judgment Bluebeard may have in store for me now that I had betrayed him and put him in a position to be mortally wounded. It was only his retrieval of me that had saved me from the Sword, but what fury must he feel for me now?

I must be practical about this. It was good to fly rather than to fall. It was good to be rescued rather than ravaged. Whatever came next, I would deal with that. I would not borrow trouble that was not mine to take.

"I didn't marry him willingly," I said to Bluebeard, hoping he would accept that small offering. Just because you are starting to realize that the current of your heart turns to someone, doesn't make it easy to bare that heart to them.

He did not reply. It was, after all, day. And he did not speak to me in the day. But he'd spoken to me mind to mind, and he could do that, so if he wasn't speaking, then he probably did not wish to.

And yet, I had things to say. Keeping secrets didn't work if you wanted to be someone's ally. Or friend. Or wife.

I swallowed.

My father always said that if you wanted to ride a spirited horse, you must seize the reins firmly and keep a solid seat.

I felt a pang of sadness at the thought. He would never say that again. Never offer his other practical, bluff advice. And I needed it now more than ever. How did you make amends with a wild man who both thought he possessed you and saw you as his betrayer?

Carefully.

You did it carefully or you didn't manage it at all.

I swallowed and took the reins in hand firmly.

"I originally thought to spy on you," I said, keeping my tone calm and frank. Emotion would not help matters. He would just think I was trying to manipulate him. Even with my calm tone, his hands tightened around me. "My king asked it of me."

I met his eyes, and he raised an eyebrow. I had forgotten that he didn't want me to call the King of Pensmoore "my king." I cleared my throat to cover my error and continued.

"It seemed reasonable at first. And then I met your people and I decided I did not want to spy on you. I wanted to work with you."

Bluebeard had a remarkably expressive face. It seemed paler than usual, nearly green, but the way his lips twisted conveyed all his distrust so clearly that he might as well have said "liar" right then and there.

"When Coppertomb suggested that I steal one of my own days, I was tempted to try. After all, having some small part of my fate in my own hands had an appeal. Would you like someone else to own every one of your days and to spend them as they pleased?"

His face seemed to soften slightly at that, but he still shook his head disdainfully as if I should have known better. And, of course, I should have. Still, he remained silent.

We were flying away from the city now, flying low over the river that divided Pensmoore from Aayadmoore. I could feel the spray of water on my face we were so close. If the birds dropped us, we would rush down the rapids and be dashed on the rocks. I could almost feel it happening, see it step by step in my mind's eye.

I wrenched my gaze away and back to him.

"I didn't plan to give him the garnet. Not in the end. In the end I decided I wanted to work with you – to be your ally. Maybe even your friend."

He remained silent.

I sighed. "I suppose that is over now."

And he did not disabuse me of the thought, he merely tore his gaze from mine and looked toward where we were flying.

The birds dipped lower and lower and when we reached the bank of the river on the other side, they suddenly let loose, scattering in a hundred different directions.

It was hardly a fall. Almost more of a stumble.

But Bluebeard's arms lost their grip on me, and I sprawled in the tufted grass along the gravel shores before I realized he was beside me, eyes closed and face paler than death.

The wings of hundreds of birds flapped around me, brushing my face and arms and hair as they dispersed and leaving behind a flurry of falling feathers in white and black, brown and gold, blue and scarlet. They fled like my hope – spooked and scattered.

When I could see again, there was Bluebeard, passed out on a thick tuft of grass, his face pale as death. His birds had fled with his consciousness.

I sat up, rustling the tall grass.

"You promised me revenge on the Sword, and yet at your first encounter you let him trounce you completely," Grosbeak complained from where he lay. He kept spitting between words as the sandflies we kicked up tried to swarm in his mouth. "Useless! You had to be saved by the Arrow! No Wittenbrand woman needs a man to save her."

"I doubt there are any who need a useless woman to carry them around or shake the flies from their mouths, either," I said wryly, shooing the flies away and setting his head upright so he could watch me. "Any tips on gut wounds?"

I pushed Bluebeard onto his back, ignoring how beautiful he was in near-death, like the memorial painting of a battlefield after a great victory.

I unbuttoned his fox-fur-lined shirt and pulled it from his trousers so I could get a better look at his wound. Flowers sprung up around him. The tiny plants pushing through the earth and tumbling up toward the sky before blossoming into white with purple hearts and purple with yellow hearts. There were a hundred of them where he'd passed out, and more surrounding him before I was able to so much as expose his skin. What did it mean to be married to a husband who did this to the land and sky? Whose very presence made it come alive?

I shook my head. Wounds didn't tend themselves and I needed to get to work. Someone had put a rough bandage around his side and even set it with silver stitches, but two of the stitches had pulled loose and his entire belly and leg on that side were drenched in blood.

"Looks like he stitched himself. That's his silver thread. For all the good it did him," Grosbeak sneered.

I felt a chill go through me. Had he been unable to heal himself because he didn't have access to my days? But no, the wound was crusted a little as if it was trying to heal.

"It looks days old," I muttered. "But it was no more than an hour ago that he was ripped apart."

"It was days for *you*," Grosbeak snorted. "Or did you not notice that time is a game for the Wittenbrand?"

"What do you mean?" I asked, trying to clean Bluebeard's wound with a piece of my dress. There were so many layers of skirts that surely one of them could be spared.

"Did you not notice that mere days in the Wittenhame were years here in the mortal world?"

"That did seem to be clear when I met my younger brother as a grown man and learned my parents were dead," I said acidly.

"Don't give me that tone, mortal. It works just as easily in the other direction. Your Wittenbrand husband must have used his key when he fled on the raven. And gone home. And there he would have dressed his wound and clothed himself before returning to bring the armies of Pensmoore directly to the Sword's door. That must have cost you."

"Cost *me?*"

"Well, it's your days he spent, isn't it? Feel any older? Maybe seeing your first grey hair?" he snickered.

"What?" I glanced at the braid tumbled over my shoulder and gasped. There *was* a white thread in it. Just one.

"I'd guess he took a whole year to make that little trick happen. Maybe even more." Grosbeak laughed. He always sounded particularly nasty when he laughed – especially when his laughter was aimed at me.

I opened my mouth to object and then snapped it tight. It was hardly sensible to complain now – when complaint would do me no good. Hardly practical to complain when he'd brought that army for the purpose of freeing me. Though the cost seemed too high for the gain. My possession of myself and my innocence – while of incredible importance to me – did not seem like something others should die for.

"Why didn't he spend them to heal this wound, then?" I asked sharply. The bleeding would not stem with my bandage no matter how tightly I wrapped it and I had no other supplies. Worry made my voice tight and annoyed.

"Well, that's the Arrow for you. Disgustingly noble at the worst possible moment. He won't take from you for himself, but he'll take and take if he thinks it will be good for you. Typical."

"He thought a war would be good for me?" I asked icily.

"They were *already* at war. It was only a matter of who took the opening strike."

"And my husband thought it should be him."

Grosbeak rolled his eyes. "Is that the Sword lying bleeding on the ground? You don't call stealing the Arrow's rib a strike? Did he steal your brain when I wasn't looking?"

I ignored him, but I couldn't keep my telltale cheeks from heating.

"If you're just about done fussing with a wound that won't heal, you should come and look at my head," Grossbeak said. "I think he fractured my skull back there."

"And what can I do about that?"

Grosbeak grunted. "Fine. Then look to yourself. You have a shiner, and a split cheek, and your shoulder is nothing but one huge bruise. And I'm being a gentleman and not mentioning that neck. Actually, if you were wondering if mottled purple was your color, now we know. It isn't."

I gave him a death glare and sat back staring at Bluebeard. He was still bleeding. I had not helped matters much. And we were sitting on a riverbank across from a war with no supplies, no shelter, and no way to make a fire. By nightfall, we would freeze to death. I was already cold in the chill spring air with only this flimsy dress for cover. I was not the kind of girl who sat down and cried when things got tough but I was sorely tempted to change that.

"What I would really like to know," I said irritably, choosing frustration over despair, "is where Coppertomb was in all of this. *He* stole the gem. *He* brought the Brotherhood. So why were they answering to the Sword?"

"Not his style," Grosbeak said. "He likes to work from the shadows. The manipulative voice behind the activity. The puppeteer. The slithering snake."

"Delightful."

"Likely, he struck a deal with the Sword to snatch you for him. Coppertomb's a new player, but he's coy as a girl trying to marry into wealth. He'll be lurking in the shadows nearby. Mark me on this. If you want to help the Arrow, you should keep an eye out for him."

A horse whinnied somewhere nearby.

I froze, wishing I could make myself small.

"Are you hiding? Are you hiding from a horse?"

I put my fingers to my lips to silence Grosbeak. There was someone there. And what did he expect me to do? Use my terrible sword skills to take them down? No. The practical thing to do was to be quiet and hide here.

"You're going to let us all freeze to death along a riverbank because you're afraid of a herbivore?"

He was right. A horse might not have a rider. It might be tied along the riverbank and loaded down with supplies. And some of those supplies might be medical supplies.

With a sigh, I scooped up Bluebeard's sword and lifted my skirts with my other hand.

"If you leave me here, I swear I'll scream."

"If I am to take you, you bodiless rogue, then you must promise silence," I whispered.

"You're starting to sound like your husband."

"Promise." I shook his chain.

"Nngh. Promise."

We stalked silently into the trees together.

CHAPTER SEVEN

There was something about being back in Pensmoore that made my skin tingle. I was only a few strides from the river – a few strides into the land of my birth and it had etched itself into my mortal fibers in such a way that I could feel the pull of it tangling into every beat of my heart. The trees leaned forward to touch me with their waving branches. The grasses caressed me. The earth rose up to meet me. Gladness, deep and full filled me just from the resonance of the land to my presence. What would it have been like if I had lived a whole life here? Raised horses? Kept a keep? Bore and raised children for … what was his name? Leonid? Already I was forgetting him – a cruelty he did not deserve when he'd given himself to save me.

It was with these gloomy thoughts that I emerged from the trees that lined the riverbank and out into a rolling field. The field was broad and deep – so much so that I could see all the way to where the river curved back on itself and to the fine bridge positioned there.

I had not been wrong about the horses. There was one tied to a tree not far from here. He rolled his black eye at us – as horses do when they have no other way to express anxiety – and stamped a foot.

He'd earned his right to be worried. Beyond the horse, filling the road beyond the field and packing the bridge to its limit before spreading out on either side, was something out of the Wittenhame.

Only in dreams do you see such mad things as this. I blinked twice to be sure I was not dreaming, but the ache of my throat and jaw told me certainly that what I saw was true. An army with inhuman, cold eyes marched up the road carrying fierce weapons. I bit my lip at the sight of them. Their bodies were flat – as if they were made of carding or parchment. When their eyes moved or features flickered, it looked as if they were suddenly painted on in a different configuration – so they did not so much move as shift from pose to pose.

I froze, my ruined throat throbbing as I swallowed nervously.

"There's a move you'll never forget," Grosbeak said, taking in their patterned red and white uniforms just as I was. They were all the exact same inscrutable pattern in a mirror image from bottom to top. "A playing card army. I haven't seen one of those in … well, never, but it was said that one was used in the Great Game of Crowns and Thrones five ages ago. It's red, so it probably belongs to the Sword. But why did he need your days if he could conjure up *this*?"

Why, indeed?

"I thought the Wittenbrand's color was blue?" I said.

"Oh, aye, but it is, but the Sword seems to think he needs his own personal color and for him, that is red as the crimson tide he drains from his enemies."

"How charming," I said dryly. "And it still doesn't explain why he wanted my days."

"He means to wound me, bodiless curiosity," Bluebeard

murmured from behind me and I had to clutch my mouth with a hand to keep from yelping.

Though he spoke to Grosbeak, his lips were mere inches from my ear. He'd snuck up on us as soundlessly as if he didn't even ripple the air. I spun, looking him up and down. How was he on his feet after losing so much blood? He was still pale. He was still drenched in blood from his wound.

He swayed slightly but kept to his feet.

"The horses are mine, Grosbeak. Left here before this little adventure. We'll race the playing cards to the heart of Pensmoore."

Ridiculous. I scowled at him and took the key from my bodice. "If you can walk, then you can walk yourself into your room of wives with me and rest there. You're in no shape to ride anything right now."

He smirked at me and took the key, but he didn't open the door, instead, he tucked it back into my dress, his fingers brushing the neckline in a way that made my cheeks hot as a blacksmith's furnace and limped to the wild-eyed horse. I watched the army warily, but they did not turn aside to us.

"Stop dawdling," Grosbeak complained. "They won't stop for us. They obey orders and there's no one here to order them to go after us. We're safe enough."

They still made me nervous. Like a snake you could see slithering in the grass not far away – no matter that it was not poisonous, there was always the fear that it might be.

Bluebeard caught my hand and drew me to the horse. The stallion stamped a wary hoof, but Bluebeard stilled him with a hand, reaching into a leather-tooled saddlebag and drawing from it clothing, which he handed to me.

"This is your horse. You put him here," I acknowledged. "That's very practical of you."

He didn't reply, but he reached into the other saddlebag and drew out a clean shirt, changing swiftly despite the severity of his injuries. I glimpsed other bruises and cuts on his exposed skin while he dressed and when he was done, he looked at me with a raised eyebrow.

"I know you can speak to me," I said, steeling myself for the worst.

His eyes tightened into narrow slits, all the more worrying in their cat-like regard. And then he did speak.

Faithless and Feckless you may be, but I am not. Though you sell me to my enemies, still I honor you as wife. But speak to my riddle, you sensible monstrosity. Why will the ruffed grouse refuse to be tamed? Why will a plant not grow in salted soil? Why does the heart refuse to trust?

Just looking at his expression left my mouth dry but if ever I wanted a chance to still be allies, now was that time. I took a long breath and said what I must.

"I have seen how you are a violent man, killing whomever you please, and dealing with each according to your own judgment."

His head cocked to the side. *And you thought that wrong? When have I ever been anything but good to you? Did I not just snatch your skin from the flayer?*

"You have been other than good to many people," I said, twisting the clothing in my hands. "But I own that I am in your debt and the debt is so great that I cannot repay it."

You cannot judge how I treat others because you are not them. Tell me, have I ever betrayed you*? Ever been violent or unjust or cruel to* you*?*

He took a step forward as if he couldn't help himself. My lip trembled.

"I cannot tell you yes."

He was inches away now, leaning in, his own lips trembling over ragged breaths. I could almost taste his breath in mine, that ever-lingering hint of mint bidding me to lean forward into it.

Then tell me no, for my ears long to hear my justification.

"You have never been cruel to me," I whispered and I gasped as his hand grabbed my waist and drew me against him so suddenly that I couldn't catch my breath before he leaned in and stole away a kiss. It was gentle but swift, sweet but bitter.

But you have broken off a shard of me with your betrayal and left in me a never-healing wound. And yet, I have purchased you with my rib, sealed our vow with my sacrifice, and made you utterly my own. And how shall you honor this, fire of my eyes? How shall you meet my fervent devotion?

"It won't heal?" I gasped. He hadn't let go of me, though his kiss had ended. I wanted more, as if one kiss was just not enough – which was insane since he was almost as dangerous to me as the Sword – whether married to me and my rescuer or not, for when this speech of his was done, he would sweep me back into his mad ambitions and this gamble of his to save my land and people.

The Sword marked me with water-tempered Wittenbrand steel. And such a mark by one Wittenbrand to another had no cure I know.

"Then you'll die?" I was aghast resting my hand gently on

the uninjured part of his waist. He half-closed his eyes, leaning into my hand as if he liked the feeling and then he sprang away, snatched his blade back from my hand, and slid it into his scabbard – so sudden that he left me reeling at the shock of his changing moods.

I have grown attached to my immortality. It would be a shame to lose it now. Dress, you sober monstrosity. I brought you clothing from home.

I changed hurriedly, confusion topmost in my roiling emotions. I was relieved to be rid of the Sword's horrible dress with its collar and imprisoning skirts and I was surprised by what Bluebeard had brought me. It was blue – as everything he owned seemed to be – but it was more akin to his clothing than what he'd given me before. There was a frothy, rabbit-trimmed shirt, a pair of dark, fitted trousers, high, ruddy boots, and a periwinkle jacket embroidered all over with little figures. When I looked closely at the fabric, I blanched. The jacket seemed to depict the Sword, sewn carefully with his scarlet coat and golden curls, but each depiction of him was the size of my first finger and in each one he was being killed in a new and more gruesome manner so that long consideration of my jacket would turn the stomach of even the staunchest warrior.

I put it on hastily, trying not to look too discomfited. At least it fit well. The fur-lined collar went up to my chin and the sleeves widened over my hands with a fur cuff that gave enough warmth to battle the spring chill. Across the waist and breast, someone had set a number of purely decorative straps and buckles in the same ruddy leather as my boots. It made me look formidable. It was a statement that I found I enjoyed almost too much.

"Thank you for the clothing," I said quietly.

Courtesy of the mirror. Bluebeard shrugged from where he

stood as I dressed, his back to me, his eyes studying the playing card army. There seemed no end to them. *He seems to love the Sword as much as I do. Though I reserve my greatest fury for young Coppertomb who thought to entomb me in my own affections. I will enjoy disabusing him of the notion of his cleverness.*

I cleared my throat and he turned as I lifted Grosbeak again.

"No clothing for me?" Grosbeak asked and we both ignored him. "Not even a hat? You stopped to get her a full wardrobe."

I faced Bluebeard squarely and drew myself up to my full height.

His eyes sparkled at that with something that almost looked like hope.

"You ask for loyalty. You ask that I match your sacrifice with my own." I nodded. "You're right to ask me for that. I promised you I would be your ally. I broke my promise. But what can I give you when you already possess everything that is mine from the clothing on my back to my very hours and days? What can I give you when I have married you, and taken your home as mine, and left the remains of my family behind? What else is there to give?"

Your heart remains your own.

"And is that what you would have of me? The one last thing that I maintain of my own?" I was proud of myself. My voice did not shake at all.

Yes, he prowled toward me like a big cat stalking prey in the high grass. *I would have the whole of it dedicated only and always to me.*

"It is not so easy a thing to do. I cannot cut it from my body and place it in a crown for you," I said dryly. "And I cannot prove that I was tricked – that I did not intend to betray you, that I will not do it again."

Prove it to me by not *being tricked again. Prove it to me with no more betrayals. Prove it to me with the gift of your heart.*

Once more, he was inches away, and I thought he might kiss me again but instead, he blinked as if coming awake from a dream, reached into his pocket, plucked out a bone whistle the length of his thumb, and played a single note.

If you cannot gift it in whole, then gift it in slivers and I will reassemble it within my own breast and guard it there in the sanctuary of my immortal soul.

I opened my mouth, meaning to answer – though what did a person say to *that*? – when a drum rolled fast and certain and out of the shadows Bluebeard's band appeared. With their arrival, the moment was lost, though not the offer or the promise.

CHAPTER EIGHT

It was Vireo who crashed through the trees first, riding one of the ghostly elk of the Wittenbrand.

"You whistled?" he asked, flicking blood from the end of his naked blade. His brow was sweat-slicked, and his elk stained in streaks of red, his feet blackened with ash and soot.

"The sacking of Aafgaard?" Bluebeard asked crisply, mounting in a single movement despite his pale face and bleeding side.

Aafgaard must have been the city we just left.

"We hit them hard and fast," Vireo said. "A raid, not an occupation. And his enchanted cards were already on the move when we hit, just as you planned." He pointed at the army of playing cards still marching by. "It will take them some time to deal with the damage and bury their dead. Enough time, perhaps to deal with his enchanted soldiers before they arrive at Pensmoore City."

My eyes widened. That army of magical … things … was headed to Pensmoore City. And they were so set on it that they had not turned back to defend Aafgaard. I swallowed. That was my people we were speaking of. Perhaps not my actual family anymore – and my heart hurt for Svetgin at the thought of that. Had he survived the battle I'd just escaped? – but Pensmoore was still my home in a way I couldn't explain and the idea of them being overrun by this playing card army upset me in a way I couldn't fully explain.

Bluebeard offered me a hand up to ride pillion, but I shook his hand away and mounted myself. He shouldn't be pulling me into position. He shouldn't be riding at all in his current state. He was going to make his injury worse.

I was settling myself when Sparrow's elk emerged from the forest, running to join us. She had a haunted look in her eyes as she crossed the field.

"You should stash her back at your house or in one of those rooms you carry around with you," Vireo said, gesturing to me, as they waited for Sparrow. His mouth twisted, his eyes on me. "You need her days, perhaps, but she's no friend to us now."

"Is she not?" Bluebeard asked, suddenly frosty.

Sparrow pulled her elk in, her breath gusting and her cheeks flushed as if she'd just ridden hard and fast.

"Will you declare that she is still your bride when she has sold you to your enemies and slain you alive?" Vireo asked, his voice full of disbelief. He did not even look at Sparrow as her head swiveled back and forth as she watched the other two speak. "You've paid in blood and pain for her treachery."

I felt my face grow hot. He was not wrong. The practical thing would be to keep me out of their way where I could do no more harm.

"Does the earth have no bones then, Vireo?" Bluebeard asked. His voice was the voice of the winter when it rolled down from the high passes. "Have the tides ceased to ebb and flow with the breath of our sovereign? Have the ages ceased to pass and fail, and the waters below the earth risen up and swallowed her whole? Is this what you have come to me to declare?"

Vireo shifted uncomfortably in his saddle. "You know I have not."

And now my husband's voice snapped like a whip. "Then understand this – that we remain one, and if she has sacrificed a piece of my flesh, then that was hers to give – for my body is dedicated to her and to no other."

Vireo's mouth dropped open, forming the beginnings of unspoken words before discarding them, trying again, and then finally settling into furious horror.

"If you're done questioning our lord, then I have news," Sparrow said, letting her elk step closer to Bluebeard's horse.

It was a measure of Vireo's shock that he let her push past him. Our horse stepped sideways uncomfortably. I patted his flank to calm him. He and I were the two mortal creatures here. We needed to stick together. Grosbeak swiveled on the end of his pole, eyes bright with cunning as he absorbed every word.

"Speak your message, Sparrow."

"I went to the drop point, but the messages there are not good. Rouranmoore pleads with us to ally. Ships from Quranmoore and Salamoore are spotted just off from the Rouranmoore coast. Either we make her our ally, or she will be lost by the next moon."

Bluebeard cursed violently.

"I was just leaving with that message when the Bramble King raised the silver flag," she continued, her face growing more sober still.

Bluebeard and Vireo froze, all other thoughts forgotten.

"I missed it?" Bluebeard asked, face white.

Sparrow shook her head, "I hope you'll forgive my ambitions, but I …" she seemed to have to take a breath to say this next part. "I stood in your place to receive the message."

Bluebeard and Vireo were so still that my nerves shuddered.

"Oh ho!" Grosbeak roared, unconcerned by our consternation. "You've a rival, Vireo! She declares a loyalty you don't feel, doesn't she?"

"Shut that garish slash you call a mouth, Grosbeak." Vireo muttered but his face was flushed, and his hand kept gripping the handle of his sword.

"What does it mean that she took the message?" I asked calmly.

"Don't tell her," Vireo snapped, his outstretched finger pointed at Grosbeak. "She betrayed us once and she'll do it again."

Bluebeard snapped his fingers and the flesh on Vireo's pointing hand crumpled suddenly as if it had aged, and aged, and then died and was nothing more than desiccating flesh on useless bones.

Vireo gasped, pulling the hand back and clutching it to his chest.

"You're a fool, Arrow," he spat, so furious he was vibrating. "She's not one of us. Not born to us. And she's done nothing worthy of us. She has no place among us. Quote your marriage vows to me all you want but I cannot fathom why you would give her your loyalty over me – me, who has been with you these past hundreds of years – or Sparrow who has done the same."

"I married her in the Wittenbrand way," Bluebeard said so quietly that I barely heard the words, and Vireo had to lean forward to hear them. "You saw it, for you were in attendance. It is a thing I have never done before and will never do again." At that, Grosbeak gasped as if utterly shocked by his words. Bluebeard's voice grew louder and became authoritative. "In so doing, I have shifted my poles and turned the tides of my heart, I have made her north star and center, a treasured treasurer, a well of souls. And those who would call me friend must honor that or they dishonor me. What say you, Vireo? Are you still among my band?"

"I am," he spat it so quickly that I barely caught the words, but I did catch my husband's snap of his fingers.

Vireo's hand was instantly living flesh again. He sagged as it was restored.

"Gather up the creature they call a king and bring him to meet me at the war camp," Bluebeard instructed. "We shall join you there as quickly as it is possible and make what plans we must."

Vireo nodded, but his face was still twisted as if in pain as he rode away on the white elk.

We watched him go, the air around us as thick as a down-filled bolster.

"In receiving the message on his behalf," Grosbeak said distinctly, breaking the tension, "Sparrow has sealed her fate with her lord's. If he fails, she will fail with him and receive the same forfeit – her immortality."

Shock is a thing that tastes of vinegar. My eyes widened as it washed over me, and I met Sparrow's eyes. She nodded curtly but she was not hostile to me as Vireo had been – merely indifferent.

"And if she succeeds?" I breathed.

"She will have a taste of the same reward," Grosbeak said, smiling in his speculation.

"Lord Riverbarrow," Sparrow said formally, ignoring us. "The Bramble King invites you and all the others to solve his riddle. He had put a personal stake into the turning of Ages this time. For while you play your everlasting game, he offers another within it."

"And what is his riddle?" Bluebeard asked.

"I am the culmination of desire, the fruit of death. I am the summit of loss, the passing of weight. What am I?"

"And was there any more to it?" Bluebeard pushed.

Sparrow nodded. "As he was closing his eyes he whispered, 'His glory fades.' Does that mean something to you?"

Bluebeard tapped his chin. "Perhaps it does. Lead the way, Sparrow. We ride for the war camp."

CHAPTER NINE

Our route avoided the card army, but at the first village we found, Bluebeard stopped and signaled to Sparrow who dropped down and ran into the nearest house. I felt a pang of homesickness at the sight of the hamlet. It reminded me too much of home. The small houses were thatched with the same steep roofs, the same type of ridgepole was stuck through the thatch with its figurehead carved on the end to protect the entrance to the house. A similar thatched roof was set on poles over the community well in the center of the village. I remembered drinking from a well just like that when my father brought me on his inspections of the outer villages. I could almost taste the goat's cheese and radishes I'd been fed.

"I thought we were in a hurry," Grosbeak complained.

"If I had to guess, I'd think she was warning people who still have living bodies to take theirs somewhere safe," I said, pushing back a wave of homesickness.

"What does it matter if they survive? They're only mortals."

I let the words hang in the air a long time before I replied. "Perhaps I'll find a new pet. One with more compassion. A polecat, perhaps, or a scorpion."

Grosbeak grunted. "Don't expect apologies from me. I neither give them nor receive them."

But I was annoyed enough to stuff his pole through the saddlebag strap instead of holding it myself. It would be a rougher ride, but I wouldn't need to apologize since he didn't accept apologies.

A man ran out from behind the house before Sparrow had returned. He flung himself to the dust in front of Bluebeard's horse and something in me tightened. He was too close to the stallion's hooves and Bluebeard had chosen a horse just like himself – arrogant and fierce. What if he kicked the man's head in? His hands were worn from farm work, but someone had carefully patched his shirt. He was loved. He would be missed.

"Mercy on us, lord of the Wittenbrand," he said.

"I am not here to judge but to warn," Bluebeard said. "An army spreads across the land, marching not far from here to the west. You should flee further east. Your village lies too close to their path."

The man bobbed his head, eyes still downcast. "Are you Lord Riverbarrow? The patron of Pensmoore?"

Bluebeard grunted. "Where have you heard that name?"

"From my grandad when I was just a tad on his knee," the man said hurriedly. "He told a story from his own grandfather of a one who had stood for our lands long ago, keeping us safe from the wrath of the earth. Was that you, Lord of the Wittenbrand?"

My brow furrowed. In my time, I had met people who feared the Wittenbrand and spoke of them in hushed tones. I'd seen them send peddlers off with loud curses because they sold blue garments. I'd heard the whispered hushes when a storyteller tried to spin a story of their lands for a night in a warm bed. But I had never met anyone who was so close as this to worship.

"What is it you ask of me, mortal," Bluebeard asked.

"Patron, help me. My son is gravely ill."

Behind him, there was a sudden commotion as Sparrow left the cottage. Spilling out behind her were children and women dashing in every direction. Heeding her warning, they were gathering what they could to take with them as they fled.

"Why think you to ask me for healing?" Bluebeard asked.

"You're the patron for our lands – you stand for them. You plead for us before your own sovereign. Won't you plead now? Are you not one with our lands?"

Bluebeard smirked. "Through my wife, I am indeed. Ask her if she is willing. I shall abide by her choice."

The eyes of the man looked up to me, pleading and vulnerable.

"My boy," he pled, his voice rough with unshed tears. "Please."

Bluebeard's eyes rested on me, too, and when I met them, I nodded firmly. I did not care what price he took and of course, there would be one.

"Bring your son here," Bluebeard demanded.

The man rose, gesturing urgently behind his back. A curtain in the window twitched. We'd been watched all along.

And then a pair of men came clambering out of the cottage, a blanket held between them. A small boy lay pale and sweating on the blanket.

Bluebeard set his mouth grimly as if he could feel the boy's twisting pains. He wiped a hand over his face and then leaned toward me and took a kiss delicately from my lips.

Gasps of relief and shock filled the air. When my head was no longer spinning, I looked down to see the little boy standing up and leaping into his relieved father's arms.

"Sparrow," Bluebeard barked. "Manage the warnings, or I'll be stripped of her days before their needs."

Sparrow bowed her head slightly as Bluebeard kicked the stallion. The great beast leapt forward, and in a moment, I'd lost sight entirely of the happy child and his terrified village. I'd lost sight of Sparrow or the people she was warning. I didn't need to see them. Their faces were engraved on the lids of my eyes, and I saw them every time I blinked. My husband had the power to heal anyone – everyone. He could heal all the world.

"I suppose one might say I'm greedy to hold such power to my breast, wouldn't you say, Grosbeak," Bluebeard said as if reading my mind. He must hate having to speak to me through our go-between, though why he didn't just simply speak to my mind was a mystery.

"I … take … every … opportunity … to insult you … Arrow," Grosbeak managed, his head pounding wildly at the end of his chain without my grip to soften the blows. Served him and his smug immortality right.

"Indeed, you do," Bluebeard said. "But still I have decided to impart wisdom to you. For I have but one wife now, and I must bargain every blessing I can from her days before they are gone and used, and I am left bereft."

His explanation was clearly for me but why didn't he say it within my mind?

"You've granted her … a … great honor … never before seen … that a mortal … would live with the Wittenbran … d … as wife," Grosbeak agreed before shaking his lips like a horse, letting spit fly in every direction.

I grimaced.

"And yet, though she is now my heart, I will spend her like water through a net," Bluebeard said ruefully. "I will spend her land and perhaps even that boy she just gave a day for. I will spend, and spend, and spend even if it takes the last drop of my own blood to accomplish what I must."

I shivered. For I knew it was true, but what could be of such value that he would give everything for it? Forget the sovereign's puzzle – *this* was the puzzle I would need to figure out. Especially since my violent husband promised me his enduring commitment one minute and that he would use me up for this mysterious purpose in the next.

But as we galloped away from the little village, a realization dawned over me. The last time I had ridden across the landscape of Pensmoore, it had been on the way to Pensmoore City where my father was bent on finding me a match and the most I could hope for then was a man who would be kind to me and if I was truly lucky, might even be faithful. I had hoped for respect. I had not thought it reasonable to expect love.

And here I was married to an unpredictable Wittenbrand who had not just given me marriage vows but had declared I was to be considered his equal and his most precious associate – though I had neither earned my place through birth nor deeds. It was a respect that was more than I could have hoped for. It was a position higher than I'd ever hoped to reach.

And what was I to do with all this loyalty? What was I to do with all this honor?

The weight of it troubled me.

Perhaps, I should try to be more than an ally. Perhaps I should consider that he truly wanted me to be his wife.

Was it possible that with respect we could have … companionship? Deep friendship? Sometimes the way he spoke made me almost think of love. And I knew my heart was slipping over the edge of it, but it would be willfully ignorant to let it. He was an impulsive, energetic person – ingenious, vibrant, and horrifically violent. Did he know what love was? Would he love as violently as he lived?

The thought of it stuck in my throat like the bone of a fish and I could not dislodge it no matter how hard I beat at it or tried to press from every side. Before I could dislodge it, I would need to know what it was he felt so desperate for that he was willing to give my life.

Bluebeard was wandering just as deep down his own mental paths – or I assumed as much for he did not speak.

Morning came and went and still we rode. He moved me to a spot in front of him so he could play with my hair again, tying little knots as we rode in silence, but though the forest acted strangely around him – the birds whirling up in the trees as if greeting a friend, the branches waving to him and flowers springing up anywhere he set a foot – still this land was to the Wittenbrand like a garment beat against the rocks too many times. The color had seeped away and with it, my sense of place and home. What was this place to me now? What loyalty did I owe it? What part of my heart did *it* have?

But thinking of that brought to mind the face of that small boy and I could not say I did not care because spikes of compassion shot through me at the thought of him fleeing with his father – healed but not safe. Someone must stand for these people. And Bluebeard had offered me the choice of how to spend my day – to offer or withhold it from the boy. What did that mean? Did it mean he was offering me the chance to be an equal with him in standing for my nation? Was I the right choice for that?

Lost in thought, I pondered all this. And Bluebeard played with my hair. We rode easily together, moving in concert, easy near one another despite our painful injuries and stiff limbs.

Sparrow would warn the villages behind us, so Bluebeard pushed his horse hard, gaining ground until we passed the marching playing cards. He winced from time to time, grasping his wounded side, but when I reached to check his injury, he shook his head, moving my hands aside.

"It's awfully quiet," Grosbeak announced when the hours grew long, and then he launched into a rowdy tavern song.

Bluebeard shut him up with a cuff to the cheek.

"That hurts, you know. I still feel pain!"

"So do I," Bluebeard said. "Your voice saws through my nerves worse than the Sword's blade ever could."

After that, Grosbeak remained silent.

We found a stream wending through the meadows at midday, a small bridge crossing it on the road. A bird trilled in the trees as our horse's hooves struck the bridge and Bluebeard cocked his head to the side. And then another trilled. He frowned, turning our horse off the road and into the trees.

"What is it?" I whispered.

He pressed a finger to my lips, listening.

We'd come out to a little clearing, and in the center of the glen on a cut stump, someone had placed an egg the size of my hand woven from grass.

Bluebeard tilted his head slightly to the side, eyes glittering. This was not right. You did not just see woven eggs sitting in clearings in the mortal world.

I looked from side to side, suspicious.

And there it was. A boat flipped over but half-submerged along the river. It should be pulled properly up on the shore. And over there, someone had hastily hidden chopped firewood behind pine boughs.

But Bluebeard was already urging the horse forward.

Ambush! I cried in my mind, trying not to alert the predators waiting for us. *Ambush!*

Nonsense.

He wasn't listening.

I turned in the saddle and shoved him backward with all my might. His eyes widened as he lost his seat, and then turned his fall into a flip and landed in the soft grass at the same moment that a crossbow bolt *thunked* into my shoulder.

Pain flared through me, roaring and overwhelming. I tried to blink it back. Tried to clear my head but I was already being dragged off the horse and into the bushes. I fought against my captor, blindly, desperately.

Easy. Easy now.

It was Bluebeard. I drew a shuddering breath, but his hands

had left me, and all I saw were his boots as he stood beside me, and then even they were gone as he leapt from sight.

I shoved down a wave of nausea fighting the pain and the sense that I needed to get up and *move.*

I pushed up to hands and knees, buckling and seeing red at the pain in my shoulder that came with that movement.

I was just in time to see Bluebeard leap like a cat onto the back of a man holding a crossbow and bolt. My husband swayed as he plunged his sword into the man's neck and then spun to land in front of a second man, sword neatly slashing his throat.

Bluebeard spun again, already on to the next attacker and the next, a whirlwind that sent out streaks of blood instead of raindrops.

And all I'd done was … well, I'd done nothing, as usual. Why did he want me along when he was better off fighting alone? I did nothing but slow him down.

"Psst … Izolda," Grosbeak said. He was lying on the grass beside me. He must have been dropped in the attack.

I looked up muzzily just as a crossbow bolt thunked beside me. I needed cover. I needed it now. I couldn't find any. The trees were all too far away.

There was a scream, and when I looked over, Bluebeard was severing a man's head from his body. He scooped it up, two heads in one hand now as he stalked forward. But his enemies were everywhere, coming out from under the overturned boat, leaping from their hiding places in the rushes, and dropping down from trees like deadly bats.

"Psst … grab me first!"

First? Before what? But I couldn't think – the thoughts wouldn't come – so instead I obeyed, snatching Grosbeak's pole up.

"The door! Go through the door!" he said.

Door?

"The key is around your neck."

"Oh. Yes." I fumbled for it, but my right arm was barely working now.

Bluebeard backed up to us, holding off three men with his fine swordsmanship and the help of the heads he held in one hand. Raising them kept blows back easier than a shield would.

"Come on!" Fear filled Grosbeak's every word, slicing into my foggy brain.

I found the key as another bolt hit the ground just a finger-width from Bluebeard's foot. My heart was in my throat, pain spiking through the rest of me in raw-mawed bursts.

"Open the door!" Grosbeak screamed.

I opened the door, remembering to grab the horse, and stumbled into the room.

"Bluebeard!" I called as I fell to my knees on the floor. Panicked breathing made my words rough-edged. "Bluebeard!"

The door was closing behind me – I didn't remember doing that last time. I'd saved Grosbeak and the horse and left the most important person behind. Horror roared through me like a forest fire.

And then he was there, crashing through the last sliver of open door before it closed, the heads he'd taken held in one hand and his bloody sword in the other.

I'd never seen anything so beautiful.

I was smiling as the world went dark.

CHAPTER TEN

I woke to gentle hands tending me. Someone had balled up the rug made from the striped creature and pillowed my head on it. One would think that would be luxurious, but it smelled of dust and dead animal. That same person had set out the three severed heads in a row beside me and put Grosbeak's on the end of the row.

"You should know that I would display very poorly," he said sourly, his eyes not on me. "Especially now that I have been hit, and knocked against walls, and used as a sword."

"You do not need to be pretty. You need only remind my enemies of my power."

Grosbeak snickered. "Is that what your mother told you?" His eyes settled on me. "Oh, she's awake."

The hands moved and then suddenly Bluebeard's cat's eyes came into view. They searched my face intently as he spoke in his mental voice.

"We've ruined another jacket. It seems I will need to employ a tailor exclusively for you – maybe even a dozen of them. You'll leave me destitute in the cost of clothing."

"It can be mended," I said faintly through gritted teeth. A moan escaped them despite my best efforts. My shoulder was radiating pain.

"Easy now. Easy." Bluebeard said, running a hand over my hair. *"Don't move until we've drawn this bolt out of your shoulder."*

"You're talking to me again," I gasped. "You wouldn't speak before."

"In the mortal world, our speaking between minds requires the use of magic, and I will spend a single one of your moments on such expressions. No thought I have is worth their expenditure."

It seemed sweet. But also very much something a man would think. As if leaving me to stew on what he might be thinking or wanting wasn't spending my time and efforts already.

"But you'll speak to me here." Little black spots danced over my vision. Don't pass out again, Izolda.

"In this little pocket of the Wittenbrand, magic lives free. I can spend enough of it to speak in your mind without spending your moments."

Well, that was fair enough. "Can you help my shoulder?"

My words came out more pleading than I'd hoped.

"Of course, he can," Grosbeak snickered. "He could heal you from any ill if he used up your days. But he won't do that. He needs them all for some grand plan of his. By the way, have you seen this place? It's creepy. And I'm saying that as someone who has a gaping wound at the end of his neck and possibly a fly infestation starting up."

"They're his wives," I said weakly. I must have lost some blood to feel so weak. I tilted my head just enough to look up at the nearest wife. Princess Margaretta with her tiny, pinched waist and her big golden curls.

Grosbeak snickered again. "And now, with you here, the collection is complete. I knew some of these mortals. Or at least, I saw him carry them into the Wittenbrand crowned with his flowers and carried in his arms."

Was that a stab of jealousy I felt at the thought? Or was it just the agony of a bolt in my shoulder. I swallowed against a dry throat.

"I'm going to draw out this crossbow bolt," Bluebeard said in my mind. "*We're lucky. It is not deep, though it struck bone and that may be a problem. But crossbow bolts are thrown like a dart with a heavy head, not launched like an arrow. People are often misled into thinking that they're more powerful than a good bow, but it's simply not true. The rogue was too far out of range and his dart hit your shoulder and penetrated through clothing and flesh but it has severed no major blood vessels and not caused the damage it would have if it had been a broadhead with a proper bleeder point.*"

"I remember how bright his eyes were with each of them – as if he had found a lost pearl," Grosbeak said, unaware of the conversation in our heads. "And now he stands them up in rows like little silver spoons in a case." I shivered but Grosbeak didn't stop as if he needed to say his piece and could not stop himself. "Did you know that we grew up together? The Arrow and Vireo and me? We tried to pull the arrow from the stone. We stole magic from open flowers and wrung little charms out of pixie wings. And now look at us."

"You betrayed me, Grosbeak," Bluebeard said grimly. "You deserve what's been done to you ten times over. A price paid in blood."

"She betrayed you, too. I don't see you claiming *her* head, though you've claimed her whole self, I suppose. What's her penalty? What's her price?"

"I paid her price myself in my own blood," Bluebeard growled, gesturing at his wounded side. "And I will go on paying it forever."

I gasped, tears springing to my eyes, and he froze.

"You've made me neglect my wife," he growled at Grosbeak. "Remain in silence or I will kick you across the room."

But my wound was not why the tears sprung to my eyes. It was his words that cut so deep. I had not known there would be a price for trying to cut myself free of him. But of course, there was. Of course. And of course, he had paid it. And wasn't he trying to pay some kind of similar price on behalf of his beleaguered people and mine?

Tears marred my vision, but I could just make out him producing a knife and stroking my hair again.

"I must cut this quarrel out. Be brave, wife."

I clenched my eyes shut as the knife sank in, and gritted my teeth together as the pain started, breathing hard and fast as he cut the quarrel free. The pain was a glass shard in my shoulder, cutting me even after the true damage was passed. It took long breaths before I could so much as open my eyes again.

"As I suspected. It may have bruised your bone, and ravaged your flesh, but this will heal. Stay still now. I've thread and needle in my bag."

"Did you see the woven egg?" I asked him, trying to distract my mind as he drew thread and needle from his bag and cleaned them both.

"It smelled of mint."

Interesting. I hadn't noticed that, but I *had* noticed his

particular fondness for mint.

"Do you think it was the Sword?"

"Too soon. We'd only just fled him."

"Coppertomb, then?"

"It was likely the mortals. Not all of them appreciate their 'patron.'"

"I don't think so," I whispered as the needle but my skin. "I think that someone plans to murder you, husband."

He froze. Had I said something wrong?

He leaned in close so that his lips were bare inches from mine, and I could feel his breath against my lips.

"Say that again." His mental voice was a caress. I shivered at the sound of it.

"Someone plans to murder you. Husband."

He shivered, eyes closed and a smile on his face. *"That, I could listen to all day long."*

"You love to hear of plots on your life?"

"I love to hear you address me as husband."

"In this place where fifteen others have done the same?" I couldn't keep the wryness from my tone.

His face fell and he returned to stitching my flesh. He'd cut my coat and shirt away from the wound and they gaped open lending to the strange intimacy of him mending my body for me. If it was a loving thing to mend a coat for your beloved, was it not more loving still to mend her flesh?

"I hate this place," he confessed. *"Each face you see is a failure of mine. Each book, the story of my dereliction. Think you that the wound in my side will never heal? This is a thousand times worse for it is the wound in my soul that cannot heal – the plan hatched a thousand years ago that has failed and failed and failed."*

"And what is the plan, exactly?" I asked, anticipation filling me. This was it, at last. I could feel the edges of it as if by understanding this one thing, I could understand everything about him.

He looked down at me and his lips parted on his inhumanly beautiful face and for a moment I thought he might answer. His cat's eyes were wide and vulnerable, and they made his tousled hair and thickened blue beard look almost boyish.

But he shook his head. "*No. Not now. I will not confess this yet. For though I have borne the sorrow and agony of your betrayal in my own flesh, I dare not open this to you, also, lest you plant your traitor blade in its back and destroy us all.*"

I gasped and he shook his head and returned to his methodical stitching, his touches against my skin gentle – oh so gentle – but his words had wounded me far more deeply than any quarrel could.

He was just to judge me. Right to protect himself from me. So, then, why did it hurt so much? Why did it wound so deeply?

I bit back tears. Ridiculous, Izolda. You have let him mislead you with pretty words. You are no more the trusted wife than Grosbeak is.

"That was a trap back there," I said, changing the subject to something where I could be helpful. "And it was not a trap laid by mortals. Nor, as you have stated, was it likely laid by the Sword or Coppertomb. Which means that one of your other rivals is trying to assassinate you and that they know the exact way to draw you in."

His mouth twisted wryly.

"*What makes you so certain?*"

"No mortal would be lured into an obvious trap by nothing more than a grass egg."

He laughed – to my surprise. "*They did not contend with my mortal wife's eyes. But you are not wrong I think.*" He lifted the quarrel with care and to my shock, the arrowhead evaporated in a puff of purple smoke. "*This is laced with Sapporous a Wittenbrand poison that saps away control over magic. You, being mortal, are unaffected.*"

"But it would have rendered you helpless," I agreed.

He shrugged – the motion of his tightening muscles reminding me that he had more danger in him than just magic – and flung the shaft to the side, drawing out a soft cloth from his saddlebag and winding it around my shoulder.

"*If they wish me dead, they will have to send better assassins.*"

"If you wish to live, you might think about knowing where their assassins will be," I countered. He needed spies. More of them and better than what he had.

He took up another of the rugs – a sheepskin dyed purple – and draped it over me for warmth.

"*Sleep now,*" he suggested. "*And in a few hours' time, we will mount the horse and gallop through the door and hopefully they will have dispersed or will be so startled that we will be free and clear.*"

"Will time pass differently here, as it does in the

Wittenhame?" I asked and he shrugged.

"Sometimes it does. And sometimes it does not."

I nodded but the gesture felt hollow. He did not trust me enough to confide in me – not even enough to tell me whether we could trust time in this place. Buying my debt to him with his own blood, elevating me to a respected position – these were gifts. But without his confidences, without his trust, what did they matter?

I shifted and squirmed, and while the pain in my shoulder ate at me like a furtive mouse with a block of cheese, the doubts in my mind ate at me more. For with every day that I stood by my husband's side, I lost the ties to my own people, to my own past. Svetgin was back there somewhere. Hopefully, he had survived the attack on the city. Hopefully, the Sword was not angry with him for my escape. I could have allied myself more fully with him. I could have chosen the Sword over Bluebeard and sealed my chance to live again alongside my brother.

But I had chosen my husband, and though he had chosen me in some ways, there were still rooms in his heart locked so far away that this little key could not open them. I could not still my anxious mind to rest with that forever chewing away at my edges.

After long minutes, a hand reached out and touched my arm and I shifted enough to see that Bluebeard had settled down in his own bundled rugs close enough to touch me.

He left his hand on my arm, and though it did not heal the gnawing or fill the hollowness in my breast, it was just enough comfort to help me surrender into sleep.

CHAPTER ELEVEN

In the tales told by mothers to their children through the ages of my land, there is always a common thread – in every happy ending there are the seeds of the next tragedy and in every deep calamity there is still the possibility to wrench happiness from the clawed fingers of fate.

I woke to my fate staring intently at me with his cat's eyes glowing like twin stars.

"Your injuries must be checked, and needs attended to as quickly as possible, and then we will leave this haunted cavern – this place that makes my belly roll and my heart lurch – and face our enemies full in the teeth."

"When you say 'haunted cavern' are you talking about this wedding gift you gave me?" I offered dryly. "If I knew you thought so poorly of it, perhaps I would not have accepted it. A husband's gifts are meant to show his regard for his wife."

My own belly was lurching, the muscles around the quarrel puncture stiff and agonized. I tried to sit and blinked back tears.

"And so my gift does, for does not laying bare my failures make me vulnerable to your knife? In drawing back my shirt and leaving you a clear path to my heart, do I not offer you what I would give no other?"

"You gave it to fifteen others," I said gesturing to those very women, still and ominous on their pillars. My face felt hot as my body fought to heal me.

He made a brushing motion with his hand as if I was missing the point and then reached out to help me sit up.

"Today's ride will be hard on you. But you are made of strong fiber and a copper will. I think you will survive it," he said as he carefully removed my jacket. His hands quick as they worked to undress me and my cheeks burned so hotly I feared they would be damaged as he stripped the layers separating us. This time their flush was not from my injury.

With a touch so delicate that I barely felt it, he loosened the ties of my shirt and slid the rabbit-lined collar down over my shoulder so he could tend my wound there. I held the rest of my shirt up with blushing modesty, watching as he unwound my bandage and then frowned.

" This wound is not mortal wrought, as you well know, or It would have healed more by now." He blew on it, startling me and sending a rush of heat through my core. *"One of my fellows has tried to assassinate me. But which one? That is the question. And it needs an answer."*

He bathed the wound, wrapped it again, and then gently turned me around so he could loosen my ties even further and let my shirt slip down my back to my waist while I clutched it to my breast with a trembling hand.

"Your back is healing, though. I will snip these silver stitches for you later, wife, but they need salve now. You should know the scars have a longevity beyond the healing."

"Scars do not bother me," I said, my voice trembling.

He leaned around me in the sudden way he had and caught my chin, looking into my eyes as if he'd find the answer to a riddle there.

"If they do not bother you, then why do your cheeks flame scarlet? Why do you tremble with every breath as if you are afraid I will set you to fire or rip you apart entirely?"

My gasp was involuntary but the way his lips parted in response to it was enough to unfurl the last shreds of certainty I still had.

"You said you do not sully yourself with mortal brides and yet here you are, undressing me piece by piece."

He frowned. *"Your innocence is safe with me, wife. Have I not told you so?"*

"Did you say the same to all of them?" I asked, gathering courage under the clouded eyes of all the other brides he'd had. "Did you look each of them in their lovely faces – so much prettier than mine – and tell them you would not share their favors?"

"Each of them heard the same from my lips." His eyes were still drinking in mine – still trying to draw something out that I didn't know was there. It was not helping with the blushing or with the flipping and spinning of my belly.

"But why?" I gasped.

"I made a vow of chastity."

"What?" I asked and now he ducked his head, as if somehow embarrassed, and he retreated around my back as if he were safer there. "For how long?"

"As long as it takes."

I felt the sting of salve as he applied it to my healing back.

My mouth felt dry. "But whatever for?"

"I have been awaiting my true bride and the wait is worthy of the maiden."

What should I say to that? What should I say, looking out over all the others, standing imperiously on their pillars, faces blank in death, eyes glazed with the passing of all their dreams, perfect bodies preserved forever?

He was not entirely the monster I thought he was. Not entirely, but still, it was there. He had not taken *everything* from them, but he had burned their days like logs in a fire. And yet, that gesture, that nod to their humanity and value – that he had not also used them for his own amusement – it made my heart ache with some emotion I could not name.

"Then I hope that you find her someday," I said in a small voice as his fingers traced the healing wounds of my back, applying this healing salve of his.

His touch was so delicately soft that it was like a lover's caress. Was it the first time he'd traced patterns on a woman's back? Was he as new to the way it pulled at his breath in the same way that I was new to it?

He cleared his throat and pulled my shirt back up for me and I felt the strangest feeling of regret as he helped me back into my jacket and all the tight tension that had filled my every muscle lessened. With the lessening, the pain in my shoulder flared hotter.

"It will be a hard ride for you, but ride we must," he said in my mind, changing the subject as if we hadn't just shared an intimacy. *"But we must ride out now, before we lose the element of*

surprise. We'll prepare, mount the horse, and then you'll turn the key, and we'll gallop from this place at full speed. My hope is that they won't be able to respond fast enough to stop us. And then we'll ride hard and fast to the war camp."

I nodded, taking a sip of water from a waterskin he offered me.

"We only slept an hour or two at most. They shouldn't have had time to gather reinforcements."

He was back to being a lord of the Wittenbrand – intense, strategizing, unafraid.

And I was back to being Izolda, not sure if I was sowing seeds of peace or reaping a whirlwind. With Bluebeard, I was probably doing both.

"I need to look at your wound before we ride," I said, reaching for him, but he batted my hands away.

"*There's nothing that can be done for that, fire of my eyes,*" he told me mentally. "*A Wittenbrand wound it is, and a Wittenbrand wound it will remain.*"

I raised an eyebrow but left him alone. If he wanted to keep bleeding through his shirt like an endless blood spring, well, he was a grown Wittenbrand and he could do as he wished.

In a matter of minutes, we were mounted again. Bluebeard set me to ride behind him.

"*I plan to fight my way free, and I don't want you to take any more quarrels for me,*" he explained as he offered me Grosbeak's pole.

My bodiless friend woke with a scream and then blinked several times. "Oh, we're still here. How disappointing."

"Where did you think we'd be?" I asked, braiding my mussed hair as Bluebeard tied the heads he'd collected to the saddlebags behind me. He was tying them by their hair, which felt far too similar to what I was doing. I hoped I didn't end up a bodiless head.

"Heaven. Hell. I know not, but not in your lover's death closet."

I glanced around at the spacious room, its denizens keeping their silent, judging watch. The hourglass at the back of the room made a tinkling sound as one of my garnets broke free and fell to the bottom bulb of the glass. The room was many things, but not a closet. I shivered, glad to be leaving it again.

"Keep your tongue in your mouth or lose it, too," Bluebeard growled at Grosbeak as he mounted. "You're traitor to your people and a blemish on your family name."

"You would know," Grosbeak said sourly. "It was you who killed my father after he cheated the Duskatain. And yet, can a Wittenbrand cheat? Is that not *who we are?* Is it not how we soar in this world? To ask us to do otherwise is to ask a leopard not to wear spots. *You* are cheating. I know you are. That's what this grand plan of yours is really – some way to cheat at the great game of crowns. Or maybe to cheat death once more. But you condemned him for the same. You were barely higher than his waist when you took his head and claimed the Duskatain as your redeemed vassals. You took half my birthright that day. You took my family name. So don't talk to me about blemishes."

Bluebeard cuffed him coldly and I froze as he growled into Grosbeak's face. "Don't talk to me at all."

And then he drew his blade and said, "My wife has named this blade true. Edgeworthy she was called, Edgeworthy she shall be. Brace yourself, traitorous Grosbeak. We've heads to free from bodies today."

"*The key, if you please, wife.*"

With a shaking hand, I drew the key out of my bodice.

Ready or not, here we come.

I turned the key in the air and Bluebeard kicked the stallion with a cry of, "Ha!"

CHAPTER TWELVE

When I was a small girl, my mother would tell us the story of the Wild Hunt.

"Deep in the darkest place in the forest," she would say, "rides the Wild Hunt. Led by the Redblood Stag and mounted on antlered wolves, the Wittenbrand ride to kill, and rend, and tear. Each visage is hard as stone, carved by the wind and their cruel acts. They sniff the wind and then they streak out in each direction. They are falling stars, wandering planets, heavenly demons bringing the gift of death. And if they smell mortal flesh they pounce, ripping, and tearing, and shredding to pieces." And then she'd pounce herself, tickling us like mad before falling restless into the blankets beside us and saying, "But I will keep you safe, little bugs."

There was no mother to keep me safe this time, no one but Bluebeard.

I turned the key and we leapt from the hidden room back into the forest clearing. Someone screamed and then men were scattering in every direction as I fought to remember to turn the key again and close our little room. It shut just in time, almost slicing one of our ambushers clean in half. He drew back, sword rattling as he drew it from the scabbard. I spun then, ignoring his cry to keep my eyes on what we were doing.

Warriors rushed in from every side, knocking over supplies and spooking horses in their hurry to get to us. Bluebeard leaned to the side, scooped up the woven grass egg that had lured him there in the first place, and tossed it back to me, and then his eyes turned on our attackers and I braced myself. I was just in time to grab his waist with one hand as the stallion reared, coming down hard on a screaming warrior.

They were not all mortal, I noted. Just as many had antlers or wings as regular mortal features. Just as many were dressed in the decadent, maddening styles of the Wittenbrand as those who wore doublet and hose or the colors of livery.

I gasped as Bluebeard cleaved the first head from shoulders – an antlered head, I noted. After that, it was a haze of spattering blood and screams, of bodies launching toward us with clawing hands, or sharp claws, or edged weapons.

My husband fought and fought with the grim determination of the reapers at harvest, hurrying to bring in crops before rain or frost rotted them on the fields. He spun the horse with a deft hand tangled in the reins while his sword arm flicked and danced, weaving like a master at his loom – only instead of weaving cloth, he wove death, and he wove salvation.

I was too occupied to watch every detail. I rode pillion, gripping with my knees as I thrust and jabbed Grosbeak's pole at anyone who slipped past Bluebeard's dancing attacks. There were few, but for me, even a few were enough to keep me on edge, heart racing and muscles stiff as I desperately swung and blocked. My shoulder burst with pain for every movement, and doubly so for every impact. I was certain I'd torn the stitches Bluebeard had so carefully set in my flesh.

The world around me was nothing but noise and people, motion and clawing forest branches in one wooden hue or another blending to a tapestry of fear and pain.

"I bite! Do you hear me, I bite hard!" Grossbeak snarled right before he sank his teeth into a mortal's ear. The man screamed, and there was a ripping sound. I did not look. I did not want to see. By the time I was swinging Grosbeak again, he was spitting out the ear.

"That's right! Run! Run back to your mothers!" he screamed as our horse plunged through a gap in our attackers, plummeting through the woods. "Oof! That was a branch! Do you know how much that – oof!"
I hurried to pull his head in closer to the horse's flanks as we sped into the hot late afternoon sun and back to the road, branches whipping us as if they were our enemies, too. The horse thundered down the road for far longer than I thought a horse could take before Bluebeard finally drew him into a walk.

He flicked the blood from his sword and paused to wipe it.

"This does not look right to me, Grosbeak," Bluebeard said, glancing over both Grosbeak and then me as if checking for injuries before returning his gaze to the ground. I suspected he spoke to my friend so he could speak aloud to me without breaking the rules.

"I see the footprints of the card army, and I expected that, but what do you see here?"

"Men and beasts fleeing the army," Grosbeak said. "Nothing to be concerned about."

"No small footprints. No cattle other than horses. Where are the villagers that Sparrow warned?"

"Perhaps they went a different way."

"Why then, do I see so many men and horse tracks?"

Grosbeak's expression was like a facial shrug. "It's a road. There are tracks. I'd be surprised if there weren't."

Bluebeard grunted but he stayed quiet as we rode, and he shushed Grosbeak when he tried to sing a ribald song.

"Something is amiss, betrayer of mine," he growled.

Our pace sped quicker with every turn until, as the sun began to burn a sulky copper, we turned on the road to where the landscape on either side opened up into a wide grassy field.

I gasped.

It was almost too much to take in.

We had emerged behind the playing card army – hundreds, maybe even thousands of small figures were spread before us in formations, but the edges of the formations bled out across the land as they thundered toward a retreating army of men on the far side of the field opposite to us.

Bluebeard cursed.

"Tell your mistress to hold onto you tightly, Grosbeak," he ordered. "It seems I must spend a week of her life today."

And then he raised a palm and a rip tore through the air ahead of us.

I balked at what I saw there, my palms instinctively clammy, my breath coming far, far too fast until my head went light and woozy. If I'd known where we were going today, I would have stayed hidden away in that little room of dead wives. If I had known we were on the path to this, I would have cowered behind their corpses and watched my days run slowly out one by one rather than be here and now.

I forced down that feeling and clenched my jaw tightly. I could see I must be practical about this. There was nothing that could ever stop Bluebeard from racing into danger and if I was his wife then I must accept that I would be forever rushing in with him. I held onto the lantern pole with a shaking hand, straightened my back, and forced myself to breathe as our stallion leapt like a trout through the slice and into the fray.

We'd emerged where the playing card army rolled over its opposing mortal army like surf on sand. The stallion barely kept his feet as a wave of them crashed into him, it was only Bluebeard's clever riding that kept us upright as he shifted and guided with rein and thigh.

I swung my lantern pole at the nearest attacker, knocking him back – to my surprise. He was lighter than me, vulnerable even to my weak attacks. But though they were vulnerable, they were deadly fast. Three more filled the gap where one had been, and now I had three to battle instead of one.

"To me!" Bluebeard roared. "Men of Pensmoore! To me! Stand with your patron!"

And as he called to them, he steered the stallion to face the army and raised his hand, a wave of air bursting from it and knocking the cards back and into each other.

They're shuffled now, my brain offered. A stunned thought, but all I could manage beyond simply reacting and reacting again as the cards gathered themselves up again and clambered forward, their focus on just one point now – us.

Their painted faces shifted so rapidly from expression to expression that I wondered how they kept them from falling off entirely and they moved with the nausea-inducing flexibility of paper and a strange, almost side-to-side movement like a snake.

Up close, the paintwork on each card was utterly incredible in both detail and design, each one a work of art and each one very subtly different.

Bluebeard flicked his hand again, such a small movement for the result. Flames erupted among them, catching their paper aflame so quick and hot it stole my breath away and leaving them in smoldering heaps around us. They weren't human – not even animals, just things made for trouble and evil – and yet I still flinched from how easily Bluebeard shredded and ignited them. He drew his sword, slashing and hacking as he roared his song, "To me, to me, to me!"

I grabbed the whistle that hung around his neck and blew.

He said nothing about my breach of his person. Maybe he had nothing to say or maybe he was simply too busy battling for our lives.

The cards fell before him, cut or hacked to bits, or trampled by their fellows.

For a long moment, I thought it would not be enough. For a long moment, I thought we would be trampled anyway, dragged under by the pull of so many thousands of bodies.

It was just us in that moment, just Bluebeard swinging his sword with business-like determination and a grim set to his mouth like he was doing something unpleasant. And just me behind him, swinging Grosbeak out to catch any cards he missed as my bodiless friend screamed at the top of his lungs.

"No! No! Not the cards! No!"

And then they were there, masses of mortals rushing up beside us, dressed in the colors of Pensmoore, weapons flashing in the fading sunset.

"For the Arrow!" Someone cried and we surged forward as one, knocking cards aside, trampling them underfoot. They were just cards, right? Just cards. So why were they a threat at all?

A mortal beside me cried out in agony and I looked to see his arm severed at the elbow, a card with a red edge plunging past. The card slid easily through a second man's wrist before two other mortals skewered it on swords and slashed it to pieces.

I was going to be ill. I needed to be away from here. Anywhere else. Anywhere else at all.

"Fight harder!" Grosbeak scolded, bringing me back to reality.

I fought down my nausea, and with all my strength, I swung the pole.

If I'd been on my own, I'd be dead a thousand times over, but my husband turned every blow aimed at me. He was like five men fighting at once, a flurry of blades and movement.

Vireo rode up beside us.

"I beg your forbearance, Arrow," he said breathlessly, flicking a pair of cards aside. "I was a fool to leave you."

"So you were," Bluebeard agreed. "And a fool to lead the mortals to battle here."

"We did not pick this place. We met them on the road, but they drove us back to the fields."

Bluebeard stiffened and by now I knew him well enough to understand. He was furious.

"How many have you lost?"

"We had no time to count. We were routed. The men are scattered."

"Forward!" Bluebeard roared, ignoring Vireo and leading the men himself.

He was right to do so. They rallied to him, hope blazing in their eyes. Man after man joined him, helping him as he pressed their enemies back, flung them to the ground, and trampled them under his stallion's black feet. He fought them, wave upon wave, a sea of enemies, but even the sea itself could not stand against my husband. He was rage and darkness, martial power and fury, death loosed upon the earth. And though his own side bled furiously, still he fought onward.

"If you'll not stand me as your brother, then bind me as your vassal," Vireo said when he surfaced again from the fray. "Give me one more chance, brother."

"Peace," Bluebeard roared, shifting his reins to his sword hand and reaching across. Vireo clasped his hand. "Round up those who are scattered and bring them to the flanks of the Sword's folly. We'll dash them against the rocks and rid ourselves of this monstrosity."

"As you say, my Prince," Vireo said, sketching a bow, but though he had clasped my husband's hand, there was still a cloud of worry on him as he rode away. I would be worried, too. Bluebeard had claimed Grosbeak's head for less loss of life.

"To me, men of Pensmoore!" Bluebeard called, "to me!"

We turned back to where the mass of cards was pushing and pressing. I was soaked through with sweat already. Every muscle ached and my shoulder was fiery pain, agony in my living flesh. Blood poured down my sleeve to match the blood staining Bluebeard's side and thigh as I sucked in deep breaths through my nose, just trying to stay upright.

But though we had the men with us, though they sped to

join their patron and fight alongside him, even so, we were outnumbered. The first stab of fear hit me when I saw a mortal beside us stumble and fall – not from the cards, but from sheer exhaustion. The fear turned to terror when ten more stumbled with him.

"Up," Bluebeard cried, "Up."

But they were beyond encouragement. They were almost beyond life. I could see what was coming, see the falling comrades, see the cards wash over us, knowing it was too late – just too late to stop it. Disappointment was bitter on my lips as I slipped a hand around Bluebeard's waist. One last touch to savor before we both fell and were sliced to ribbons by the raging cards.

A horn sounded on the far slope ahead of us and to the left. A second horn matched us, ahead of us and to the right.

But horns could not save us now.

And then there was movement over the left hill. I squinted at the sight and gasped. Mortals. An army of men thundering toward the fray and at their head was Sparrow, her sword arcing before her in a bright crescent.

"Sparrow," Bluebeard breathed, relief strong in his voice, too.

On the other hill, Vireo thundered down, the men he'd found thundering with him.

"We're saved," Grosbeak said – sounding almost as if he feared for his life, too. Though how he could fear when it was already taken, I didn't know. "We're saved."

But he was right. We cut them down like a field of grass before the mowers.

Until there was only one. Standing alone before the Arrow.

His drawn mouth worked across his card surface and then – in a way that sent chills down my spine – the Sword's voice spoke through him.

"What have I done behind your back while you were killing this army, Arrow? Where is the knife planted and how are you bleeding?"

Then the card crumpled to the ground, still and lifeless and across the landscape, every ruined card disappeared. What manner of magic could have sustained them and then ruined them?

Around me, a cheer went up from ragged throats and heavy hands – so tired they could barely lift up in salute. No one else was looking at such good news with sideways eyes. There was only relief and gratitude.

"The Arrow! The Arrow!" they roared – one name on a thousand tongues.

"Let's go find that missing human king," my husband growled. And I did not think he meant to congratulate him.

CHAPTER THIRTEEN

If I'd imagined a war camp, I would have imagined a grim set of low tents with little to eat perched atop a hill where a watch could be set on every side. I would have imagined a few stoic men clutching weapons and dreaming of home.

What we found when we rode into this war camp bore little resemblance to what I had imagined. There were tents and fires to be sure, but the tents were made of fine canvas and painted with the crest of Pensmoore – a black horse galloping over a field of green – and trimmed with careful stitching.

Where I had expected grim conditions, instead there were roaring fires and servants bearing trays of food and wooden chairs on which to sit and tables on which to dine.

Certainly, there were pickets – fine lines of well-bred horses I couldn't help but approve of as we walked by – but they were tended by grooms. And certainly, there were apothecary tents where moans and screams were common, but they were pushed off to the side and away from the boisterous clamor of the celebration going on in the camp when we arrived. Indeed, one would hardly know a devastating defeat had only narrowly been escaped just a short ride away from here.

We were on foot, Bluebeard insisting that our horse was too weary to carry us after the mad dash and then the battle – and he seemed correct, though our horse held his head high and did not stumble despite his sweaty flanks and neck and the heavy gusts of breath stirring the black hairs in his nostrils.

Night fell moments before we reached the camp – sudden as an ambush – and Bluebeard leaned in close so that I could feel the brush of his rough cheek against mine as he whispered. It sent a little shiver of pleasure through me that almost disguised the teeth-clenching ache in my abused shoulder.

He whispered so low that I could barely make out the words. Certainly, they could not be stolen by ears not meant to hear them.

"I must dance a pretty jig here, fire of my eyes, for it is a fine line between respect and resentment, adulation and abhorrence and I must keep to the former and fend off the latter. I fear I shall be distant to you as I tend to this, but fear not, you remain my wife and ally. And so, I beg you not to speak mind to mind unless we must. I fear you tap some unknown source with this strange speech we share, and I do not wish to waste it, or it will not be ready at hand when it is most necessary. Simply stay near me and when all this is passed, I will take you from this place of war and to a better nest in which to rest."

I opened my mouth, and he laid a finger over my lips. I nodded my agreement instead, remembering belatedly that now that the sun had set, I must not speak to him. The inability to argue voice to voice – or even just discuss chafed like a wet strap against the skin.

I had no desire to speak to anyone else. Seeing so many dressed in the colors and sigils of my people made my heart sick for Svetgin.

More than that, the sight of my people – sharpening the

shorter, stouter blades of home, their beards trimmed in the way of Pensmoore, their accents ranging from the roll and sway of the east to the quick clip of the west, the scents of their foods as much like home as my mother's keep – drew from me a homesickness that turned my heart in my chest. I felt deeply the years that had passed, and they left a blackened scar across me that was so tangible I felt sure that were I to expose my skin I would see it somewhere upon the pale expanse.

I watched the men with a heavy heart – my people, and yet not mine. I watched the shadows just as carefully, certain that at any moment I would awaken in Bluebeard's house and this place would all be a fitful dream.

I was still thinking that when a groom came and took Bluebeard's horse. I disentangled Grosbeak from where his pole had been propped in the saddle. He was fast asleep – snoring in a way that seemed inconceivable in a dead man, but who was I to say how the dead ought to sleep? Certainly, they slept the deepest of any of us.

Bluebeard snatched his trophy heads from the saddle before the groom led the stallion away, and in the commotion, the people nearest us noticed who he was and the battered army marching at his heel.

A cheer went up through the people left behind.

"Arrow! The Arrow! Patron Saint of Pensmoore!"

When had they added that part? They said it with such conviction, as if each of them had known it since birth, and yet I had been raised among these people and though I'd known to avoid the color blue and that the Wittenbrand stole people away and soured milk and were the source of every stillborn calf and foal, I had never heard one of them called "saint" or "patron." I had never heard anyone shout in joy at their arrival. Indeed, had they not all cowered back from him when Bluebeard came to take me for his bride?

It was that moment of adulation, that cheer that was still echoing, repeated again and again as we entered their midst, that glassy-eyed worship – it was that which severed a string I did not know was tied to me. Was it loyalty? Was it belonging? I couldn't put a name to it yet, but even so, I was certain that something had broken that was once strong. Something was flapping loose in the wind that had once been tightly bound. I prodded at the feeling in my heart as a tongue might prod a missing tooth, feeling the pain of the loss but also the sense that something new was emerging where it once had been.

There was a movement in the crowd like a rolling wave, and then, emerging with lantern-bearers on either side and a gaggle of older men in kaftans and trousers – and even one in a long robe – following behind, emerged the King of Pensmoore.

He had aged poorly.

His eyes were rheumy and his dark hair a hoary, yellowed white. His face twisted with what I read to be suppressed fury.

"Who leads my armies into battle? Who makes demands of me and mine?"

Everyone froze, the inner layers first and then, slowly, whispers rippled outward as the celebration stilled and all paused to see what would be said next.

Bluebeard pulled something small from his pocket and bounced it on his palm. The action unsettled the King so much that he wobbled, catching the arm of the man next to him for support.

I strained my eyes to see what had caused his discomfiture and Bluebeard paused, opening his palm before him so that we could see what was in his hand.

It was the tiny king figure he had pulled from the molten lead at the start of the game. He bounced it one more time on his palm and the king's face blanched under the redness of cheeks and nose.

"What devilry is this?" he gasped as the tiny figure stilled and then arched in agony, twisting and squirming in Bluebeard's palm, his tiny face twisting into the most precise lines of agony. No sound came from his open mouth, though the flesh of his face seemed to strain back from what must have been a tortured cry.

The king's eyes were transfixed on Bluebeard's palm, and he was not alone. Everyone who could see – or strain to see – that little figure was staring at it breathlessly. I felt a knot forming in my own throat. They were going to murder us.

Grosbeak snorted in his sleep.

"I hold within my palm the future of this nation," Bluebeard said in a low voice – a voice that was barely loud enough to be heard.

I could hear the people around him swallowing as he spoke, all their gazes looking toward his. His cat's eyes glimmered with bright moon-like reflections in the lanterns.

"I hold the fate of its king in my grasp," he continued. "And here we arrive, blooded and parched from a battle. We slew, on behalf of Pensmoore, the playing card army sent by the patron of Aayadmoore. But we were victorious only after it slew five villages, leaving not a soul alive or even enough of one person to bury and be sure it was them." I gasped at this and heard my gasp reflected in the gasps of the crowd. How had I not heard that? "Would you have preferred that army marched across the breadth of Pensmoore, slaying all that came in their path? Slicing them to shreds like cabbage for sauerkraut? Is this your wish? Do you envy the cabbage his due? Does the carrot catch hold of your envy?"

Someone snickered in the crowd, but others shifted uncomfortably, eyes wide. They were watching, eyes sweeping back and forth from the king to my husband, and I caught the moment when they seemed to be teetering in the middle, as if their loyalty perched on a fence post.

"I do not spend freely," Bluebeard said, and his words were met by whispers as they were passed back through the crowd. "Not lives. Not men," he gestured here to the men in the column behind him. "Not kingdoms," here a vague wave to the king. "Not even wives."

And though he did not point at me, all eyes turned to me.

"She's one of yours, if you'll remember," Bluebeard said. "Your blood, your kin."

He beckoned to me, and I came forward. He caught my hand in his and looked into my eyes considering, as if deciding whether to do a thing. We were allies. He should know that by now. I nodded to him. Whatever it was, I was ready.

And like that, quick as a serpent, he moved. The tiny king figurine was flipped into the air so that it tumbled end over end like a juggler's ball, while he drew his knife and slashed my palm, tucking the knife away before he caught the tiny king again. He tucked the king in his pocket, too, scooped up a handful of dirt from the ground below, and rubbed it into the wound on my palm and for a moment I felt utterly woozy. The ground around me tilted and then came up to meet me and it was only a pair of strong hands catching me that kept me from falling flat on my face.

Bluebeard spoke – and yet it sounded as if his voice was layered with another voice, as if two voices spoke at once in unison. And with it, I heard the sound of a great thrumming, like a long, deep, throaty heartbeat.

"Blood to earth, branch to bone, she holds your heart, she holds your home. Within her lies your fecund earth, within your hills, her blood brings birth. Now two are knit and one there be, the roots below the flowering tree."

And then the words passed, and my vision cleared and when I blinked back to awareness, I realized I was held up by Bluebeard's grip alone, clasping my upper arms. Around our feet, vines wrapped up to waist level and silky flowers the size of my hand hung in white decorative bells.

I could almost hear them tinkling as the heartbeat faded with the earth. I sucked in a long breath and once more, Bluebeard's beard tickled my cheek as he whispered so low, I could barely hear him.

"Take a moment to recover yourself. I have spent nigh on a year of your life in sealing the land with you. Surely, you must feel the loss."

I did feel the loss. But why would he spend so much on *that*? What was the point of it?

My lips thinned out into an angry line. When it was my turn to speak again, there was going to be a pointed discussion about the spending of days and exactly how much could be spent without at least consulting me. After all, they were *my* days he was spending. *My* years. And maybe he'd given a rib for me, but he'd have to ask if he wanted to carve decades off of me like the breast meat of a roasted goose.

But his action had certainly done one thing. There was only a pause for a single moment and then the roar of approval from all around him was so loud, so overpowering, that it immediately made my head ache and ears ring. The king flinched back from it, quickly smoothing his face to hide expression.

"Come, patron," he said with false gladness when the thunderous approval died enough to hear his words. "You'll dine with me tonight – you and your lovely lady wife."

And for the first time since my arrival, his eyes shot toward me and the look in them was not happiness, nor approval, nor welcome at all but a baleful fire that might have scorched me to the ground if it were not for my powerful husband and his mercurial favor.

"As you say," Bluebeard said lightly, turning slightly so he could share his wink and smile with all the onlookers. "Provided there is no shredded cabbage on the menu."

CHAPTER FOURTEEN

Entering the king's tent as hot food was served brought back memories of eating at his table in Pensmoore City. The scents were identical and little flashes of my father's proud visage, and the excited energy of my brothers' movements kept stealing over me. I had to brace myself against them in an effort to keep from being overwhelmed. My best help was Grosbeak.

"Pitiful," he muttered as we entered and were seated. "Mediocre. The ways of mortals turn my stomach."

"You have no stomach," I said idly as my eyes tried to take everything in at once. There were almost no women and what few there were bobbed and curtsied, serving the tables, eyes downcast. Those in the tent must not have heard the commotion without, for they were deep into their cups, drinking as if it were a race to the bottom of a keg.

I shifted painfully. The ride and the battle had not done me well with my injury and I was lightheaded and exhausted as well as in constant, throbbing pain just as insistent as the words of my bodiless friend.

"Then it turns my sense of taste," Grosbeak grumbled. "I still have that, do I not? The ability to judge ridiculous and pathetic from noble and worthy."

"I should hope so, or you are of no use to me," I said, but my brow was furrowed because the scene in the tent didn't look quite right to me, and I couldn't figure out why. Perhaps it was only pain clouding my mind.

Silence seemed to blanket me, and I paused, realizing belatedly, that the king and his council were regarding me with wide eyes, frozen in the act of entering the tent.

"You speak to a severed head," the king said, as if each word was being spat from his mouth. "You. A Savataz of Northpeak. You have no proper decorum. You are no lady of this court."

The censure in his voice was grim and with it, something inside me rebelled. What did I care if he judged me? I judged *him* for selling me to a man he both feared and hated to save his own daughter's skin. I'd been grateful to him up until now – thankful for his insistence that I be properly married when Bluebeard had come for me, but I saw now that it wasn't from a generosity of heart.

"How *is* Princess Chasida these days?" I asked, my face and voice a blank canvas. "Did she marry? Is she well? Has she children?"

The king's face flushed red. It seemed he was still capable of hearing my meaning. But the flush drained from his skin after a moment and he shook himself as if waking for a dream, paused, and there was a calculated gleam in his eyes as he said, "Indeed. And we should speak of it, as you were such dear friends. Please, go on without me, beloved advisors. Eat and be merry together and show our patron guest the pleasures of my table."

His advisors entered as they were bid, my husband coming up on their heels like a wolf behind geese.

Bluebeard's eyes narrowed and he looked at me. I lifted an

eyebrow. The king was not very subtle. If he wished to pretend I was friends with his daughter as an opportunity to tell me something, surely we must both want to know what that something was.

"Stay where I can see you both," Bluebeard ordered, shooting a daggered glance at the king.

The way the king of Pensmoore's face turned to a light maroon told me he was biting down fierce retorts and maybe even fierce actions. He should bite harder. I'd seen Bluebeard take a head for less than the insults the king had offered so far.

Speaking of which, my husband set the heads he was carrying on the table before him as he turned to speak to one of the kaftaned advisors. They were looking worse for wear. If he insisted on ragging his trophies around, he should take better care of them.

I was curious about what he would say to an advisor. Was it simple pleasantries, "Oh, yes, I have more at home, but these will be an excellent addition to my collection" or was it more serious talk such as, "Since I'm your patron saint, I think a monument is in order"? I couldn't listen from here, even if the king wasn't drowning out my eavesdropping with his hissing words but I was curious about how Bluebeard spoke to mortals when he wasn't taking them as wife or removing their heads.

"You were sent as a spy to his house," the king hissed.

"I was sent as a tribute," I corrected him, coldly.

"But the note I sent and the mirror – "

"Were worse than useless." I turned away from my husband to face the man who ought to have been my sovereign and my protector. "And what shall I tell you, my king? That the

Wittenbrand have carved up the world and they will fight now using the nations as the playing pieces on their board?"

"I'd prefer you didn't lie or make up wild stories," he hissed. "I'd prefer you acted as a loyal daughter of Pensmoore. Did I not tolerate your father and brothers in court all these years because of you? Do you not owe me now more than this?"

We were pressed against the tent wall, lost in the crowd of people, even though he was king, and I found my eyes straying from his face as if he were no more important than a nattering neighbor rehashing the same gossip he'd already told me thrice. There was something odd about the room. It was bothering me. And yet I couldn't identify what it was.

"Tolerate?" I asked, keeping my voice as cold as I could. "This is your message for me? That the sacrifice of my life for our nation bought my family a mere grudging tolerance? I thought you were going to tell me about Princess Chasida."

He waved a hand. "She's well of course. She has four children who are healthy. She married a prince of Ptolemoore and our trade has been beneficial. She's fat with fortune and health."

I let that hang in the air as I studied the crowd. It was the serving girls, I realized. They were too beautiful. Far more beautiful than me, though that wasn't the point. The point was that they were extremely comely and yet they were out here tending the army instead of safe at home. They were covered from head to foot, so it was doubtful they were camp followers. Why, then, were the most beautiful women I'd ever seen – with the exception of the Wittenbrand and Bluebeard's other wives – serving the king's table here? There was not a dull face in the mix. Not a single one. Surely that was odd.

"You can hardly blame me for selling you for peace," the king said, grimly. "What is it if one woman dies for the sake of an entire nation? What is her life worth when stacked against those others? What loyalty do I owe her or her family for merely doing their duty?"

It's strange how quickly a strong root can wither and die. I had thought I was rooted to these people. I had thought that root could hold and feed me all my days. An anchor to my past and to my self. I thought to shelter in its shade and sleep in its embrace, safe from the horrors of the world beyond. But now, it had crumbled to chalk in my hands. And though Bluebeard had tied me to the land and the land to me, I felt no kinship to this man, or his ways, or his court. I felt only a deep antipathy. Any loyalty within me for Pensmoore was long lost.

I was about to say something cutting to him, when Bluebeard lifted a drink from a tray carried by the most stunning serving woman I'd ever seen.

I left the king and ran towards him, screaming in my mind.

Don't drink it! Don't drink!

To my relief, he set the drink down. Now that I looked, I realized that the men around the table were not so deep in their cups as I had thought, but rather that someone – or several someones – had been serving them something … off. One of the nobles clambered onto the table, eyes glassy, a song on his lips. He laughed wildly as I reached Bluebeard's side.

"What is it?" my husband asked at the same moment that the man fell from the table and lay there, motionless in the ground.

"What manner of mortal madness is this?" Grosbeak echoed.

"Poison, Grosbeak," I said. "The kind only the Wittenbrand have. The kind that makes you mad with emotion."

A second man was already clambering on the table to the shouted horror of the guards. But I didn't look at him as Bluebeard turned to me and then back to the chaos around me and then back to me again.

"Brilliantly noticed, fire of my eyes."

Vireo joined us, emerging from what had been a peaceful crowd only moments ago but was now bubbling with fear and aggression.

"Watch yourself!" a man nearby warned a chair was thrown across the room, breaking with a crash.

"Take my wife away from this madness," Bluebeard said, shoving me into Vireo's arms. "Take her somewhere safe until I call you. She is right – as she so often is. My enemies are plotting my death. This time, with poison. We must put an end to this underhanded deceit before they take something more valuable than my playing field or the ribs in my side."

I wanted to tell him to be safe. I wanted to tell him that I hadn't given the king any new information – that I was still his ally and wife. I had to settle for silence as he tucked a stray lock of hair behind my ear and whispered.

"Obey me in this one thing, wife. Go with Vireo and do not fail to follow where he leads you. Swiftly now, all is unraveling."

And then Vireo seized me by the arm, drew his sword, and led me into the night.

CHAPTER FIFTEEN

"Where are you taking me?" I asked Vireo. He had led me through the chaos of the camp, his sword drawn as if he expected an attack at any moment. I saw no reason for such concern.

The poison had been grim, but it had been in the king's tent and surely such a poison would be costly and limited to where it could do the greatest damage. Out here in the camp, no one would spend their resources on a few common mortals. Most were already in their tents, sleeping or moaning in pain from the injuries dealt them. Those who remained had strung chunks of witch's hair moss over the entrances to their tents – a sure sign that patron saint or not, Bluebeard and his small band made them nervous.

We could easily join them, huddled by a campfire, and no one would notice. I could even moan in pain quite genuinely. I was already blinking back tears as he tugged on my hand. Each tug pulled at the wound in my injured shoulder.

Those mortals we encountered looked up from sharpening swords or eating a savory stew. The scent of it wafted to me, making my stomach rumble and clench. It had been more than a day since I'd eaten.

As we passed a ring of men eating around a fire, Vireo snatched up a chunk of bread from a communal bowl and a skin of water and shoved them roughly at me. The fiddle one of the men had been playing squealed to a stop.

"Eat," Vireo ordered me, glaring at the men as if to demand that they insult him so he could return the favor. "Continue with your music, mortals, this is none of your affair. Something quick and joyful, I think. I loathe your dirges."

The violin stuttered back to a start – a stumbling, leaping melody that was half jig and half terror.

I stuffed the bread into my mouth, eating as quickly as I could as struggling to swallow down the water while holding Grosbeak's lantern pole. I would not put him down. If I did, he'd be lost to me and I would be alone with Vireo and I did not trust the Wittenbrand, even if my husband called him brother and forgave him for his temper.

I was just glad not to hold his hand anymore.

"Yes, that's how to feed her," Grosbeak sneered. "Bread and water like any other prisoner. The Arrow won't like it if you care for his wife so poorly."

"Bread and water can't easily be poisoned," Vireo said, and then turned to me, his voice snapping like a flag in high winds. "I'm taking you somewhere safe as I promised. I have no silver key to take us straight to the Wittenhame, so we will ride as we have ridden before."

"Is it safe to go back?" I pressed. "Time passes differently there."

He snickered in an evil way. "What does it matter to you, mortal wife of the Arrow? You are but a treasury of days for him to spend as he wishes. My only fear is that he will reach for one and find it is missing."

"Then perhaps we should not spend my days in futile travel," I said dryly. I had only just returned to the mortal world, and I did not want to go back to the Wittenhame. Especially not without my husband to guard me against its many horrors.

"Time marches on with or without you. You can no more stop spending days than the sun can stop rising. Perhaps the sun stands even a better chance than you do, being a great light of heaven when you are only a wisp of mortal life."

We were well into the tree line now, and the dark branches crowded out the last scraps of light so that I stumbled often, barely catching myself.

I was not certain I should follow Vireo into the darkness, but when I weighed my options, there were none better. If I turned back, I risked falling into whatever revenge Bluebeard might be setting out on the Wittenbrand who had attacked him, or on the court of Pensmoore, or whoever else he blamed. He would think me safely away and could easily harm me by accident. If I managed to find his side without harm, he may very well turn me around and send me back again with Vireo by stronger means and feeling all the while that I had betrayed him once more.

There was no place for me among my mortal kin. The king had made that certain in his speech to me. And there would certainly be no place for me in Aayadmoore with my brother – unless I wished to be at the mercy of the Sword again.

There was no way forward but through, so through I must go.

Vireo grunted each time I fell, but he did not turn to help, and he did not slow his pace.

"If you kill me in this forest," I said calmly, "I do not think it will go well for you with your master."

He spun and grabbed me by the throat. It was already bruised and aching from the last man to do it. My heart sped like a rabbit caught in a trap, as if the heart itself knew time was short and was rushing to beat as much as possible before the end. But underneath that fear was a cold fury at the feeling of his fingers around my neck.

"Do not presume to tell me what is best for me and do not call the Arrow my master."

Grosbeak snickered cruelly. "You could be a head on a pole, too, Vireo. He likes collecting heads from anyone who bothers her, and he didn't stop her from claiming me. He'll smell the truth. You know he will."

Vireo cursed and released me. "Just stay close," he growled. "Are you not glad to be free of him?"

I was not glad, I realized. I was likely safer away from him, no longer a bargaining chip or tool, but leaving his side felt like being wrenched from my home.

We reached a clearing a few moments later where three saddled and antlered elk stamped in the moonlight. Tiny bells tinkled from the chains hung between their antlers. A pang of remembering shot through me – the memory of the last time I was stolen away on a frosty elk. But that time I had been mounted with my husband.

"I will not share a mount with you. You ride alone," Vireo announced, to my relief. The longer I knew him the more wary he made me. I did not trust his jealous looks or calculating eyes. Did Bluebeard not see in him what I did? Was he blind somehow to a man who clearly was oriented due self?

"Are we riding those misty paths all the way to the Wittenhame?" I asked as I mounted the elk. The elk stood very still, allowing the trespass, though he snorted crystal breaths into the air through his twitching nostrils. I found his huffing quite charming.

"I know a shorter path," Vireo growled. "You'll need to stay close on my flank, so we reach it in good time."

"You have no key," Grosbeak reminded him. "So, what shortcut do you speak of? You don't mean a colossus? That's madness, brother."

Vireo spun despite being mounted and slapped Grosbeak so hard that his head swung on the pole, and I had to hold on with all my strength not to lose my grip. My mount shifted uncomfortably under me and then lowered his head and bellowed.

"We ride," Vireo said and put action to words.

My elk followed but now my mind was full of questions.

"What's the colossus?" I asked Grosbeak.

"A huge statue. Have you heard of them? Figures of Wittenbrand who have fought as patrons of the nations in the past and won. They usually leave a colossus behind to mark the spot and then the colossus serves as a key to and from the Wittenhame."

"Then why didn't Blue – " I caught myself, "the Arrow use one last time? He was in a hurry then."

"They come out in odd places – sacred places where the Wittenbrand are vulnerable. Had he done that when he was rescuing you, then you may have died before he took a single day from your life."

"I thought Vireo was supposed to be bringing me somewhere

safe. That's what the Arrow told him to do."

"I thought so, too," Grosbeak said ominously.

It didn't take long until I realized we were headed south toward Aayadmoore. We charged down short roads and then cut across country to hit them again.

"Vireo," I called after several hours of him riding ahead of me, circling back to urge me on when I fell behind. I considered if I should try to lose him, but even the smallest hesitation was immediately noticed and I did not have reins on this elk, it merely followed Vireo's mount wherever it went. There would be no riding off on my own. "Are we going to Aayadmoore?"

"We're going to the Wittenhame. I did promise the Arrow to keep you in a safe place, didn't I?"

His smirk worried me, and I remembered how he chafed when Bluebeard had brought me to the various events in the Wittenhame, how he'd stormed off when Bluebeard hadn't listed to his advice, how he'd somehow been losing that battle only for my husband to win it when he wasn't looking.

"Should I trust you, Vireo?" I asked him calmly.

In fairytales, the girls never ask that question. Maybe it's because they know they will be lied to, so why ask at all. Or maybe it's because they fear the answer will be exactly as they expect. Or maybe because they have other things on their mind like spinning straw into gold before everyone they love perishes. But I have always found you can learn as much from lies as from the truth, so I asked.

He shot a sharp glance at me, and I could tell he wasn't sure what to say next. And then a look of cunning crossed his face.

"Bargain with me, wife of the Arrow."

"What bargain would you strike, you who calls himself my husband's brother."

He made a clicking sound of disapproval from the side of his mouth. "I call myself nothing that I do not have the right to claim. But now heed me, mortal woman, for I shall offer this only once. I do not know what madness has seized our prince that he has chosen you. You are not lovely like his other wives, and yet he has married you properly. I would think he would want to choose a woman who would distract his enemies more fully."

"I suppose beauty does serve a purpose," I said calmly. I did not need it rubbed in my face that I was not beautiful, though people seemed to think that bringing it up put me in my place. I knew my place. I did not require reminders and it was not where people thought it was. "The beautiful are meant to be looked at while the rest of us get on with the business of making a life."

There was an arrogant tilt to his head when he answered me. "We Wittenbrand do not prefer to work. We'd rather bargain or fight, steal or kill."

"So it would seem. And do you think this makes you our superiors?"

"I think our long lives and magic do that. The only good a mortal serves is as a pawn. And you've been a poor pawn to my prince, the Arrow. Already, you have lost him a move in the game and a rib. I would see better things for him."

It might have been a valid point if he hadn't stolen my girlhood, my future, my prospects, and my days. It seemed an even trade to me.

"And so you are pleased to see us separated," I pressed, still suspicious.

"I am pleased to see you out of his way. Don't you think that is for the best? Don't you think he is better off without you?"

"I think that if I am out of the way, I cannot help him. Was it not I who saw the drinks were poisoned by those very beautiful women? My skills have helped him more than once. Perhaps *you* are the one who sent the poisoners, since you seem so taken with beauty. Are they not who you would have chosen to deliver your draught?"

He pulled his elk in so quickly that the poor creature rose on hind legs, pawing the air before settling again. Reaching out, Vireo seized the front of my jacket and pulled me in close.

"Don't think to blacken me in your husband's gaze. It will not happen. I am no rival of mortals."

I refused to succumb to fear, not even when his belt knife flicked up and scratched at my throat.

"None can be your rival unless you let them, Wittenbrand. Do you call me rival? Is it not you, then, who has made me so? I have only the power to terrorize that you have gifted to me."

He huffed a frustrated breath and released me, and I tried to be subtle in how I checked my throat. Only a small nick. It was bleeding, but not badly. It stung, but only enough to remind me that I must be very careful with this Wittenbrand. He was not my friend. Whether he was a friend to my husband remained to be seen.

"You can be killed and snatched from him, and then what will he do for days? How will he win his battle?"

"He's encountered that problem fifteen times and had no problem finding a solution," I said dryly. "Here in the mortal world, it should be easy enough to find a girl to greet their patron saint."

He grunted, but I was worried now. There was no reason for him not to kill me.

"Do you wish to bargain to see your brother again?" he pressed.

A stab of worry filled me. Was that where he was taking me?

"If you bring me to him, you will betray the Arrow," I couched.

"How disappointed the mortal man must be to have spent his entire life seeking you only to be abandoned by you in the final hour. I am given to understand that gratitude is considered seemly in mortals."

The final hour? Worry gnawed at me at his words. Did he know something I did not? Had my brother died there with the Sword?

We burst through the tree line to where the river flowed before us, only here there was a guarded bridge not far upstream. The soldiers patrolling there wore the ruddy uniforms of Aayadmoore. How did he intend to cross it? He could not fly on the backs of songbirds as the Arrow had.

"What would you have of me, Vireo?" I asked, hoping we could finish this talk before he took me somewhere truly dangerous. "What would you bargain for?"

He stopped his elk, suddenly, and my elk stopped with it. The moonlight limned them both in bright edges and their breath was matching ghost-like gusts hanging in the air with every breath. And for the first time since the day I'd met him, Vireo reminded me of Bluebeard. It was the vulnerability, I realized, the way he seemed to be baring himself to me.

"You asked for a real marriage, and he gave it to you, and now it is killing him. He ought to have burned through you and made his move and remarried all over again, do you understand? Can you follow this reasoning with me?"

An image of Bluebeard stripped naked, his rib torn from his side came to mind and I swallowed, my throat too dry for it to be any relief.

"Yes," I whispered.

He leaned in closer. "I would not see you humiliate us before mortals, but you make a laughingstock of my prince. His other wives never did that. It is this that drives me forward and bids me appeal to your reason."

"I don't care what the others did," I said, putting as much defiance into my voice as I could. But I did care about not humiliating him. I was surprised by how much the thought of that stung. Was he flinching inside with every choice I made? I hadn't noticed that, but then again, he was opaque to me as clouded glass.

"Hear that?" Grosbeak taunted from the end of his chain. "She doesn't care what you think!"

"Ignore the ghast," Vireo said, his voice low and trembling. "He's dead. Nothing he says can be something new, he can only regurgitate old things."

"You're a regurgitated old thing!" Grosbeak spat.

Vireo ignored him, and now all of him seemed to tremble and not just his words as he pushed his argument. "The Arrow says you are practical – that you have the magic of seeing things and knowing their use." That was magic? "Would you not employ that for him? Would you not wish to serve a purpose his other wives did not? To be more than decorative? To be helpful? A benefit?"

And now he was striking close to my heart because I *did* want to be useful. But I did not trust Vireo and I did not want to work with him. He would betray me – of that I was certain. He would knife me in the back, given half a chance, or push me from a cliff. Or … well, the Wittenbrand had many ways to kill. I did not need to imagine them all.

"Is that what all this is about? You want me to be useful? You want me to help you help him?" I pressed, because I needed time to think about what to say. Bluebeard had urged me to follow him. He'd urged me to obey this one thing.

I gritted my teeth against how that stuck in my throat. I didn't want to trust Vireo. I didn't want to follow him anywhere. But I also did not want to betray my husband's trust a second time.

"I wanted to give you these hours we've been journeying to think. To realize what has been happening. It makes me sick that he doesn't trust me anymore," Vireo said in a low voice. "Sick to my very heart. Do you know what I have done over the years to purchase his confidence?" He shook his head wildly. His breath was coming too fast as if everything depended on this. "Surely, you must want redemption, too. Are we not the same, you and I? Are we not both proven unreliable? Proven treacherous? Don't you want to wash that stain from your hands? And you can. You could spy for him in a way that no one else could. You could gather information. You could use the false expectations of others to hide in plain sight."

"The king of Pensmoore asked for the same thing, but I was of little use to him," I said, still cagey. I could follow him without truly trusting him. I was a practical girl. I could do this practical thing.

"Were you really trying?"

I shook my head.

"The next time someone tries to assassinate him, you'll know in advance. You'll know before anyone else. Wouldn't you rather be useful than a decoration? Wouldn't you rather prove your worth?"

I remained silent. He seemed to talk enough for two of us.

"Then bargain with me. We both have so much that needs forgiveness," he pled. "Give me your word that you will come with me willingly to the place I am taking you and that you will trust me and stay with me until you are shown this useful path, and in return, I will make you useful. I will give you a better understanding and a powerful role in this Game of Crowns and Thrones. What say you, Izolda Savataz, wife of the Arrow?"

"I wouldn't do that," Grosbeak warned, his voice rising in pitch as if he was catching Vireo's desperation like a disease. "You can't trust a traitor."

"I'll follow you without a bargain," I said coolly, unwilling to be swept away in their drama.

Vireo leaned in close. "Bargain with me, or do not follow at all."

I bit my lip. I'd been given one order and one only. To follow. Did I dare make this bargain in order to obey? But I did want to prove to Bluebeard that he could trust me, and I wanted to trust him. And the only way I could do that was by following his one request.

"You'll live to regret it!" Grosbeak warned. "Or worse yet, you won't live at all."

"Yes," I agreed, ignoring my friend. "I accept your bargain."

And I couldn't have said why, but Vireo's answering smile worried away at the edge of my mind like a puppy on a fresh bone.

CHAPTER SIXTEEN

"Then we are in agreement," Vireo said, pulling a key on a light chain out from within his shirt. It gleamed silver in the moonlight. "And we have no more need of hours of pretense at riding across this dull mortal land."

"Where did you get that?" Grosbeak gasped, horror in his voice as his eyes watched the key.

Vireo turned it quickly in the air and a door leapt open.

"Don't go through the door, Izolda," Grosbeak said with trembling lips. "Ask him where he – "

His words cut off as Vireo cuffed him so hard that he spun in a spiral on his chain.

"Come, wife of the Arrow," Vireo said, his voice suddenly cold after the warmth of his arguments. "You promised to follow until the plan was revealed."

I could not have done otherwise. The pressure of our bargain clamped down on me and bid me move as he had ordered. I did not so much as lift a finger to protest, though my skin crawled as he led my mount behind his and stepped through the door.

The key had looked just like Bluebeard's key into the Wittenhame. Had he stolen it? Had Bluebeard given it to him in order to more easily spirit me away?

All question of the provenance of the key vanished as the elk took a second step and the madness hit me.

The world stretched and pulled like rope under tension, and I was unmade and remade in a blink of an eye, my mind seeing a thousand tiny visions like slivers of mirror that reflected a world I did not know and then were jammed directly into my brain. Agony filled me and I tilted my head back as I screamed.

It was over as fast as it began, but though we stepped onto the other side and through the madness, I couldn't help the endless whimper shuddering through my lips or the way my hands both clung white-knuckled to Grosbeak's lantern pole, or the way I was shaking like the earth when it quakes and nearly breaks apart.

I hardly noticed the arrow jammed into the stone, for there was no music this time and no golden light. No singing or petals falling from the sky.

There was nothing that greeted us as it had greeted Bluebeard – as if the Wittenhame rejected our entry. I clenched my teeth and forced myself to stop making such terrified sounds as Vireo pulled my elk along behind him – not toward where Bluebeard's house had been last time, but in the other direction.

Around us, the carpet of leaves and moss on the floor of the Wittenhame seemed to rustle and crawl. I watched it, half curious and half trying to claw my way back from madness. It wasn't until long minutes had passed, that I realized there was something under there following us as we moved. I thought I caught a glimpse of a slug, but after a moment, I realized they were white roots.

I opened my mouth to ask about it but was cut off when Vireo cursed under his breath and kicked his elk into a run. We ran

– the roots running alongside with us – until the forest opened itself wide and I realized that ahead of us the land dropped off abruptly and I could see far into the distance where the land rose to meet the horizon in that familiar blur of land kissing air. There, in the vague shapes so far past sight that they had forgotten they could be seen at all, a thousand small rainbows glinted and danced, and my eyes played tricks on me that told of faerie dust and faerie gold.

"I hate this part," Grosbeak gasped as we thundered forward.

We weren't stopping. We were going to plunge right over the cliff.

I gripped Grosbeak's pole and tried to gauge how to leap from the back of a moving elk, but I saw no way to jump without my momentum carrying me over the cliff. I'd have to jump without the assurance it would work. I tensed my muscles, prepared to leap – and then the elk was in the air, I'd missed my chance, and we were flying through the air, off the cliff, over the valley of waterfalls and rainbows.

A bright light flashed across my vision, and we landed hard on rock.

The elk scrambled, his hooves trying to find purchase, and then he crumbled under me like a sandcastle washed away by the sea. I gasped as my feet hit the ground, my mind bending to try to see what was happening. One moment an elk had been under me and the next thing I knew it was gone.

The injury in my shoulder flared hot and painful and the smaller cuts in my back echoed the pain, leaving my mouth opening and closing like a fish drawn up from the depths. Catch your breath, Izolda. Just one good breath.

Just in front of me, Vireo had his face in his hands, little sobs sawing out of him.

“What did you see in the valley?” Grosbeak asked me in a rusty voice – the kind of voice that sounded like he'd buried his entire family.

“I saw,” I said, pausing to lick dry lips. “Waterfalls and rainbows.”

His laugh was snapping sticks and broken bones. It went on and on. When he recovered himself he snorted. “Hear that, Vireo? She saw rainbows and waterfalls.”

“What did you see?” I asked, catching that breath finally and letting it fill me and ease some of the pain.

“Everyone I knew burning and blackened by the flames of hell,” he flung the words out like a curse. “And though I doubt our Vireo will tell us what he saw, you can see it was not rainbows by the way he holds his shoulders so tight."

I blew out the long breath. More Wittenbrand magic. I didn't want to guess at what it meant.

And now we were here. On an island made of fierce slabs of upturned granite and dead, white trees like pillars smashed into place by the hand of an angry god. Pale lichen etched itself across the rock faces and tiny evergreens tried hard to replace their dead and worn brethren above. And all around, as far as I could see, there was only grey water and grey sky. The water was in a temper, dashing itself against the granite shore as if it, too, wished to leap over a valley of rainbows.

“What is this place?”

“You don't want to know. Or maybe you do. What do I know? You're the one who made the soul-forsaken bargain with him.” Grosbeak sounded sour.

"I saw the key," Vireo rasped, looking up at us with his startling blue eyes, madness as thick in them as cold lard the morning after a feast. He scrambled over and grabbed me by the hair. "And as I thought, it's you. It's *you* all the way through. Come."

As if I had a choice. He dragged me by my long braid over the rocks which were more vertical than horizontal. He was half-frantic in his stumbling climb, his free hand grasping at rocks and bushes as he tore a path through the landscape. We were following the lapping waves, skirting the edge of the rocks where someone had scraped strange runes into the black lichen that grew along their side next to the water. I could not read them, and I almost thought that I should not try.

"This," Grosbeak said grandly as he swung on the end of his chain, narrowly missing small, gnarled cedars and jutting deadwood, "is the Isle of Burning Guilt. Any who make a vow here are bound by the denizens of this place to fulfill it or die trying."

How charming.

"Are we still in the Wittenhame?" I asked, "And could you stop dragging me by my braid, Vireo? I don't see how I could escape this place even if my mount hadn't melted like spring snow."

"Yes," Grosbeak said at the same time that Vireo said, "No."

And so, I was half-dragged along the rocks as I fought to keep my feet so that my hands and knees were scraped, my shoulder wound was open again and bleeding hot against my skin, and my temper just as damaged.

We only slowed when we stumbled upon a Wittenbrand sitting on a rock by the edge of the water, his eyes hollow, white hair flowing down his back to tangle in the pale, dead reeds that rustled along the bank. On either side of him, two sharp-eyed Wittenband stood, arms crossed, eyes looking in every direction. They were his guards, I realized, as I recognized him from the Great Game of Crowns.

"Bargain with me, rock," Lord Marshyellow croaked. "Bargain with me for your fate and you shall be as men who live a few days and then weep for eternity."

He looked up, suddenly, and his eyes lit as he saw me.

"I did it," he said, a vague smile lighting his empty face. "I made a mortal."

"That's the wife of the Arrow, Lord Marshyellow," one of his guards murmured. "And look, here is Vireo of the Arrow's band, here to turn his coat as promised."

Turn his coat? A stab of fear shot through me – I'd been right about Vireo – but it was Marshyellow who looked panicked.

"Then the poison didn't work. But I thought that certainly he would be tempted by more pretty wives. And what is this you wear, wife of Arrow?"

I looked down at my clothing, ripped and torn from being half-dragged over the rocks. It seemed fine to my eyes otherwise. I was dressed. Certainly, the clothing was blue, but Bluebeard had given them to me himself. They should not cause offense.

"Is that the Sword depicted thus upon your jacket?" He shuddered. "It is, it is, I remember now."

"It's just decoration," I said carefully. I was uncomfortable around those who were already mad. They made me doubt my own sanity.

“No, the memories! Stop the memories! I cannot take them.” He closed his eyes, clutching his head as if he was in pain and Vireo made a frustrated sound in the back of his throat.

“Take off that fool jacket, Izolda,” he snapped.

I looked back and forth between them. Vireo was here with another competitor for the game. And already there was talk of him turning coat. I gritted my teeth, irritated that I was right about Vireo. He’d pushed me into a bad bargain and even if I’d gone into it with open eyes, knowing what he was, I still didn’t like playing the pawn. They meant to use me as they wished and I would not bear well under their usury.

It was time to draw a line. I’d promised Bluebeard I would follow, but I was not a child. I was not a slave. I would not be treated as such.

“I plan to wear it, Vireo, and wear it with pride. Would you have me do otherwise?”

Vireo cursed.

But before he could bring me to heel there was a call from within the forest.

“If you plan to bargain with us, then join us. And if you do not, then flee this Isle while you still can before your souls are bound forever.”

CHAPTER SEVENTEEN

"It's too late now. Your fate is on your own head," Vireo hissed as he led me to follow the voice.

"Good thing we have an extra head between us, then," Grosbeak muttered.

Behind us, the two guards were helping the distraught Lord Marshyellow up so he could follow us.

We clambered through a tumble of rocks and found ourselves on a huge, roughly level, expanse of dark granite. It was ringed by broken white trees, long dead, forming what looked like a ring of broken teeth or a crown made of broken bones.

Perhaps in another time, I would have considered what it meant to meet inside a broken crown. Today, I was too intent on who waited for us there. Through the broken spikes, we saw two figures. One, I expected after seeing Lord Marshyellow, but one I did not.

If I had told the king of Pensmoore about this meeting, he would not have believed me. He would have thought it was fanciful musings of a foolish girl. If I had told him that he and the other kings and queens of man were nothing more than pawns – that the real fate of the world and everyone in it lay in the palms of a scarce few Wittenbrand and that every tiny move they made left the fates of our nations tumbling into chaos, ruin, and death – he would have thought me insane.

The knowledge should have meant power for me. Power to stop it or twist it or … something. But knowledge is not always power. Sometimes, it is only the marker over the grave of the future you thought you had.

A throat cleared, and I returned my thoughts to what was before me – the meeting of four allies. That they were here for something of import was clear from the fire burning in the center of the ring – a strange orange fire edged in thick smoke that poured like milk, heavy into the air and across the rock, and then vanishing. The Wittenbrand stood equidistant to each other as they waited and Vireo took his place easily in the ring with them, Marshyellow being herded into his place, as well.

Lady Tanglecott was one of the two waiting for us, her white-winged mist lions flanking her on either side and her golden oak crown reminding us that she was battling for the place of sovereign just like the rest. It was her who surprised me. I had expected her to be the type to fight alone.

Coppertomb, on the other hand, did not surprise me. My betrayer sat tidily on a small folding stool made of carved bones and a swath of black silk. The bones appeared to be femurs. I did not want to think too long about where they came from. Perhaps, he had tricked their owners into giving them up as he had tricked me. Betraying their very limbs as I had betrayed my own heart.

"You are late, Vireo," Coppertomb said calmly. "You promised you could get the job done and done quickly."

"There were complications," Vireo argued.

"After I handed her to you? Threw her into the mortal world for the taking?"

"The Sword was there," Vireo complained. "You said nothing about him."

"You couldn't handle dancing around him? You couldn't think to use his endless rage to fuel your desires? And yet you tell us you are fit to sit at our table, to take your prince's place as Lord Riverbarrow."

I gasped, freezing in place. But why was I surprised? Why was I shocked when I new what was at his core. Simply saying it out loud did not make it worse.

"Told you," Grosbeak grumbled.

"Silence, ghast. You were not invited here. The Arrow should have put your head with his others," Coppetomb said with a twist of disdain to his mouth.

Tension filled me. Bluebeard told me to follow – but how far would he expect me to go? Had he meant me to serve as a spy for him or had he truly trusted Vireo? Did I trust *him* enough to carry this ruse out all the way? I clenched my jaw so hard I feared it might break. I'd have to see this through. It was only sensible to gather what knowledge I could about our enemies. It wasn't sensible to trust that they wouldn't kill me afterward, though. Was a meant to follow that far? To let my own throat be cut in sacrifice? I hoped not.

"I'm not the Arrow's pet. I'm *her* pet," Grosbeak grumbled.

"I said, *silence*." The words were whisper-quiet. "Now that we're all here we must be quick. If any of the others catch word that we've formed an alliance – that we have means to remove them from this Game – then they'll form their own alliances, and the Game will quickly devolve into a blood sport."

"Isn't that what War is?" Vireo asked sourly. "A blood sport?"

"It can be," Coppertomb agreed. "When it is fought poorly."

I looked away from his blazing eyes, my heart sinking because he'd beat me once before and used me to set a trap for Bluebeard and if I was here before him again, then he must want to use me again. Had Bluebeard realized what position his edict would put me in?

Vireo kept a tight grip on my braid, but as I looked down, I saw something small in the grass by my feet – a tiny grass-woven egg the size of a quail's egg. It was so close to my foot that I was surprised I hadn't accidentally stepped on it.

I tried to stoop to retrieve it, but Vireo hauled up on my braid.

"Still, Izolda," he hissed.

"Can I not fix my boot?" I asked quietly. "Better now than when you want to move."

He grunted, releasing me just enough to let me bend. I fussed with the boot and scooped up the egg when I was done, hiding it in the palm of my hand. Maybe Vireo hadn't fully lied to me. After all, I was getting information for Bluebeard, wasn't I? If not in the way I'd expected.

"I prefer to fight my wars on my own terms," Coppertomb said with a smug smile. "I prefer to poison the enemy before I sneak into his tent."

Was it he who sent the poisoners to Bluebeard, then, and not Marshyellow? Or perhaps they had worked together – as much as Marshyellow worked at all.

"Then it's time that you explained why you've sent this dog to fetch the Arrow's latest wife," Lady Tanglecott said, looking bored. "I'm not as amused by posturing as you are. Do you want him to chase after her?"

"I had hoped to seize his power from him," Coppertomb said, hands steepled under his chin as he watched me. "Killing her will only give him the opportunity to marry again."

"The Sword tried to marry her, and that did not break the bond," Vireo reported.

"But if we keep her from him, perhaps that will be enough," Coppertomb mused. "He must have some proximity, must he not, Vireo?"

"I believe so," Vireo said solemnly. "And he seems to be more powerful when she is by his side. Keeping them apart can only help. The Sword is determined to sever their tie."

"Then send her to him," Lady Tanglecott said smoothly. "Let the Arrow and the Sword squabble over her like dogs over a bone, and while they fight, we will pick over their holdings and over their carcasses."

Coppertomb smiled and then Marshyellow began to laugh and laugh as if the greatest joke had been told. His attendants rushed to him, but he waved them off.

"Back Yarrow, back Frost. I need not your aid," he gasped. "Still laughing."

Coppertomb sighed. "That's well enough with me, Lady Tanglecott, but we must bind her lips then, too. We'll seal our pact as it always is done and seal her with it. And if she fails, Vireo, then she fails on your behalf. You'll not sit with us at the table. You'll not sit at all."

Vireo frowned, his unhappiness apparent, but he still rolled up his sleeve with the others and Coppertomb carved a rune into each of their arms with the tip of his dagger – a rune that looked a lot like the writing in the lichen on the rocks. The fire flickered and the milky smoke poured out of it, sweeping around our feet, pooling there and then flowing upward to wreath the broken crown.

"The girl?" Vireo asked when Coppertomb did not carve mine.

"The blood oath doesn't work unless she means it and she won't. The wraith will be enough," Coppertomb said as if speaking to a child. "Come now, let us make the vow."

And then together they spoke – Marshyellow a beat behind the rest. And as they spoke, I thought I saw figures and faces in the strange milky smoke.

"We swear by blood and smoke, on pain of guilt and fire, that we four are bound now to work as one, to overthrow our enemies until none are left, and to keep this pact sacrosanct to us. Or may the mist consume our souls. And we swear by the denizens here to be bound to their rule in secrecy, silence, and purpose."

And as if their words had triggered something, five figures detached from the smoke – ghostly wraiths with human faces and open mouths, their eyes white and opaque. They drifted, one to each of us, and the girl who stood beside me was thin as a wrung cloth, as flickeringly translucent as the smoke, and horrifyingly cold.

"And may the Bramble King have mercy on us all," Lady Tanglecott said, and then she blew into the fire and strode away through the shattered tree crown. Flames danced in her path and the wraith attached to her broke away from the smoke and hovered over her left shoulder, hanging down across her back like a nosy relative watching her every movement.

"Bramble King. Mercy." Marshyellow had barely spoken

the words when his attendants took his arms and guided him through the trees in a different direction, the flames licking across their path, too. His wraith spun around the three of them like a skein of wool.

"Bramble King have mercy," Coppertomb intoned, making a two-fingered pious gesture, and then blowing into the fire. His eyes were cruel and cold when he turned to Vireo. "Get her to the Sword by tomorrow at noon or I'll take back that key and turn you over to your master."

"I don't respond well to threats," Vireo said, but his voice was weaker than it should have been.

"Then you shouldn't have made an oath on the Isle of Burning Guilt," Coppertomb said with a shrug, and he turned on his heel and strode in a third direction, flames spreading out from his path like licking tongues. His wraith danced a jig behind him and turned to make a rude gesture at us before he disappeared into the smoke and flame.

"Our turn now," Vireo said grimly. And he seemed shaken when he blew on the fire and then spun, hauling me through the tumbled rocks to the water's edge. "Hurry. Bramble King have mercy. We must put distance between ourselves and the flames. The entire island will burn to seal our vows."

"What have you bound me to, you viper?" I asked him.

"I've bound you to silence, nothing more."

"And you're selling me to my enemy as bait for a trap. A trap for the Arrow!" I said as we scrambled across the rocks, the fires licking at our heels. I shouldn't have bargained with him. I should have ried to follow some other way. Coldness filled me, deep and oppressive. I'd bungled things again. Even in trying to follow whatever plan my husband had for me, I'd opened myself up to this. "You said I would be useful. We bargained for it!"

"Think back to what I said," he answered as he grabbed my braid again and pulled me with him into the grey waves.

Behind us, the entire island was a conflagration as the dead wood embraced the cleansing flames. I had a sensation of cold on my left shoulder and when I shifted to look, the ghastly face of the smoke girl was looking right back at me. I screamed, and her mouth opened wide in imitation. The scream echoed out over the waters.

"Wraiths," Grosbeak grumbled from his place on the end of the chain. "I hate wraiths."

My breath was coming too fast. I tried to twist away from the spirit, but she bent around me, following the way my head turned so she was still in my peripheral.

I was going to scream again. I could feel it bubbling in my throat. I fought the sensation. It was not practical to scream. Screaming only opened my mouth and left me vulnerable. I needed a plan. I needed a way to reasonably deal with this Wittenbrand madness.

Vireo tugged my braid again, dragging me deeper into the water so we were knee deep and then hip deep and then chin deep.

"I said you would be useful," he gritted out as we fled the flames. "I never said *who* you would be useful to."

CHAPTER EIGHTEEN

Fortunately, we didn't have to go deeper into the water than that, for the lake was no more than chin deep. Vireo dragged me through it by my braid and I had to keep all my concentration on not stumbling, and holding Grosbeak's head up over the water, and so I passed through that dark lake with only a few glances over my shoulder at the burning island or the wraith who hovered over my shoulder.

We reached the other side and began to rise up from the water, Grosbeak spitting weeds out from between his teeth – I'd dunked him more than I thought. We slid over algae-coated stones, slowly climbing from waist level to knee level, and I tried to speak.

"Back there," I gasped. "You swore me to secrecy about – "

But before I could finish the sentence, the wraith wrapped an icy hand around my mouth and twisted so that her huge, dead eyes looked into mine as she shook her head.

I shivered and then retched, fighting to push her off of me so that I could vomit. In my frantic fight, I lost Grosbeak for a moment and had to recover him, dripping, from the lake.

Vireo watched it all with a stony face, not even letting go of my braid as if I were a horse that might spook and run.

"You were bound to silence at the island," he said when I was left, panting, gasping, and clinging to my lantern pole, one hand thrust out to try to hold the ghast at bay. "Were I you, I would not try to speak of it again."

I stood completely still, frozen into place, the only sound the trickle of the water running off me and whisper of the wraith right behind me.

I watched him for a long moment and then I shivered.

"Why are you trying to replace –"

The hand covered my mouth again and I gagged on my own words. I wanted to bite it. I wanted to scream. But I had a terrible feeling that if I opened my mouth the creature would reach right down my throat.

"Vireo's a cold devil who was meant to be the Arrow's closest companion," Grosbeak informed me. "You stood over my grave, Vireo. Do you not see the irony? I turned on a man I once called friend, and tried to kill his bride. You've turned on him the same way and yet you stood over me and spoke words of remembrance as if my death was justified. Should I speak some over you now?"

Vireo's reply of, "Silence, revenant," seemed half-hearted.

But Grosbeak's words were putting steel back into my spine. I'd survived the wound he'd inflicted and now he was my creature. Surely, I could do the same with Vireo. I held my back straight as we emerged from the water.

"He was good with a blade and better with a lie," Grosbeak intoned as if he really was at Vireo's funeral. "He had no patience for the dead though they'll be required to have patience for him now."

"I bid you silent, and silent you will be on this matter, or I'll carve out your dead tongue," Vireo threatened, but he seemed shaken, and as I looked at the crumbling cliff along the shore of the lake, I could see why.

We were not alone. We were being watched by the cliff – for deep in its sandy wall, half-hidden by slides of sand and tumbles of wildflowers, was the dreaming Bramble King. His eyes eased open, watching us, and Vireo froze and then bowed jerkily, terror making his movements choppy and abrupt.

"His glory he fades," the Bramble King said barely audibly. "His glory. Fades."

And then he closed his eyes again, shook himself, dislodging a fall of sand, and opened them again intoning, "I am the culmination of desire, the fruit of death. I am the summit of loss, the passing of weight. What am I?"

"I don't know," Vireo said through thick lips. He stumbled backward, losing his grip on my braid. "Come, Izolda," he hissed. "Come away."

"What is your riddle for?" I asked the King, tilting my head to the side.

He winked at me, and his eyes glazed over with white, and he ceased moving.

I thought I might know the answer to the riddle. I thought I might have an idea of what he was offering, though I did not think he was offering it to me.

"His glory fades," I muttered to myself just as Vireo managed to snag my braid again and drag me away.

I was still pondering his riddle when we clambered up the beach and made our way deeper into the Wittenhame, leaving lake and beach behind and entering the tall wood until we were lost among the roots of the trees that stood higher than the sky.

Last time I was here, there seemed to be magic everywhere. Now, there were armies everywhere. And though flower petals fell down from the sky in a constant fragrant rain – as if this was the wedding of Spring and Summer – still this world felt empty and dark compared to the last time I was here. Some sweet magic had been torn away just as my husband's rib had been torn from his side.

"This is what your husband ought to be doing." Vireo's eyes were poisonous as he looked back at me. "Look at Lady Tanglecott's mounted Lions."

He gestured to where a column of Wittenbrand mounted on actual mist lions rode out from a tear in the sky. They rode four abreast, their white mounts clawing at the air and snapping at anyone who got in their way. White fur lined in the burnt gold of an orange blossom heart was striped jagged charcoal lines but neither light nor shadow disguised the power of bunching muscles and the way their lips curled up in black arches and revealed the scimitar curves of ivory teeth. My back twinged at the thought of one of them getting near me again. I couldn't believe that the men dressed in flowing purple and seated on saddles of gold were not immediately consumed by their own mounts but they hardly seemed to notice the beasts under them. They rode with eyes ahead and voluminous banners flying behind them.

And then we were descending into the chaos.

A group of Wittenbrand wearing Coppertomb's drab colors drilled in firm precision around a long cylindrical device. One end of the device smoked and sputtered, but it was not that end they were avoiding, but the other. They worked in perfect synchronicity as if they performed a dance.

I barely had time to gape before Vireo spun us in another direction and we were nearly crushed against a party of Wittenbrand marching to a steady whipcrack. They cracked their whips in unison, taking a step behind the whips, spinning, and then cracking again until they leapfrogged each other, jammed naked knives between their teeth, and then spun again. They smelled of sweat and onions.

I was struck dumb turning from one group to the next.

"But are they not at war in the mortal world?" I whispered to Grosbeak as we wove through the crowd. I barely had time to digest one sight before another filled my vision.

"Of course they are. This display is for intimidation. A reminder of what you go up against. A reminder of how strong and brave we are – we will not merely spend our mortal pawns in battle, we will fight ourselves. Or, most of us will." He sounded proud. "You wanted to play the game, Izolda. You wanted to break free of the Arrow. Now you see what that means. The rules are death by drowning, by fire, by enchantment, or by sword. What choose you, now?"

"I choose not to die," I said between clenched teeth.

"That was my choice," he replied, nodding sagely – though how he did that when he hung from a chain, I did not know. "It worked out well for me, as you can imagine."

I bit back a curse.

Okay, Izolda. Think. You wanted to be a spy. You wanted to find practical ways to defeat your husband's enemies. So. Do it. Watch and learn. Find ways. What would a mortal learn from this that a Wittenbrand wouldn't see?

I kept my eyes open as we whirled between displays, watching fire-breathers spout like baby dragons and a series of knife throwers strike targets the size of wine corks hanging from their friend's ears. And I knew the answer to my question.

We were in trouble – we mortals. So much trouble.

I swallowed down heavy despair, thicker than cold grease in my throat.

What hope had we against the powers arrayed against us? Who could deliver us from this coming death?

Someone stepped in front of Vireo – a familiar figure with antlers and shaggy green moss all over his body. That was one of Bluebeard's people, wasn't it?

"Stand aside, Cornelis," Vireo growled. "I've no time for you."

"The rumors say you plan to take the place of the Arrow as our prince, and yet you have no time for us?"

"Neither now nor if I ever take that place."

I was so distracted that I didn't notice there was someone standing behind me.

"Feeling misty-eyed?" a voice whispered in my ear. "No, don't turn. He's busy now. Just take this message."

I felt something slip into my palm – the same palm that held the egg – while Vireo shoved Cornelis aside.

"Know your place, Cornelis. You're folk. Underfolk. That's all you'll ever be."

"That's not how the Arrow sees us, Vireo," Cornelis called after us as Vireo pressed back into the crowd. "He sees us as people. He cares about our peace."

Vireo stopped and whirled back to shout at Cornelis, which gave me a chance to see the whole band of them there – the strange folk I'd seen in Bluebeard's house. Some were walking, shambling trees. One was a fox in a vest and hat. A few had antlers or hooves or tails. They seemed smaller out here among the Wittenbrand. Dimmer. As if they'd lost their life just a little.

I stole a look at the paper in my hand.

"We're with you," it read. "For the Arrow."

And I could see it was true, shining out from their eyes as they watched Vireo with restrained fury and me with pity.

"And is he here?" Vireo roared. "Is he raising an army? Is he vanquishing his foes? Or is he saving mortals? Did he spend all his resources on peace for his *folk*?" He spat the last word. "You. This mortal girl. The mortal world. You're all his undoing. He's a soft fool and you've killed him with your own hands."

And then he was storming away and dragging me with him and this time I went willingly because I couldn't look into their crumpling faces without crumpling inside myself. We all meant well – these folk and me – and we all weighed on him against our wills. Even my obedience felt like a betrayal to my husband.

"And how do you like the Wittenhame on your second trip here, Izolda?" Grosbeak asked as if a cheery conversation was the right choice when Vireo was glowering and tugging me by my braid so that I feared it might come out at the roots.

"I wish I had a fairy godmother to whisk me away like in a tale for children," I said, my eyes stinging. But even if she did, there was no fleeing this. "This place seems dimmer and darker than the last time I was here."

And it was true, for while it was still violent and bloody – I was relatively certain that one of the vendors was selling jackets made of human leather and there was a card game going on that we'd walked by where the competitors were betting fingers and toes – it had lost the sense of purpose and wonder that had been mixed throughout that violence before.

"Hear that, Vireo? She says it's darker. Less magical," Grosbeak said.

Vireo grunted.

"Would you say it's *lesser*, Izolda?" Grosbeak pressed. "Pathetic, even? In comparison, of course, to what you saw before?"

"Perhaps," I said, drawing the word out in my uncertainty. "Certainly, less lively, less vigorous."

Grosbeak laughed nastily.

"I can still sew your mouth shut, revenant," Vireo muttered, but he seemed preoccupied as we finally emerged from the press of bodies and pushed toward a building that looked like a tangled crown sticking out from the forest floor. It was the size of a palace and gilded from top to bottom as if the owner had said, "Try for blindingly ugly, but I'll settle for merely gaudy if I must."

"The Wittenhame, my dear Izolda," Grosbeak said, as if he were delivering the most delicious gossip, "is much like the valley we leapt into to find the Isle of Burning Guilt. You, as a mortal, cannot shape it, though some features like the valley reflect the inside of your mind. But the rest of the Wittenhame is affected by those mortal souls residing there. As the prisoner of Vireo, you are seeing *his* Wittenhame, just as when you came here as wife of the Arrow, you were seeing *his* version of this place."

Oh.

Oh.

Well. That explained Vireo's attitude.

"Shhh," I warned Grosbeak. He wasn't making us any friends.

"I'll be rid of you both soon enough," Vireo growled. "And good riddance, for I have plenty more that needs my attention."

Grosbeak nodded gravely. "Like proper grooming. Or dying messily on the Arrow's blade."

"Laugh all you want, you two damned souls. It matters not to me," Vireo said as he tugged me roughly forward and knocked on the gilded door. It was made entirely out of hundreds of interwoven blades. "You're the Sword's problem now."

CHAPTER NINETEEN

The Sword, it turned out, did not answer his own door, nor was his home as welcoming as Bluebeards for while Bluebeard's ceiling seemed to reach up endlessly into the starry sky, the Sword's castle seemed to reach *out* endlessly into one gallery after another.

He was a collector. And were I not in fear for my life, and if I did not have such utter disdain for a man who would snatch away my innocence just to test a theory about a rival, I would have been deeply impressed.

We were led by a silent butler through the Sword's halls, passing through a gallery so long it could hold the entire palace in Aayadmoore within its walls. It was decked out, floor to coffered ceiling, with portraiture. Tiny miniatures no larger than my palm were side by side with portraits so large they dwarfed me, their elegant gilt frames thicker than my waist. And while one might think that no one could take time in thinking of the place for each one of so many thousands, there had clearly been careful intent regarding the positioning so that a fierce expression was followed by one that countered it with disdainful arrogance and then that again was belied by a face of such virtuous innocence that I found myself pausing to wonder if it could be real or if the designer had intentionally revealed the hypocrisy by placing it beside that particular counterpoint.

I leaned in closely to examine one, and to my horror I realized that the curling hair around the face was real hair set into the paint and the frothy lace around the neck was made of human teeth.

And that was only one gallery.

"Ohhh. Fancy," Grosbeak commented appreciatively. "I've never seen such a collection of death portraits before. A sheer delight."

Somehow, his comments seemed to cheapen each room as if his very admiration lessened them. I was grateful for any distraction that might turn my mind from wandering how a "death portrait" was made and with *what.*

No better was a room of gnarled, shrunken bodies that Grosbeak claimed were called "mummies" arranged in various poses with blades stuck through them as if they had died and then been frozen in the pose of their deaths.

Our legs tired and our eyes wore dim from seeing horrors by the time we reached the heart of the palace. Were a connoisseur granted both access and a pair of scribes to assist, still he could not have cataloged the room of tiny miniatures crafted to look perfectly lifelike in expression and fashion – and posed in such a way that made me shudder and close my eyes, begging whatever merciful god there may be to take the memory of what I'd seen away. He would have been just as put upon to try to catalogue the hall that was a series of waterfalls falling from one tier to the next with walkways weaving between them and trees dripping with flowers leaning over the paths as if trying to catch a lover's whisper. Interspersed among the flora had been gold-cast statues of Wittenbrand and when my eyes had widened at the sight, Grosbeak had snickered with delight.

"The Gilded Falls. There's a legend about how he trapped those and brought them to his house. I thought it was merely a story."

"I would think he'd want to display those golden statues somewhere more visible," I said.

Grosbeak snickered. "They stay where they are. That's the beauty and horror of it. The waters turn any living thing that touches them into gold. If you creep closely you can see schools of fish at the bottom of the pond – but I wouldn't recommend getting close enough that the spray could touch you."

Perhaps, were I another woman, I might find such grandeur impressive. Perhaps, I might be flattered to find myself mistress of it – married to the owner of all I surveyed.

But just as in fairy tales told to children, I had an inkling that as easily as this wealth had been accumulated, it could be snatched away, and with it, no happiness had been bought, no joy fostered, no longevity purchased for the heart. Just as the false marriage the Sword had forced on me was hollow, so these horrifying luxuries were hollow with it.

And though the butler was well dressed in clothes far finer than those worn by the King of Pensmoore, and though he looked mortal to my naked eye, but for the greenish tinge to his skin, still anxiety knifed its way through every nerve of my body as we drew closer and closer to the Wittenbrand who had made himself my mortal enemy as surely as he had made my husband such.

We found him in the middle of an enormous ballroom, directing his staff of hundreds as they prepared what appeared to be a feast.

"Ah, you've brought my wife, Vireo," he said casually as if I hadn't been ripped from his grasp and then stolen away from Bluebeard's. "I believe the price of retrieval was my support on your bid for a seat on our council, hmm?"

"As you say, Prince of Wittenhame," Vireo said woodenly, and I was surprised by how still his face and body were – almost as if he were petrified in fear.

"I'll throw in an invitation to dance here tonight," the Sword said, sweeping a gracious bow – but a very shallow one that was almost mocking in how he sketched it. "After all, you were prompt, and she seems to be as unharmed as any of us. All of Wittenhame will dance at my Petal Ball tonight for the dawn of the Second Move."

His grin was toothy and dangerous, and I realized that within the spills of flowers and ornamental flowers his staff was arranging, there were a variety of traps – some large clamshells with spiky teeth like the cruel ones meant to catch the leg of a bear and some tiny little things barely larger than my fingernail. I was no fool. Those tiny ones were likely just as deadly as the large ones.

Take note, Izolda. Do not stop to smell the roses.

My heart was racing so quickly that I couldn't quite control it. Little spots of blackness danced over my eyesight, and I knew I must calm myself or risk fainting. But I needed a plan. I needed it now. It needed to be practical, and it needed to keep the Sword from molesting my person.

I could think of nothing. Reaching for thought was like trying to hold air in the hand.

"You're outdoing yourself, Sword," Grosbeak said, breaking the tension.

"I've raided a thousand gardens over a thousand centuries for these," the Sword said with a satisfied smile as he waved an elegant hand at the sprays of flowers draped or wreathed or carefully woven over every surface of the room, even including the many arched doors. "But none compare to the flower who will walk in on my arm into the Petal Ball tonight."

"Like you, I often find an enchanted partner to be the best," Grosbeak said but I knew there would be a barb by the tone of his voice. "A woman spun from a rose blossom has skin softer than a petal and she doesn't stab you in the back. Wise choice."

"My choice is wise indeed," the Sword said coldly. "For I shall display to the Wittenhame how I have stolen the Arrow's wife and made her my own. You may go now, Vireo. And mind the traps. It would be a shame to attend my ball with only one leg. It would set us one partner shy for the dancing."

He waved a lace-cuffed hand idly and then turned on me.

I could stay silent. I could refuse to speak or to cry or to run or to show my fear, but I couldn't keep my breath even and calm. Not even though I fought it with all my strength.

"You've played the coy and blushing maiden, mortal girl, but now that time is passed," and with shocking speed, his hand darted out and pinched my ear and with even more surprising strength, he wrenched me off my feet and began to drag me over the marble floor by the shell of my ear.

Pain filled me, pounding through my head. I caught his wrist with one hand, holding tight to keep my ear from being torn off, and with the other I clutched Grosbeak's pole as he was dragged along with me. Tears stung my eyes, but I would not scream. I would not.

I needed an opportunity. Some chance to get away.

And then I saw it.

We were passing an open door of what must be a library. All I could see was a wall of books. But libraries were always huge and this one would have plenty of places to hide.

With a quick twist, I hurled Grossbeak's head into the open door and then flipped hard, rolling to the side like a pickerel on the line and flipping from the Sword's grasp – the fish spitting the hook.

I tumbled, rolling across the slick floor and through the door. I could feel each bump and bruise, but I refused to acknowledge them as I scrambled to my feet and slammed the door shut before the look of shock had left the Sword's face.

With quick hands, I locked the door. There was a bar, which I set quickly into place before the first knock hammered against the thick door.

"If you think a door will keep me out, little mortal, you should think again," the Sword drawled.

It would be okay. I had time. I just had to hide in the library.

I scooped up Grosbeak's pole.

"Nnngh. Why did you throw me like that? I'm a head, not a stuffed ball for children to throw!" he moaned.

I ignored him. This was our chance to escape. Spying was not a good fit for us after all, and we'd seen plenty enough to tell Bluebeard.

I ran down the shelf of books – it was barely two strides long – and turned into a tiny padded alcove for reading.

"There's only one shelf in this library," I gasped, shocked.

Even my father's library was bigger, and we had not money for many books with our horses to care for and a keep to manage.

No. This couldn't be right. The ache in my healing shoulder intensified and when I pressed a hand to it, it came away wet. Flinging oneself across a hall to bounce and roll was not a winning strategy for healing wounds.

The Sword pounded on the door again, making the lonely books quiver on their shelves.

"I'm sorry, did you take your second husband for a reader?" Grosbeak asked sourly. "He struck you as the type to contemplate life and consider the nuances, did he?"

I gritted my teeth. My plan was failing fast.

"Let me in, Izolda Savataz!" the Sword roared. "For I will make you my wife this time and no cloud of birds will swoop in to stop me."

The monster was outside my door, clawing his way in. How would I keep him out? How?

"He's going to get in. He's going to get in," Grosbeak chanted and I didn't know which of us he was cheering for at that point.

The frame of the door splintered with a chilling crack.

"If you can't keep him out, let him in, let him *in*," Grosbeak screamed and then burst into hysterical laughter. You'd think the one who had only his head left would learn to keep it in a crisis.

I rolled my eyes at him, but as the bar across the door broke in half, I seized on his suggestion and drew the little key from my bodice.

He was right. This wasn't the only place to which I could flee, and if I couldn't keep the Sword out, then I really should let him in – all the way in.

I drew out the key, twisted it to unlock the room, and fled inside.

It was only when I glanced over my shoulder to see if he was following that I remembered the ghast riding just over my shoulder. She winked at me and that alone was enough to make my breath gasp harsh and raw in my lungs.

CHAPTER TWENTY

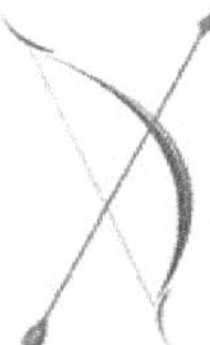

"Here he comes, here he comes!" Grosbeak shrieked as I ran down the line of wives, looking up to their impassive faces as if they could see, as if they could guard, as if just by having them there as witnesses I could derive some kind of strength from them. They had each been where I was before. In a manner of speaking. Certainly, the Sword had not stolen them from Bluebeard, but that had not saved their leaking days.

My days trickled down from the top bulb of the hourglass, the garnets ringing like tinkling bells as they fell and hit their fellows. My husband must be spending my days even as I ran toward them. I could only hope that he was spending them on something useful and not on trying to rescue me.

And just like that, steel snapped my spine straight and I felt like I could breathe again.

I was a practical girl.

I could deal with this sensibly. So, what did a sensible girl do when confronted with an enemy bent on her destruction? She found a way to dissuade him.

I took up a stance in front of the hourglass and crossed my arms, trying to look like I knew what I was doing. Like I belonged here. Like he didn't. And it was easier to do because it was true.

"What manner of mausoleum is this?" the Sword asked as he slunk into the room, hand on the hilt of his sword, his eyes wary. He stepped like a cat in a new place, his graceful movements so close to my husband's, that my traitor heart beat double for a moment. I forced it back to calm.

"Behold," I said, grandly – because he was grand and I was beginning to realize he could respect nothing else, "The brides of Bluebeard. And what, lordly Sword, do they have in common?"

"They have all passed this life," he said, awe in his voice and something that looked like enjoyment. It took me a heartbeat to identify it. It was admiration – one collector admiring the collection of the other. "I see the charm."

"And what else do you see? Surely, you, a great collector, can see the similarities," I said.

"They're each more lovely than the last," he said, his voice distant and wondering as he reached out and touched the edge of Princess Margaretta's dress.

I flinched. It felt almost as intrusive as if he'd touched the hem of my own garment. My fellow brides were not here for his amusement. My thoughts stuttered for a moment as I realized that perhaps that was why Bluebeard kept them in this room that held the hourglass. Only another bride could know what they had suffered. Only another bride could pay them the honor they were due.

The Sword lingered over Corinnian, a particularly lovely bride whose full figure gave her an air of majesty I would never possess. He paused, arrested, and then his eyes whipped to mine.

"Except you. You are an aberration in a perfect set."

His brow furrowed in confusion.

"Do you note their books?" I asked, drawing him in with my mild tone, setting my own trap among the flowers. If only it would work. If only he did not see it before it was sprung.

He laid a hand on the closest one and I flinched as he flipped through the pages.

"They speak of their lives with Bluebeard," I told him, my voice smooth as a storyteller's. "Of their secrets. Of the one thing you don't know about them."

I was betting that he wouldn't read them. A man with such a pitiful library wouldn't read, would he?

"How he takes their days as his own," the Sword breathed in reverent wonder, hunger in his tone.

It took every bit of my self-control to keep surprise from my expression. He must be desperate indeed to reveal himself to me so.

"They are virgins one and all," I say, my voice low and calm, hoping he might forget it was me talking at all. "Untouched by Bluebeard, despite his marriage to them. Untouched by any man."

He looked up sharply at me and I was surprised as his expression turned from suspicion to hope. He flipped through the book in his hands – and I knew which one it was. It would tell of the wife who tried to tempt Bluebeard into her bed, failing again and again.

He read it as a starving man eats a dinner laid before him – devouring it without pause. And then he looked up at me and the relief on his face was stark.

Had he feared what he would do to me as much as I had feared it? The thought made him seem more human to me. More vulnerable. More like someone I could understand.

"And so, I have a choice," he said and all the compassion I'd just discovered in my heart withered away at his words. "A choice on which weighs so much."

He tapped his lip with one finger, regarding me and then regarding the other brides again before returning his eyes to me.

"If I defile you, I will rob him of his secret power, rendering you useless. But if I do such, I will also keep that power from my own grasp."

He tapped his chin.

"Perhaps it was that you were married twice." He was nodding now to himself. "You will have your marriage to him annulled. We will see a priest. And then you will marry me again. It is only the vows that keep your enchantment from my grasp. I had not thought that they must be removed before others were added." There was certainty in his eyes now. "Yes, this is so. And you will return to him the key to this room, for it is not yours and it never will be." He smiled. "Yes, that will work. That will suffice."

He put down the book and started to stride away, spinning in place to say one more thing to me.

"You'll attend the Petal Ball with me tonight and I expect that you will show your loyalty to me with your eager feet in the dances and your eager smile at my side. Have not a fear for what you will wear, as I shall provide that. Think instead of resting. The rings around your eyes are dark with sorrow and you are not one of those women in whom grief works beauteous wonders. Don't leave the library. I will retrieve you at dusk."

And then he was gone – out of the room of wives, and out the door of the library, and I heard the sharp snick of bolts being thrown and the heavy *thunk* of the bar on the other side of the door being set in place.

I leaned heavily against the hourglass as if embracing my own days might make them last just a little longer – or run out right now – and I hardly knew which I wanted more. I simply let the cool glass against my cheek give what comfort it could.

"Well, that went smoothly. Who knew you were such a savvy negotiator," Grosbeak said. "But you'll need a plan before the Petal Ball. When Bluebeard sees you on the Sword's arm, he may well behead you both. Trust me, it's not as glamorous as I make it look."

My eyes went wide.

"He'll be there?" I asked, my voice choked with worry.

My battered friend grinned.

"Of course. Like the Sword said, half the Witenhame will be there."

"And I won't be able to tell him about the isl – "

The specter wrapped her hand around my mouth, frowning as she shook her inky head.

"Exactly," Grosbeak said, almost smugly. "I've gotten to like you, Izolda, and yet I've always been a passionate admirer of melodrama. I believe you're about to deliver for me tonight. I can hardly wait."

CHAPTER TWENTY-ONE

I seized upon this opportunity to finally examine the egg. There was really nothing else to do.

It was woven of grass and light as a feather and though I held it up to the light and peered at it from every which way, I could not determine what might be within the weaving for there was neither shadow nor profile to hint at it and it was not heavy, nor did it make a sound when shaken.

"Where do you pick that up?" Grosbeak asked curiously. "'Tis an odd little thing."

Eventually, I resorted to breaking it open – a difficult thing to do with an egg so tightly woven. I had to grasp each side and pull – and when I did that, it flattened the woven egg so much that I was certain there could be nothing inside and I was ruining this uncanny bit of craftmanship for no reason at all.

Eventually, though, the strands of grass shredded and the egg tore in twain, and from its hollow grassy depths arose the smell of fresh-turned fields and a voice that sounded so much like the Bramble King's that I looked around the room, thinking he might be right beside me.

It sang,

"Fly with the Arrow,

Dance with the Sword,

Give your heart to the barrow,

Die with your Lord.

"And if ever you be broken

And gasp on the ground,

Hold up your fine token

And join with the sound,

"Sing for your sovereign,

Bow to your Dream,

Make haste for the fallen,

Rise in esteem,

"And if ever you be broken,

And gasp on the ground,

The word may be spoken

And salvation found."

It was the song I'd heard from the crowd when the Arrow arrived for the opening of the Game of Crowns. And now that I heard it again, different words and phrases stood out to me than they had last time.

Perhaps, it was because when the words faded a very tiny item was found in the scraps of grass after all – a tiny golden bell, as small as the nail on my forefinger and forged with such precision that all I could think of were tiny jewelers hammering it out. It hung from a little clip meant to be fastened into hair and after a moment of thought, I clipped the tiny bell into my dark locks.

It did not ring when I moved. It made no sound at all. And there was something about that so immensely chilling that I shivered with the thought of it.

"It's only an egg from a Springtide Hunt," Grosbeak said disappointedly. "I'd hoped there would be something special inside it."

"Isn't the little bell something special?" I asked, surprised by his reaction.

"Not really. It doesn't even ring. And the song is just that old folk ditty. Who would ever give their heart to the barrow? No one falls in love with the dead."

"Aww, Grosbeak, don't give up so easily," I said lightly, troubled even more now by his words and trying to hide it. "I'm sure there's a bodiless lady out there somewhere."

"Yes, in your husband's vaults," he said sourly. But I pretended to be absorbed in repairing my braid in the reflection of the hourglass because I didn't want him to see what was churning in my brain.

I saw this place differently than the Wittenbrand did. What was normal to them was a wonder to me and that gave me an advantage because since all of this was new to me, I did not overlook any details.

Which was how I was sure that the Bramble King's little riddle was simply understood.

I am the culmination of desire, the fruit of death. I am the summit of loss, the passing of weight. What am I?

It seemed obvious to me what he was saying. He meant this game that they were all playing to be a hunt for his successor. After all, did they not all want to reign? And could that not only be accomplished by his death? And inheritance was, indeed, a passing of weight at the very summit of loss.

But it was more nuanced than that because I was certain that he had left these eggs to be found along with his riddle and while his riddle told us *why* this hunt mattered, *why* this game mattered, it did not mention how it was to be achieved. And while that might be as simple as winning all the wars and wiping my mortal brethren from the maps of this age, it might be something that was more obvious to me than to them. It might be contained in that song. That simple, folksy song they thought nothing of. After all, why else would the Bramble King have sung it? And what could this bell be but the token in his song?

I would keep it close just in case. I would hold it fast. And if no one – not even Grosbeak – realized why, then all the better. It was more beneficial for me to be thought a child wearing a trinket than to show that I understood.

The nice thing about being beneath notice was that nothing else was beneath *my* notice.

But though I turned the second riddle over and over in my mind, I had no answers when the Sword came to retrieve me. For while the first riddle that opened the second was simple enough, the second riddle was far more complex to decipher.

The Sword was decked out even more splendidly than he had been before. His jacket was made of the actual open blossoms of red roses, the scent of them filling the air and clinging to his finely wrought face and curling gold hair. He'd even twined contrasting white roses around the scabbards crossed over his back and hanging from his left hip.

"My blossom," he said, offering me an arm with a smile as if he was my husband in truth and not my tormentor. "Let us see you dressed."

I did not take his arm. "I'm fine in the clothing I wear," I said, not even looking at my torn and bloody clothes.

"I think not. I am not bringing Death's scrub maid to the Petal Ball, but rather my delicious trophy of a wife. Come." He raised a challenging eyebrow, his arm still held out.

If this was a battle of the wills, perhaps it was better to surrender now and fight back when he least expected it. Holding in all the things I wished I could say to snub him, I instead took his arm, careful not to crush the roses as I let him lead me down the hall.

I closed the door of Bluebeard's chamber of wives behind me and carried Grosbeak's pole in my other hand. The Sword scowled at my friend's head swinging back and forth.

"If you are to be my wife, you must give up such pedestrian accessories," he said in his arrogant drawl.

"If you think you are my husband, it would do you well to give up thinking you can determine my actions," I said and I hated that I sounded a little breathless. He was a powerful Wittenbrand. He could slash me apart with that sword. He could take my life in an instant. I couldn't stop him.

But I could stop him from taking my dignity. I could, at least, do that.

He brought me to a small parlor decorated in scrollwork panels of white and gold. The room was empty of furnishings except for one full-length mirror. And for a moment, I startled, because the mirror looked very much like Bluebeard's mirror except for the moon-shaped face gilt on the apex of the mirror rather than a gargoyle. It yawned dramatically and then opened its eyes.

"Dress my wife in a gown that bares her soul to all," the Sword drawled.

"I'd really rather not," I said sternly.

"Well, aren't you a fearsome bore," he huffed. He turned back to the mirror. "We'll compromise. Dress her as the fearsome bore she is but make it elegant. And captivating. I'll have no wife of mine look the drab."

I stared at him. Compromise? From the Sword. If he could compromise in this, could he be reasoned with on the field of battle?

"What are you staring at, mortal?" he chastised me. "Walk through the mirror!"

I startled at his fierce hiss and then pulled myself straight and strode through the mirror. I closed my eyes at the last second, not daring to look when I crashed into the glass, but there was no crash and I found myself on the other side feeling – heavier.

I looked down and gasped. The mirror had given him exactly what he'd asked for – at least in its own way. The dress was of a fine dove-grey silk that buttoned with tiny black buttons right up to my chin. Tight sleeves reached down to loops that fitted over my middle fingers. There was hardly a breath of flesh exposed anywhere. Modest. Boring. Totally inappropriate for something called the "Petal Ball." Or it would be if that were all.

It was not all.

The skirts of the dress were very full, and they pulled up at the front to be so short they were barely decent, exposing the edges of frothy cream petticoats – and three snapping grey and white wolves. They seemed – somehow – constrained by my skirts so that they could not leave the bell of the full skirt. They could not move more than a few inches to lunge and snap at anything nearby.

I should have feared they would turn on me and devour me, but my first thought was for Grosbeak, and I barely pulled his pole up high enough in time as the middle wolf snapped at his head.

"Go back through the mirror!" he gasped. "Nothing with wolves, mirror! Scars and sires! It's for the forest-forsaken Petal Ball, not a raid on the north peaks!"

But the Sword had already looped his arm around mine again.

"Perfection," he said with a suave smile. "We're the beauty and the beast of legend. I, of course, am the beauty."

"Of course," I said dryly, but his grin seemed to take it for a demure.

"'For none could learn to love a beast,'" he quoted smugly.

But I wasn't listening. My attention was entirely taken with the door at the end of the hallway.

"Your party must begin soon," I said awkwardly. "But where are the guests?"

For the hallway was utterly empty without even a servant in sight, though blossoms hung in garlands along the hall.

I would not want to be those servants tomorrow. My arms felt tired just thinking of all the work of hauling the flowers away and sweeping up the petals, filling sacks with them, and bringing the sacks to carts to haul away. Even an army of servants working until their arms and backs ached could hardly clear away so many flowers before they began to rot, and the stench of rotted blossoms would fill this palace from bottom to brim. It seemed, somehow, a fitting tribute to the lord of these halls.

"They are arriving through other doors. My palace has many," he drawled, playing with the hilt of the sword at his side. "Be not anxious, I have timed our arrival to perfection."

And when he hauled the woven-sword door open – a door taller than three of me standing on each other's shoulders – he was proven correct. His ballroom was almost filled to the brim.

Where once there had been a sweeping expanse of marble floor, now there were costumed people in gowns and suits so grand I could hardly take them in. A woman near me wore a dress made of a hundred doors and whenever one opened, a tiny mouse would pop out and scurry to another door, opening it in turn, and disappearing inside. Little hints of her flesh or underthings peeked out at every open door and I was already blushing for her when I tore my eyes away to the next costume. This was a Wittenbrand man with a very tall hat of ringed-tails sewn into a tall, flat-topped contrivance. Thunder made his whole hat quake and then every so often a tiny burst of blue-white lightning would crackle out from the hat and into the crowd causing shrieks and laughter in equal measure.

I ripped my eyes from him, too. There was no time to take in every outlandish costume, my wolves seemed almost tame in comparison, except that they kept the crowd back from me. I ought to wear such a dress at every social outing for just that effect.

I forced myself to take inventory of the room. The doors that had been shut before were open now, and each of them was as high and wide as the one we'd arrived through. The vistas they displayed in their open portals stole my breath more than the fashion, for each seemed to enter a different world – one a pale beach with white sand and azure sky as far as the eye could see. Another a thick jungle of heavy fronds and howling creatures, still another showed a rocky coast at midnight with the high moon full-blown and shining and another still rippled with the yellow glare of the desert.

But here, in the great room decked out for the party, where drinks both iced and steaming were flowing freely and flirtation mixed with challenge and laughter with the occasional pained scream, here, the room was so overflowing with blossoms that petals in pinks and purples and whites rained down on us, a fragrant blizzard with drifts to match below.

"My kingdom," the Sword said proudly, sweeping his arm to display the room to me, and just when I was beginning to realize that one wall – made entirely of petals – showed the figure of the Bramble King half-submerged in petals as he drifted and dreamed, the Sword added, "And those who will soon be my subjects."

And a chill rolled through me because that meant he knew what the riddle meant, too, that he knew this game was a game for winning the Bramble King's throne and he was playing to win just as my true husband must be.

That alone should have been enough to freeze me in place and burn me to a black cinder – but it was nothing compared to the jolt of terror-laced delight I felt when my eyes tripped over a gaze across the room – a gaze of light blue cat's eyes above one single streak of scarlet blood staring right at me as if it could pin me in place.

I froze and beneath those javelin eyes and one corner of a mouth turned upward as its owner rang a tiny golden bell – the bell he'd scooped up when I dropped it at the moment of our first meeting. Like magic, the crowd grew silent – all except the Sword who was growling in the back of his throat.

The Sword's face had gone scarlet, but my husband, my daring, wild husband looked down on him with a smirk as he announced to the room, "The flower, lovely in her grace and delicate in her scent is but a promise. I care not for the promise, but for the fruit of it."

And with a strange sign made by twisting the fingers of one hand and drawing them down before his face and then a flick of his wrist, he turned every flower in the room into bursting ripe fruit.

My breath caught with all the others, but not in wonder over fat blushing fruit, but in guilt, as I listened to the words he spoke, for *I* had promised him the world and fruited nothing but bitter betrayals.

CHAPTER TWENTY-TWO

The Sword muttered a curse. "One day I will make him eat refuse for every time he has upstaged me."

But then he forced a bright smile on his face as he seized my hand and led me to the very center of the room. He plucked a small comb from his breast pocket – the delicate thing I'd seen before made of mother of pearl and inlaid with emeralds. The teeth of the tiny comb were no straighter than a crone's. He ran it through his curls for a moment before tucking it away and as if the action had gained him courage, he spoke with a voice both loud and carrying.

"Friends, enemies, Wittenbrand," the crowd turned from Bluebeard to him, their eyes bright with what I thought must be a glimmer of Grosbeak's taste for melodrama. "Welcome to my halls and I hope you don't feel the need to change my décor so dramatically, as some have." Around us, the crowd laughed nervously. "The Second Move is upon us and with it, a time of celebration. And so, I beg you to be my guests this night and abandon all that is beyond these walls as we dance the night away."

He extended his free hand in open welcome and then snapped his fingers. The music started, though I could not tell where the pipers and players were hidden.

"Lady," the Sword said, bowing to me. One of the wolves tried to snap his arm off, but the Sword kept far enough back that it could not reach him – a feat since the three wolves were positioned across the front of my dress, joining in the music with the steady thrum of their growling. "We will dance, of course."

I opened my mouth to refuse him, but he leaned in close, avoiding the wolves, and whispered. "I still think divorce is for the best, but the other ways of dealing with you have not been removed from the table. Humor me."

I glanced at him, as he leaned toward one of my ears, glanced to the other side to the dark wraith settled there with a finger over her lips, and then back again. In the stories, a person had a devil on one shoulder and an angel on the other. No one had ever told me a story about a person with two devils competing, but it seemed I would be the central character in this one.

"Do you know the *akul*?" I suggested, but he only laughed and slipped himself behind me, clasping his spread hand over my belly in a way I found far too familiar and then taking my free hand in his.

I gasped, my cheeks heating immediately. But then I realized that the dancers around us were positioning themselves likewise.

Beside us, Lady Wittentree paused with her partner, her skirts whipping and snapping around her like a ship's sails in a storm. Every so often a black, white-tipped breaker would roll out from them and crash like surf upon the ground around her, leaving a brackish trail everywhere she went. She seemed to wink at me, though it was hard to be sure when she had only the one yellow eye.

"I asked for the *aconda*," the Sword said smugly, "both because I prefer not to be unmanned by your wolves while I dance, and because I have a feeling that a certain fruit-loving prince may not like this dance."

"Of course, you chose that dance," Grosbeak said from his place on the end of the chain, "since it involves hiding behind your woman."

"Silence, pet." The Sword adjusted his crown slightly, as if to emphasize the rib contained within it.

"Will the next dance involve you dramatically leaving those you vowed to protect out on their own to be cut off from their people?"

"I'm afraid I don't know that one, cursed specter," the Sword said coolly.

I ignored them both and looked up again, letting my eyes steal a quick look at Bluebeard. I gasped all over again as his eyes pierced into mine. I'd been using the common expression "steal a look" all my life, but this glance, this gaze, really felt like theft. I felt I robbed him of something private to him, for the look in his eyes as I snatched my glimpse of him was the look of a man bereft.

Without breaking eye contact, he held his hand to the side, and Lady Tanglecott took it, swaying to position herself – and her accompanying snow lions – in front of him for the dance.

A stab of jealousy burned through me. Lady Tanglecott wore a dress made entirely of white feathers and every so often a band of double rainbows appeared around her waist or arm or thigh as if she were an angel from the heavens. If our apparel reflected our souls, what did that say about her? Or me, for that matter.

The music began, and the Sword stepped me through the dance. It was easy enough to follow with him leading despite the twisting feeling in my guts. His body pressed up against my back, his hand tightened across my belly. I felt more of him than I would have liked against my back and his nearness gave me a queasiness that highlighted how this dance was yet another betrayal of mine against my furious husband. Yet another dagger in his etched back. It should be for some purpose at least.

"Have you planned your second move?" I asked the Sword, as if making conversation.

"I planned all of this decades ago, before your father's father was making sons." He jogged me to the side with the other dancers.

To my shock, I realized this was no court dance. Beside us, Lady Wittentree spun suddenly, pulled a comb from her hair, loosening the sharp blunt locks, and then stabbed it into the side of her partner. He gasped, doubling over the wound as she tossed him to the side and then with an eager smile, found a new partner to spin her through the dance.

She was not the only one. I caught a glimpse of a pair locked in what first appeared to be a passionate embrace, but I realized after a moment that the lady's eyes were rolled back, a tiny dribble of green fluid falling from her parted lips. Poisoned.

Just as many dancers escaped the fate, though the dipping and spinning and weaving and ducking were not all part of the dance, but part of a more deadly dance between partners. A dance of life and death, celebration and destruction rolling in a tide of horror.

"And is it going according to your plans?" I asked, a little breathlessly as laughter and a teasing tone rolled over us from nearby. How did they laugh and flirt in the middle of … this?

"There was only one thing I did not have – but that fault is mended now," the Sword said slyly as he guided me out from him and spun me in a whirl, my canine protectors snapping at his knees and groin as he danced both with me and away from my wolves. I was piteously glad of them. The only defenses I had were these skirts and my bodiless token. "I required only a powerful bait. A way to lure the incorruptible. Who would have thought she'd be a grim-faced mortal?"

"I surprise even myself sometimes," I said dryly, but my eyes were wide as I watched the dance unfolding around us.

"First time dancing with a Wittenbrand?" the Sword drawled. "It's a spectacle no mortal court could contain."

"If by spectacle you mean an embarrassment," Grosbeak complained. "No one is putting in much effort. I'm seeing injuries and illnesses but where are the guts strung like garters? Where are the rains of blood? You'll have to replace your whole staff after this debacle, Sword. I almost think people are enjoying themselves."

To my horror, I thought he might be right. When I looked around us, the people dancing and fighting – blocking blades, turning blows, and still keeping a tight rhythm, a steady stream of careful steps and spins – seemed to be enjoying themselves. There were as many passionate kisses as there were attempted murders. As many winks and laughs as poisoned dusts flung in the face of the other. Was this just how they danced in this mad, mad place?

But it was impractical to kill off half your court every time you had a celebration … wasn't it?

I found the question disturbing. The Wittenbrand seemed to set as much value in life as in anything – they only saw its worth for how they could make use of it. It bore no intrinsic value on its own.

"It's the Second Move, dead man. We need every player alive for the fun to come," the Sword drawled to my best friend. "Don't rush me. There will be rivers of blood in good time."

"Psst. Izolda," Grosbeak whispered as the Sword whirled me again. It was hard not to hit people with Grosbeak's pole as we danced, his head swinging wildly toward the other dancers. Hard to avoid their blows and stabs and strikes as they danced and fought with wild looks in their eyes and lips parted with delight. "Your bridegroom comes. Him with the wounded side and fiery eyes."

And then, as the spin landed me neatly with my back against the Sword again, I was suddenly face-to-face with Bluebeard – almost chest to chest with him. My breath came so fast that the little black buttons on my dress strained in the effort of holding my lungs encased.

"Do you mind? We're dancing," the Sword said drawing out the syllables slowly, but the laughter in his voice told me this was the exact outcome he had hoped for in using me as bait. "And the mortal dances so well."

Bluebeard reached out and for a moment I thought he might be about to draw me to him. I started to melt, to sag toward him, but I was wrong. He snatched one of the roses from the Sword's jacket and as he brought it to his lips it became a strawberry.

"I thought I turned all the flowers to fruit," he said. "Perhaps yours have not the ability to be more than decorative, Sword."

He bit into the strawberry with his fine white teeth and my breath caught at his nearness. Oddly, one of the wolves whined, sitting back on its haunches and despite his very close proximity, none were trying to bite him. Perhaps they, too, recognized his reign over me.

"Too sour," Bluebeard declared. "Unripe. Callow."

"That you came all this way to insult me is flattery enough," the Sword drawled. "Had you no one else to feed you, Arrow?"

"Not for the hungers that drive me, Sword," Bluebeard said, but his eyes were not on the Sword, they were on me and if my heart was racing before, it was thundering down the track now. He reached up and touched my cheek with the gentlest touch of a single fingertip. "Enough of this dalliance wife. Come back to me. I've missed your somber face."

The Sword laughed nastily. "She's within my embrace right now, Arrow. And possession in the Wittenhame is the law. She belongs to me."

"Mm." It was not assent, and he still wasn't looking at his rival. His very gaze made me feel hot all the way through. "We are not our own – any of us. Come, dance with me, wife."

He took Grosbeak's pole from my hand and offered his other hand to me.

"I don't much fancy being passed about like a party favor," Grosbeak complained as the dancers ebbed and flowed around us, no more interested in this conflict than the dozens of others breaking out across the ballroom. "I'm trying to *see*! Do you know how hard it is to keep score with this chain swinging me about like a drunken sailor?"

"Is that wound of yours still bleeding, Arrow?" the Sword asked with delight in his voice, and I realized that in offering me his hand, my husband had exposed his bleeding wound. It still seeped a fresh, angry crimson.

A tiny shudder of protective fear ran through me. Always, I made him vulnerable.

Bluebeard leaned in close so that his forehead almost touched mine – almost, and yet not quite – and I wanted it to touch mine. I wanted to feel forgiveness in the touch.

"I'll ask again, and then I will leave if you give no answer," he whispered. His hot breath gusting over me like the winds of spring, carrying away the last resistance of the ice. "Dance with me?"

I grabbed his hand before he could take the offer away.

"Always," I mouthed.

And then suddenly, I was knocked to the side, only keeping my balance by the hand Bluebeard held. Pain blossomed in my face, my head, my neck. I wrenched my hand from the Sword's and put it to my split cheek, cradling the ruined flesh.

In his hand, the Sword held a dagger, the pommel dripping with blood.

I gasped, stumbling, my wolves snarling and snapping, and almost dragging me back toward my attacker.

"There, now do I have your attention, Arrow?" the Sword asked, his voice smooth and venomous. "Take her if you want. Dance as you will, but I know I'll leave my marks on her, too, just as you have. I'll snatch her back when I'm ready and I'll dance this dance of blood and passion with you until one of lies entwined with death at the feet of the other. And it will not be me, for I have not given my heart to the possession of a rotting mortal, already dead in the view of centuries. Dance with me, Arrow, for you are weak and soft and your white belly is showing with the hole where your rib once graced it."

"I already have a partner," Bluebeard said smoothly, drawing me close to him – chest to chest instead of with me in front of him, and he moved so that his wounded side was exposed to the Sword, guarding me with his broken body. My wolves calmed at this. "And she's prettier than you, Sword, so you're out of luck."

"You won't heal from the wound I gave you," the Sword snarled. "And you won't leave this room with your mortal talisman. I've enchanted every door against her escape, so roar all you want, but you have no bite here in my palace."

And then he strode away flicking blood from the pommel of his dagger, and I was left in Bluebeard's arms. He spun me out, slowly, watching me through eyes I could not read, and then spun me back to him, but while those around us fought a dance of passion and power, his handling of me was almost tender in its gentleness, achingly sweet in how he moved me so that it was his own back that was exposed to the other dancers and not mine.

He danced silently, his eyes on mine, his lips parted slightly, as if he had so much to say that he didn't dare say anything at all. And never, not for even a moment, did he stop looking at me, as if he were reading me like the most enthralling of books.

We were clear across the room, dancing slowly toward the huge fire that burned in an alcove along the wall, when the voice of the Bramble King cut through the festivities. It was barely more than a whisper and yet it sliced through the noise like cutting puppet strings.

"I declare the opening of the Second Move," he said, and then his eyes closed, and he retreated, vanishing into the flowers.

Where the Bramble King had been only a moment before, a tear formed in the wall and Coppertomb strode out of it. He was tidy and dapper and well dressed – not at all decadent in his choices. And his crisp appearance sent a chill down my spine. And though I wanted to be still and watch what he did next,

I found I could not stop dancing – almost as if my feet were enchanted to dance until my slippers wore out like a girl in a tale.

"Tanglecott," Coppertomb announced, and for a moment I thought he wanted to say something, but he only pointed at her and then stepped aside and through his tear in the wall a bright streak leapt forward that looked almost like a dog, except that it had six heads, growling and snapping.

It lunged forward, scooping up the nearest screaming dancer and shredding her between the snapping jaws of two heads. And oh how I wanted to stop dancing, but my feet would not still. My heart would not calm.

"To the hunt!" Tanglecott cried in return from her side of the ballroom and then her snow lions leapt toward the six-headed dog and the party – such as it was – devolved into screaming, flight, and the drawing of weapons.

A sound filled the room. Screaming cicadas. And then, with the horrific sound of a hundred thousand sets of wings, they were everywhere, filling the ballroom in a mad cloud of vengeance.

"These parties always seem to end like this," Grosbeak said, but it wasn't a complaint, it was pure delight in his tone. And that tone turned my stomach.

"It's time we left, wife of mine," Bluebeard said mildly. "Unless you wanted to dance more?"

I met his eyes with mine and my eyes must have been doubled in size.

He nodded gravely as if I had replied, and then snapped his fingers and the room grew and grew until it seemed the dancers around us were giants and their screams made the whole world shudder. We barely dodged away from trampling giant feet as he danced me toward the flames – double my height now.

Just when I feared we would be burned up he called out, "My fire!"

"My master," said the fire.

And the world went red, red, red, and hot as shame.

CHAPTER TWENTY-THREE

A hand led me gently through the licking flames and then, with a sound like fabric tearing, we stepped out of the fire and into my husband's house.

Home, home, home my mind sang as the raven croaked and swooped down toward us, landing on Grosbeak's head.

"Love of forests and dales, would you get that thing off of me?" he protested.

Home, home, home, my heart sang as Bluebeard turned and said, "Thank you, my fire."

"A pleasure, my master," the fire growled, sparks spurting upward as he spoke.

Home, home, home, my heart sang as Bluebeard spun me to face him and raked my body with his gaze. I opened my mouth and he closed it with a single finger laid across my lips.

"It's evening, fire of my eyes. Your silence is required." One of my wolves snapped at him and he reached down and shut its mouth, pinching its snout together with his hand just like he'd closed my lips. "Hush now, pack of the night, wolves of my wife, guardians of my princess."

They obeyed immediately.

"That was the best Petal Ball I've been to in years," Grosbeak said with a happy sigh. "It's a shame we had to leave just when the fun was beginning."

"Say the word and you may return, O my enemy," Bluebeard told him distractedly, but his eyes never left mine. He gently touched my split cheek and I winced. "Days or silver thread, wife?"

I pointed to the thread in its hidden place, and he made a smug sound that might have been a rueful laugh. Now that he was here with me again, I couldn't help the almost intoxicated feeling I had at his presence. He sang to me like a song only I could hear. And it was brighter and stronger now that I'd seen his world without him – vicious, washed out, and blood-soaked – and seen the love for him in the eyes of his folk.

"Sit, while I do the honors," he said, and so he cleaned and stitched my wound, and as he did, he spoke to me. "I hope that you learned something of value, wife, so that your ill-advised dalliance with the Sword – or should I call it what it truly was? – your attempt at *spying* did not go to waste."

My eyes widened and he gave me a saucy half-smile as he threaded the needle with silver. I had only been there because I was following *his* order to follow Vireo. Did he really believe I'd betrayed him? And yet it had felt like a betrayal even though it was not.

"Speak to my riddle, wife," he said, looking up through the fan of his eyelashes. My breath caught in my throat. "What arrow sits better in the quiver than flies in the air? What spirit is better bound than set free? What sword is better kept in the sheath?"

"*None,*" I admitted in my mental voice.

"And you are better left to fly free and seek your mark," he murmured. Touching the sleeve of my dress which was wet with blood. “We will tend this a bit later, I think.”

“She’s a great spy,” Grosbeak said his words snapping like my wolves. “Wasn’t at all in danger – again – when the Sword tried to steal her virtue. Again. You don’t seem too worried about that, Arrow.”

“Why should I worry with you to defend her, Grosbeak?” Bluebeard asked, cleaning my wound with gentle hands. I tried not to flinch. “Why would I worry when I know my very sensible wife is craftier than the trickiest of the Wittenbrand?”

“You *should* have worried,” Grosbeak argued. “Vireo betrayed you! He dragged her into a conspiracy. We thought you would blame her for that!”

“And he will be punished for what he did,” Bluebeard said coolly as he set the first stitch. Tears stung my eyes. “But think you that I did not know what was in his heart? If I did not, would I have charged him with her care? Would I have asked her to follow him where I could not? He was most certainly planning to betray us. I hope only that my wife saw what was needed.”

Grosbeak and I both gasped at once and my husband quirked an eyebrow.

“You thought so little of me, wife? You thought I’d send you away to be protected by a traitor? To be watched over by a twisting reed? That I had misjudged both him and you by so far a distance?”

I shook my head, stunned. He was making no sense. He knew all this? Then why did he not prevent it from happening?

“I did think so. And like Grosbeak said, I thought you would blame me later even though I was only obeying your request. I

thought you would feel betrayed."

"Not so," he breathed as he set the second stitch, sending a little shiver over my bruised skin, and then he spoke this part into my mind so that it would stay between us. "*I have given you my trust, wife. And though I cannot yet entrust to you all my purposes, I do trust your heart and value your loyalty."* He switched back to speaking aloud. "My enemies plot and plan and think I do not know, but now my austere aspect, my sober visage, you can tell me all they have sworn you not to tell. Now, you can tell me what ways they threaten you and what means they use to try to tempt you into their arms. I would know the fullness of what we face."

I saw – I began, and then the specter was there, leaning around my shoulder and wrapping her clammy hand around my mouth, and to my shock I could not speak with my mind, either.

"Back creature," Bluebeard said, flicking the wraith away. She sulked over my shoulder but pulled her hands back in close.

"They've sealed you with a wraith." Bluebeard's eyes were bright with excitement. "Now, why would they do that unless you had something interesting to tell me? But you cannot tell me, or she'll choke the life out of you. Not even with your mind." He bit his lip in an inviting way. "That does complicate things. It wasn't the Sword, I gather. Secrecy is not his style. Nor Vireo for that fool would not think to seal you so."

"Not the Sword," Grosbeak confirmed. "And I grow weary of waiting for my revenge on him. Why will neither you nor your mortal wife slay him and get it over with?"

"You know as well as I do that if I slay him by my own hand, I will forfeit the game," Bluebeard said, sparing a quelling look for Grosbeak. "Is that what you'd have me do? Give up my immortality for your petty revenge?"

“Revenge is better than a thousand days of life.”

“If you say so. I suppose you would know best, dead as you are.”

“Then treat with Izolda, and convince her to kill the lout,” Grosbeak muttered. “She is remarkably peaceable, even when pushed.”

In answer, Bluebeard set the last stitch on my face, picked up Grosbeak’s pole, and set him on the bookshelf across the room from me. “I am done speaking with you, corpse. I have a wife to attend.”

He threw a cloth over Grosbeak’s grumbling head and returned with a little pot of salve, leaning in close so that I could feel his breath as he spoke.

“I’ve had enough of your pet for the time being, wife, and there are things we need to say to one another.” He ran a hand over his short beard nervously before meeting my eyes with his unsettling cat’s eyes. “I seem to be forever short on time. But I must spin more time for this. Somehow.”

He took my hands in his calloused ones, as gently as you might take a child’s, but I saw him wince as he turned, the wound in his side soaking the side of his clothing. I flinched as I looked at it and he met my eyes.

“Never mind the blood. It is no matter. Listen, wife, my enemies gather around me. I know not who to trust. Tanglecott has offered me an alliance, but should I agree?” He shook his head as if he was confused and I opened my mouth only to have the wraith clap both her dark hands over it. Bluebeard flicked them away irritably. “She seems now to be at odds with Coppertomb, but this could be a ruse. I cannot know yet.”

He drew me down to sit on the hearth with him as the fire crackled merrily behind us and a tiny clock on his wall burst open while a bluebird sang out from it to tell us the hour of the night.

"But there are things I *can* tell you and I must tell you some of them now. Give me your ear, wife. I have planned this turning of the ages for a very long time," he said and as he spoke, I could almost feel him weighing every word, deciding what he could trust me with and what he needed to keep to himself. "It's my one chance to get this right. The only chance there will ever be. I think I have my pieces in place, my moves chosen with care, my strategy firm, but now you are here, and you change everything, bringing order into my chaos like a pole jammed through the spokes of a wheel."

He shook his head again, but whether it was to clear it or out of denial, I didn't know.

"*Then you trust me still?*" I probed, disconcerted by this turn of events. I'd expected anger. I'd expected hurt. I had not expected admiration and plotting.

"Why would I not when you have not betrayed my trust?" he asked, seeming as confused as I was. "I know well enough your limitations, my mortal ally, but you wanted to work with me and I have decided to have faith that you can – nothing can grow if fenced too tightly."

"*Oh,*" I said with my mental voice. It seemed far too small a thing to say for the enormity of what he'd revealed – that he had accepted me as his partner in this so fully that he was willing to let me try to work at his side. I swallowed down a sudden dryness in my throat. This trust – unexpectedly vulnerable – touched something in me I hadn't felt in a long time. Family. It felt like family.

His next words came out in a rush.

"You must understand. I have people depending on me. I did not grow up like other Wittenbrand. I was abandoned, alone. Taken in by kindness from time to time but just as often kicked in the teeth. When my time came to become a man, I carved out for myself lands in the Wittenbrand by deception and sword and arrow. And to those lands, I invited all who, like me, were without a place – the wild things, the forgotten things, the things of strange innocence. But to command a thing brings the necessity to care for it, and to care for it brings the necessity of command, and if I lose this strange gamble every Wittenbrand I have ever sheltered, each one I have succored – down to the smallest and last – will be without shade again – hunted, slaughtered, tortured for fun. Do you understand why I must fight so hard? Why I must not fail them?"

I nodded.

"Too much rides on this, Izolda. Too many souls look to me. I cannot fail them. Have you seen this land through the eyes of the Sword who wishes to snatch you from me? Have you seen how he would remake the Wittenhame in his image?"

"*I have,*" I said, and my words just didn't seem like enough. I wasn't gifted in speeches as he was.

He sighed, as if frustrated that his words, too, were simply not enough. He ran a hand through his hair.

"I was a boy of fifteen, shaggy-headed and dreamy-eyed, when I found this house and the fire took up residence here. And what did you say to me, fire?"

"Feed me, my master," said the fire in his deep, rumbling voice.

Bluebeard placed a piece of wood carefully on the fire and kept speaking. "And so, I did. And so, this house was made, bit by bit, hope by hope, in simple requests granted and simple hopes made new. And when I took my first head at sixteen, I kept that head to advise me, and so my Vault of Wisdom was crafted. And when I was a daring youth of seventeen, coming now into my ambition, seeing for the first time what I might achieve if only I dared, I stole for myself the first of my blushing brides. And now here we sit, you, this fearsome wife of mine, you, this traitorous heart that will not simply rest, you who constantly runs headstrong into every danger – here you sit with me. And here I pour out my heart to you in hopes that for once, instead of returning it to me in shards, you will return my hopes with a little of your own heart."

My breath caught in my throat.

"You love your people," he said thickly, and his eyes shone a little too brightly, though he wasn't looking at me – almost as if he couldn't. "Love them enough to give yourself as my bride. Love them enough to keep giving even now when they have traded you away and treated you as chaff on the wind. And surely you, my severe partner, my stalwart bride, surely you will understand what it is to let your life's blood seep out with every beat of your heart for your people and your land."

I blinked back a tear that was trying to form because I did understand. Even now, with my parents gone, and Svetgin so confused, and my king showing his hatred of me – even now, I wanted my people safe and well. And I would, indeed, give what I must to achieve it. I felt in him a spark of recognition – two fires knowing they burned on the same fuel.

His voice trembled as he added, "Surely you must see how I will give of my own flesh to have you, to keep you, to buy you back from treachery. Surely you understand that you are without price or equal to me."

I could not speak and even if I could, I was not so eloquent and I did not know what he was to me – only that when he was not there the world felt dull. And so, instead, I leaned forward and kissed him gently.

His answer to my kiss was so violently delighted that my breath stuck in my throat. He caught me up, crushing me to him, his kiss devouring my lips as if he could not possibly get enough and when I had been so very kissed that I was not sure I could breathe at all – that I thought perhaps my stitches may have torn, that the wolves of my dress chased each other's tails snarling and snapping, he finally let go and drew back.

"If anyone can light the Wittenhame ablaze, fire of my eyes, it will be you," he said and he sounded almost despairing. "What have you done to me? You have broken what was whole and torn down what was walled up."

I bit my lip, not sure what to make of that. I'd thought to seal our alliance. To show my willingness to remain his wife. Instead, I had somehow invited a fire into our friendship just as he had once invited a fire to live in his home and this fire – like that one – had one thing to say: "Feed me."

"Come now," he said, his voice husky and breathing ragged. "Let us free you from this wraith that blocks your sweet lips and think together on how we shall fit your straight lines and sharp edges in my serpentine tide. We will adjourn to my vault and consult those who came before."

And he seized my hand and pulled me along after him like a boy bent on showing me his collection of frogs. And I hardly knew what I would say when it finally was my turn to speak again because he had surprised me and surprised me until I hardly seemed to know what manner of man I had married at all.

CHAPTER TWENTY-FOUR

"Bring your pet," Bluebeard suggested as I walked past Grosbeak and I snatched him up as we went by. "It would be good to remind him how fortunate he is to have been adopted by you."

Bluebeard leaned down and picked up a leather sack that had been placed by the front door, balancing it easily on one palm despite the heavy look of the thing.

"Oh, I know this already, Bluebeard," Grosbeak said happily. "The drama she brings is exquisite. I have never tasted the like."

"You will not call me that," my husband said with a scowl.

"Why not? It's her name for you," Grosbeak said lightly.

One of my dress wolves whined like a dog being disciplined and Bluebeard reached down to caress its head, settling it. Leaning down brought him closer to my face and he leaned in so that all I could see were his pale eyes and teasing smile.

"Is that your name for me, you somber visage?"

Yes, I said with my mind.

"Then I shall wear it with pride and grow this beard you are so fond of to my knees."

I'd rather you didn't.

"No, it is settled. I never go back on my word," he said, pulling me to the staircase. To my surprise, they were sloped into a descent instead of ascending into the stars. Which was crazy since this house had no cellar. Even so, we began our descent down the dank-smelling, moss-fringed stairs. "I shall grow it long and with pride."

But you didn't give your word! I protested in my mind. *Please, reconsider.*

Although why I was asking him not to hide his pretty face, I couldn't have said. Wouldn't it be good to have it hidden, to be able to disguise himself from his enemies? To be able to disguise his beauty from me where it wouldn't make my stomach flip and my breath catch at the worst possible moments?

"I like the look of your pouting lips, wife. I will, I think, defy your wishes more often simply to provoke so stirring a sight."

I shook my head at him as he laughed and then put his shoulder into a heavy wooden door at the bottom of the stairs.

He heaved and the door opened into a high-ceilinged room. Dusty light filtered down in beams and to my surprise, green moss coated the walls, and long vines curled around anything they could, swathing it in emerald and giving this place a curiously fecund look. Tiny blue flowers sprouted on the vines. A comfortable-looking tufted chair and ottoman had been placed facing one wall. They were well worn, as if someone had sat here, again and again, looking up at the wall. To one side, the fire burned bright and hot, though not hot enough to dry up the wet air or bright enough to light the shadowed corners. It was a homey place that felt like curling up with a good book and a hot drink on a winter evening.

The wall the chair faced, however, was completely occupied with shelves carved straight from the earth and rock. They were rough-hewn and as my eyes slowly adjusted to the low light, the occupants of the rough-cut shelves were finally revealed.

They were heads. And more heads. And more still. Rows and rows and rows of them reaching up to where I could no longer see them, they were so high.

I struggled not to gag at the sight, though I should be used to decapitated heads by now.

It was like a witch's cottage in some grim tale, or a cavern where a gorgon might rule, or the cave of treasures in which a single coin must be searched for to pay death his due.

I shivered at the sight of them, for it seemed my husband had not been exaggerating when he said he collected heads. And he had not been merely acting on a whim when he animated Grosbeak's head, for he drew from his leather sack a new trophy and placed it, almost reverentially on the shelf at shoulder height. And as he set it in place it shivered and woke.

I gasped as I saw who it was.

Vireo.

He'd been alive only hours ago and now here he was, being placed on a shelf with hundreds of others. A chill shivered through me.

"Did you ask Vireo to care for your bride after all?" A head off to one side asked. It was a greenish color with dark matted hair and lower incisors that stuck up past the upper lip. I gasped at the sight of him.

"You can't do everything," Bluebeard said lightly. "Sometimes you have to send someone to do it for you."

The speaking head snickered. "And has that ever worked out for you?"

Bluebeard laughed ruefully. "Never even once."

"And yet you still offer villains chances and blackguards second tries."

I moved to place Grosbeak on the ottoman but stopped when he gasped. "Please. Don't set me down. I fear you will not pick me up again. Please. I see my father there on the shelves."

"You fear joining us, son?" the green-faced head asked, snickering. "You fear the fate you earned for yourself? How did *you* betray the Arrow?"

Grosbeak seemed choked when he answered. "I tried to kill his bride."

This time, the laughter filled the room. Every single head laughed, except for the scowling Vireo.

"Are you all traitors, then?" Grosbeak asked, terror lacing his voice with sharp edges.

"Every one of us," the green-faced head said. His accent was thick and coppery. It made me think of rolling hills and tan-colored skies. "As you well know."

But though his voice was warm, my skin chilled to goosebumps. Because I was a traitor, too. I deserved this wall, too.

And when my husband turned from his task and faced me, my eyes strayed to the wound in his side – the ever-present evidence that instead of taking my head, he'd let them take his rib. That instead of giving me what I deserved, he took my treachery in his own flesh.

I swallowed, fighting not to feel faint.

"What do you think of my councilors, wife of mine?" he asked.

I held his gaze, but I said nothing for I was bound to silence, and I did not speak with my mind for I was afraid that any word I said might condemn me. At another time, I could have claimed I had acted for my parents, for my land. At another time, I could have claimed I had never meant to act, that my wavering indecision could not be held against me even if it had offered opportunity to my enemies. But I could not argue that looking back at it. From this new vantage it seemed, at best, poorly thought out and unfounded and at worst, true betrayal.

I licked my lips, nervously.

"They're a sight to see, Arrow," Grosbeak said with a nervous laugh. "A sight that chills the bones. But why seek their counsel when clearly you were the wiser man?"

"Clearly? Bluebeard asked, but his eyes were still on me.

"Well, ha ha." Grosbeak really must be worried he'd be put on the shelf. I'd rarely heard him so obviously pander to anyone. "They're the ones on the wall and you're the one talking to them. If they were wiser than you, they wouldn't be dead."

"Mmm," Bluebeard said, and it was neither agreement nor approval, but his gaze was unwavering as if bidding me here and now before these fearsome visages to make my case for what I did or join them. I had no case to make. The only sensible thing left was to offer what I could.

Surely, there is some way I can atone for what I did, I said in my mind, bound up in sudden fear.

His eyes softened, and to my surprise, he kept our

conversation private.

I have already made atonement for it, bride of mine. Speak no more of treachery. Wear not a dress of shame.

He stepped forward and to my utter shock, he took my hand and raised it to his lips, tickling it with his light beard as he kissed my palm.

"Sit with me, now, as I take the wisdom of my councilors," he said softly, guiding me to the chair, and offering me a hand to settle into it. He pulled the ottoman to the side and perched on the edge of it, side by side with me. His breeches, soaked with his own blood, began to stain the light tufting of the ottoman.

"Speak you, my enemies," he said, addressing them. "Speak your wisdom to me, for the Second Move is upon me and I fight to see my way forward."

"What is your dilemma?" a female voice asked. I peered up into the darkness to see a woman with golden hair and a silver crown speaking to him. Her eyes were closed as if she slept.

"The Sword seeks to divide me from my wife and my power, to take it for himself and to snatch up her lands as he does so, for she has been married also to the land and what mars her, mars her country, what breaks her with shatter it, and what heals her, mends its ills."

"An interesting problem," another head replied, snickering. "You could not have prevented this by hiding her away as you have done before?"

"He married her the Wittenbrand way," Vireo's head said, filled with scorn.

His words were greeted by laughter – but not I realized, directed at Bluebeard. All the eyes of the heads on the wall were slanted toward Vireo in the middle. There was one that struck me as odd. It was the beautiful head of a woman with flowing green hair tangling around her head and flowing down to the shelf below. Over one ear, her hair was held back with a single mother-of-pearl comb decorated with emeralds. She looked as though she had been drowned.

"You who were friend to the Arrow, first in trust, first in esteem – you betrayed him over this?" one of the heads said.

"He betrayed me for my place. To win royal blood for his own veins," Bluebeard explained. "But his treachery is no matter now. Speak, Vireo, and tell me what it is you vowed on the Island of Burning Guilt."

But even now, when Vireo opened his mouth, a dark spirit burst forth, spinning around his severed head just once and then pasting both hands over his mouth.

"He's warded," the green-faced head said, certainty in his tone.

"As is my wife," Bluebeard said, frowning. "And together they know who the conspirators are, but I cannot make either speak or the specters will destroy them before any answer can slip out. Which means I must find other ways to detect my enemies and run them afoul. Who now will prophesy and what will you say to me?"

They look at one another and then one of the heads speaks, "If you wish to remove the specter, you must break the tie that binds the conspirators."

"I've already killed Vireo," Bluebeard said coolly. "Would death not break the conspiracy?"

"It would seem not," the same head said. It was long and thin with a yellow cast to its brown skin. "It would seem the conspiracy stands without your former captain."

"Hmm," Bluebeard seems unhappy. "Does anyone else have a word to speak?"

A female head cleared her throat and when I found her head on the shelf, she was a square-jawed woman with a tangle of red curls around her head. Her eyes were glazed and white as if she had been blind in life as well as in death.

"Keep your token close," she intoned. "Keep it at hand."

"Is that a prophecy?" Bluebeard asked when there seemed to be nothing else coming.

"Yes," they agreed in unison.

He looked at me, licking his lips. Did he think I had to do with that token? I shot a glance to Grosbeak. I thought that if I had something that could be called a token, it would be him. He was, after all, my symbol for defeating enemies and finding friends. My symbol of everything both gruesome and magical in this strange Wittenhame.

"I must ride out to battle the Sword and his mortal armies once more. Have you advice for that?" Bluebeard asked and there was a formality to his words that made me wonder how they made prophecies and gave advice. Did he come down here often and keep them informed or did they have their own ways of seeing what was happening in the worlds beyond this dank cellar?

"Make an ally of Wittentree," one of them said. A man missing an eye with a grievous scar where it once had been.

"Can I trust her?" Bluebeard pressed.

"Who can say?" the man asked with a laugh. "It matters not. She is to be your ally in this or the threads will not wind the pattern and our weaving will collapse unformed."

Bluebeard grunted.

"And the battle?" he pressed.

"The woman, the wife," the redheaded seer said, her cloudy eyes seeming to light from within. "She must lead your troops in the Battle of the Bairn."

"How will I know this battle?" Bluebeard pressed.

"It will come in red. Scarlet in sign, crimson in cast. It will be apart from where you are."

"Have you no more than this?" Bluebeard pressed, and his eyes looked pained as he spoke.

"No more," they intoned together. "Even our wisdom has bounds."

"Mmm." Again, he sounded neither approving nor content.

He rose, offering me a hand up from the chair.

"Then I'll bid your leave until next time, Vault of Wisdom," he said, bowing elaborately. After a brief pause, I bowed, too. It was always best to remember your manners, after all.

"I'll have my revenge on you, Arrow," Vireo wheezed, finally finding his voice again from his place on the shelf.

"Will you?" To my surprise, Bluebeard did not seem to share the chill I felt at those words. He tilted his head slightly. "Do not take my mercy for weakness, Vireo."

"Mercy?" his former friend growled. "You call this mercy?"

"Your death was fairly earned. You'd scorn it now?" My husband's voice was cold. "That I kept your head and invited you to my council, offering entertainment and the chance to be of use instead of the burning fires of hell – that is the mercy. I have given it. And I can take it away."

And with that, he spun and swept out of the vault, and I found myself hard-pressed to keep up with him, even though I ran, my wolves howling under my skirt all the way to the top of the steps and into the front room beyond.

CHAPTER TWENTY-FIVE

I stumbled, breathless, as we reached the top of the stairs, my cheek aching, my shoulder aflame, and my legs tired. How long had it been since I last slept? I felt as if I could hardly stay upright anymore.

Bluebeard steadied me, taking Grosbeak's pole from my weary hand and jamming it into an urn close to the door that housed a collection of long items. I glimpsed a walking staff with a toad on the top of it, a pair of unstrung bows, and a shepherd's crook. The toad winked at me with a leering smile on its amphibian face.

"Sit. Stay," Bluebeard ordered Grosbeak. Grosbeak scowled back but said nothing as Bluebeard drew me to a place near the fire and began to strip off his party clothes, throwing them into the flames.

"Thank you," said the fire, puffing a little black cloud for each item. "Thank you, master."

He was down to his breeches when he stopped stripping and seemed to realize what he was doing.

"You're shivering," he said, scratching his beard irritably. His movements were impatient, like he was holding himself back from acting. "We need you fed, the stitches removed from your back, need you bathed, and given time to sleep." He blew out a long breath. "There's no time. There's never enough time."

I laid a hand on his arm. He was wasting more than enough time with this litany when we could just be getting on with it.

"*There's time enough for what matters,*" I told him mentally.

"Every day of yours is precious," he protested, shaking his head as looked up into the vaulted ceiling and snapped his fingers.

A raven flew down and landed on the desk. Bluebeard looked at the raven, tilting his head one way and then the other, and then stepping back as the raven leapt into the air. Bluebeard hurried to brush his parchments aside to form an empty space on the desk. But despite his haste, I caught a glimpse of one that read,

"Solemn visage, somber stone,

Your steady gaze anvil to my sword

Wrench from me now my steady home

And to your breast press this . . ."

I wished I could have read the rest. It had been on the top of the papers as if it had been recently written. Had he been writing poetry while I was with the Sword? The thought was . . . odd. Not planning? Not fighting? Writing poetry? When would he have found the time to do that?

And was it ridiculously conceited that I thought it might be about me?

"And because your time is precious," he said, snapping me out of my thoughts, "wasting even a moment of it seems to be a luxury I cannot afford and dearly wish to avoid. So. We must cram every bit of what is needed into these few hours we steal."

There was a muffled cry and the sound of furious flapping of feathers, and then a pair of ravens descended carrying a heavy cloth between them. They set it on the desk, screamed, and flew back up into the star-filled sky in a flurry of black feathers. Even the arrival of dinner was a dramatic production here.

I opened my mouth and shut it again with a click as Bluebeard untied the knot at the top of the cloth and opened it, revealing fresh-baked bread, rounds of cheese, and a variety of fruits and roasted vegetables.

"There's never meat if you ask them for dinner," he said, looking slightly chagrined. "I hope you don't mind. They find the idea of delivering cooked meat offensive and if you insist on meat, they bring you what they would eat, and trust me, it will make you wish you had not asked." He grimaced. "Don't even think about asking for eggs."

He must have taken my shock for disapproval. His cheeks burned hot under their layer of beard.

"Here," he said, gesturing to a cleared off spot on the desk. "Sit. Eat. I will remove the silver stitches from your back as you eat, and I will talk to you about what we will do next." He sighed." Three things at once. Surely that must satisfy even the most stringent of task-masters."

I had no idea why he was so worried about my days. Had he not spent them as often as he liked? And now he was obsessed with using each minute well? But I was very hungry, and the bread smelled of home and of snatching little loaves from the hot pan while Cook scolded me, so I took my place on the desk and tucked in. He rummaged in a desk drawer and came out with a little pair of sewing scissors and a large knife.

I froze.

"The scissors are for the stitches," he explained as if this made perfect sense.

I swallowed the mouthful of bread and gave him a level look.

Don't tell me that the knife is for the cheese, I told him with my mind. *Because if you do, I won't believe you.*

He'd already clambered up onto the desk and settled himself behind me, crouched on a stack of books and papers as if he were an oversized raven about to scold me for requesting a dinner of eggs.

The knife flashed in the firelight and then suddenly, he seized the back of my collar, and I heard a ripping sound. My back felt cold.

"The knife was for the dress," he said as if it were perfectly obvious.

I liked that dress.

"You may have all the dresses you like, fire of my eyes, but not if they are given to you by the Sword," he said and there was a glimmer of violence in his eye when I turned to meet it.

I held that gaze and silently fed a piece of cheese to one of the wolves curled up around my knees. He returned my silent stare for a half a beat, and I wondered what he would do. Would he be angry?

His sudden laugh made me want to laugh, too. He shook his head and then carefully moved my braid over my shoulder so he could look at my back. It felt better. It didn't pain me anymore.

Not like my face.

"These need to come out. They've done their work already," he whispered, and his breath made the hairs on the back of my neck prick up.

Perhaps, were I a different kind of girl, I might have had thoughts of lust at a beautiful, well-set-up man crouched behind me, shirtless and running gentle fingers over my back – especially knowing he was my husband and nothing was forbidden to us.

I did not feel that way.

Rather, I felt like pulling away.

It was not that I didn't trust him with my safety – I did. Not that I didn't believe he was trying to help me by taking out the stitches – he was. Not that I thought he would take advantage of me – I did not. He'd proven again and again that he was nobler in nature than that.

No, my sense of wariness came from fear that anything between us could not last. He claimed he had some masterful plan in this strange dance of crowns and thrones but we'd both come close to kissing death. And even if we both survived, what then? Could a Wittenbrand live peaceably with a wife as a mortal man did? Could he come home to eat and settle in to speak of the day with her? Would he not grow bored of my mortality day after day? That would only lead to heartbreak for me and humiliation. Perhaps it was better to avoid it completely.

What should I make of this man who had given me his hand in marriage, and his rib, and his loyalty, and his vows for seemingly no good reason?

I peeked up through the curving branches of the multi-tiered chandelier, looking past the glowing eyes of the cats strutting through the waterfalls of candlewax and up even further to where the raven had returned and I thought back to another raven long ago who had sat by my window as I spoke aloud my lack of hopes and prospects.

One raven was much the same as another. It would be foolish to think it was the same one. More foolish yet to think that such a one could report to my husband.

And yet.

And yet, I had stood there, looking out over the sleepy city, and told the world that I would prefer to be married off for some kind of good and not just convenience. And if someone had heard, then they had answered, because what greater good could there be than saving your nation?

"*Were you there with the raven when I confessed that I wanted more from this life?*" I asked him tentatively with my mind.

He bent around me to meet my eyes and he winked, disappearing again to work on my back.

"Why did you think I was pleased when you greeted me, Izolda Savataz?" he asked lightly. "We shared a kinship, we two. Both of us want our lives to mean something. Both of us want more than comfort or ease. Both of us married for something greater."

"*And is that why you married me in the Wittenbrand way?*"

I felt an unexpected touch on the back of my neck, soft and warm. A kiss. A shiver of surprise drifted down my spine.

"Among other reasons, my solemn monstrosity. That, and your judging eyes,and your sober refusal to bend, make you the straight line to my wanderings, the plumb to my troubled depths, the anchor to my bucking ship."

His hands left their work and drifted, taking liberties as they combed through my hair and ran down my shoulders and arms, lightly, softly, in a way that made me think of where else I could allow them to go. I swallowed and held myself tighter.

I picked at the last crumb of bread and winced as Bluebeard pulled a particularly tough stitch out.

"Easy now, easy," he whispered. "Almost done. Have patience now."

All the kinds of things you breathed to children, to hurt animals, to troubled souls. And yet there was a solidness to his voice that went deeper than iron, deep into the veins of the molten earth.

"Let me tell you a story," he said as he worked, and it made me think of the way he'd told me a story when he'd put these hundred stitches in place. "Of a time when the world was new, and she grew life by the word of the creator and sprung from his chest as he lay on his back in repose among the stars. And as he breathes, her oceans move, her tides come and go, her stars spin and set her courses. And when he smiles, she feels warmth and sunshine, and when he cries, she feels it in the rain."

I flinched steadily as he worked, but he knew what he was about because the story soothed the bite and pull as he worked.

"And one day man began to dig, dig, dig, deep into the mountains, down, down, through the caves, seeking the heart of the earth. And when they reached it, they went further still, for it was not gold or iron, silver or diamonds that they dug for, but for power. And when at last they found the hidden pools of midnight power in the belly of the earth, they dug them out and pulled them loose, and thus they dug out the rib of the creator and wrought in him a grave wound, a mortal wound, a wound edged in evil and self-focus so that it may never heal, and always until this day the creator bears the festering mark of man's pride. From it have spread all the evils of this world and the land has been washed over a thousand times a thousand with the tears of those who have felt it and the tears of him whose body was broken by them."

"*And what happened to the men who dug?*" I asked with my mind because I did not want to say, "Just like me." Or to ask if there was any saving of those who had done the digging. I knew without asking that there would not be.

He moved from the last stitch on my back to work on my shoulder, restitching the stitches I'd pulled there and binding the wound. It felt hot and angry where he touched it.

"They were consumed by their own hearts."

"And is there any hope for the creator, or will he die and the world with him?" I did not know why I was taking this so seriously. It was only a story. It was only a myth. So why did I feel a chill greater than his breath on my back as he worked, more than the shiver of stitches coming loose from my flesh? Why did it feel so real?

"There is always hope," Bluebeard whispered, and I felt almost as if I could feel his lips pressing against the skin of my back and his shadowed chin scratching against the delicate skin of my neck where it met my shoulder. "There is always redemption."

"*Even for me?*" I whispered in my mind.

"Especially for you. But I would think you would stop musing on worthiness and on whether you must pay for your betrayal. Is guilt sensible? Is self-recrimination a practical skill?"

I felt my cheeks growing hot. He was right. I was being

ridiculous.

"If I have forgiven you, who can say otherwise? If I have set you free of these impractical burdens, are you not free indeed?"

And this time I was certain it was his lips I felt pressed up against the wing of my shoulder.

And for just a moment we both kept perfectly still and let ourselves rest in that moment.

"*Why do you kiss me so often?*" I asked with my mind.

"Because every kiss may be the last," he whispered before he shook himself and said, "They're out now and we have much to discuss. Come now, you must bathe, and we must speak before you can sleep, for I fear that you will be snatched from me again before I have had the time to confer with you. Always, time is our worst enemy, stealing away what is most precious to me."

"*Don't you have less of my time to spend, the more of it you stay with me?*" I asked, wondering if he'd make sense of those jumbled thoughts. What I meant was that he could spend all my days and marry again quickly and have more days at his disposal. But I paused for a moment, because hadn't he suggested that I would be his last bride?

"Were I to spend them with no constraints, I would spend them all exactly like this," he said, and he leapt from the desk in a sudden burst of energy, swept me off in a flurry of papers, and then carried me up the singing nightingale stairs with my wolves howling all the way.

CHAPTER TWENTY-SIX

"You play the His Nibs' seven in this hand if you want to save your queen," Bluebeard said as he laid down a King's Nibs. I was struggling to keep up with the cards and the conversation at the same time. I'd played a little before – mostly with Svetgin and Rolgrin when we were younger. It wasn't fashionable in the Pensmoore court to play at cards. But playing cards seemed to help Bluebeard think, so he had us spread across the wide bed, playing a hand as he talked to me.

It was not what I'd expected he would want to use his bed for. The sense of that hung heavily between us – as if, while we played cards so innocently, both of us were thinking about what games could be played that required no cards at all.

The stairs, of course, had taken us back to his room. No number of protestations would take us anywhere else – though I did not think Bluebeard had his heart in his threats.

I had bathed hastily in private, minding my many wounds, and then – while Bluebeard fed my poor wolf dress to the fire, howling and all – I had drawn a new outfit from the mirror. The mirror spat out a nightdress of silk lined in fur. But it was not to be outdone by the Sword's mirror and it had produced a nightdress with a mink collar. The mink's eyes moved like it was alive. I hesitated to put it on, but it was that or sleep in my underthings – and besides, the mink was in a staring match with the dead girl hovering over my shoulder. I didn't mind if they both wanted to keep an eye on each other.

"I'd apologize that there is only one bed for two people," Bluebeard had said dryly when I finally made my way to it, "but seeing as you have brought two more with you, I can hardly see you objecting."

"When can I get rid of this horrible dead specter?" I'd asked with my mind. "*It's not like –* "

She had put her hand over my mouth even though I was speaking with my mind. I tried to bite it, but she tasted of rot and grime, leaving me choking and trying to spit with her hand still over my mouth.

To my shock, she was ripped away and I could breathe and clear my mouth of the taste of her. Over my shoulder, I had seen my husband shaking her by the scruff of her neck.

"Play nicely, specter. I could make you wish you were not attached to my wife. I could make you wish it with every last wisp of that scrap of a soul."

The specter had drawn back, lifting her hands and then very obviously clasping them together as if to promise good behavior and the shaking had stopped.

I played a different card than the one he was coaching me to play. I didn't like having my moves dictated to me.

He shook his head as he played his next card and snatched my queen away. "You don't want to lose the queen," he said meeting my eyes. "Ever. That's the first rule."

I felt a strange shiver at his words. He meant them to mean more than advice at cards. He meant he was planning to keep me safe. Or maybe just keep me. Or maybe both. Which was very practical of him. This steady cycle of finding and marrying wives must have taken a lot of time and effort. If he could learn to be more careful in using up my days, he could save himself a lot of wasted energy.

"In the mortal worlds," Bluebeard continued, laying his discarded cards face up and arranging them off to the side to illustrate his words, and then taking up strands of my hair to play with as he spoke, "we are lining up for battle. The Sword has marched the Aayadmoore straight across Salamoore, which he could only do if Coppertomb had allowed it. He appears to be making for Rouranmoore. But why? Why drop his never-ending siege of Pensmoore simply to chase after Wittentree's holdings? It's a wild thrashing move and I don't like that I can't see what is behind us. But two things are certain.

"First, that we would be fools not to rush down the west coast of Aayadmoore and secure it in his wake. Second, that we must help Rouranmoore to hold. Wittentree has offered me a bargain to work together and with her close on our eastern shore, we cannot afford to make an enemy of her. With the blessing of my wise council, I must make that alliance."

He tucked the hair back behind my ear and leaned over the cards to kiss my forehead almost reverently. I felt flushed by the attention.

"Why do you trust the heads so much when you defeated them?" I asked with my mind, laying my next card out carefully. He was distracted and I took the trick with a small self-satisfied smile of my own.

"A man knows himself best through the eyes of his enemies. They see the things I cannot." He laid his card swiftly as if he already knew what I would play next and then caught one of my hands in his, making it harder to play.

"But why would they help you when you are the one who killed them?" I pressed as he opened my hand, tracing each finger with his and then pressing a kiss into my palm and then my wrist and then the crook f my elbow. The blush in my cheeks was growing hotter and it was getting hard to think straight. *"It does not seem reasonable to put so much faith in the bitter dead."*

"I don't know why they are so compliant, so willing to work with me when I ended their lives. Perhaps, it is merely familiarity – a face they know when all others have passed away. Perhaps they were better people than I acknowledged. What I do know is this, they have only once misled me."

I cocked my head as I took yet another trick from him. He must be truly distracted. His next kiss was in the crook of my neck and it did dizzying things to my midsection. I swallowed.

"It was in the matter of the Sword," he said musingly.

"*Was it?*" I pressed. I nearly had this game won even with my struggle to think straight. I placed my card with seeming indifference.

He swept the cards aside and settled where they had been between us.

"It was," he said, lifting an eyebrow and grinning at my breathlessness. I cared not that I'd been prevented from winning the trick. "They told me his doom would come from the tides of his heart. But the Sword loves nothing. I have searched and searched for a thing he might love and found there is nothing but himself." He smiled ruefully as he spun his fingers through my hair again. "Perhaps that was what they meant. That his doom lies within." He seemed to shake himself. "But we were discussing strategy. We must move an army down the west to seize the coastline as we also rise to the defense of Rouranmoore along the east coast."

"Leaving our middle unguarded?" I was barely holding onto my wits well enough to discuss this. His fingers tangling in my hair lit up every nerve in my scalp.

His mouth twisted sourly. "I do not like that part. It leaves Pensmoore vulnerable. But with the Sword occupied on both fronts, will he be able to spare troops for such an assault? I do not think so. The only other person who could drive a force in between ours while we were distracted is Coppertomb and one might think that this is why he has allowed the Sword on his land, but that little display at the end of the Petal Ball tonight was proof of the rumors I have been hearing – that Coppertomb has set his sights on Ilkanmoore and will be much occupied with the taking of that land and happy to let the Sword watch his back as he finishes off Lady Tanglecott's thin army."

I opened my mouth to tell him how wrong he was, how they were allies, but the ghastly hand was there at once, blocking my mouth again.

Bluebeard tugged the hand free, irritation on his face as he flung the wraith aside a second time.

"Don't bother, wife," he said with a sigh. "I know you can confirm that Coppertomb and the Sword are working together. I know they are tied up with Vireo and his betrayal. No need to make yourself uncomfortable just to tell me such."

My gut felt heavy as if I had eaten a meal of stones. There was a wide flaw in his plan – right down the middle – and I could save him from grief if only I could tell him. The ghast shook her finger in my face as if she could guess what I wanted to say.

"But we will need to prepare you. As my advisors said, you

must lead one of the armies."

I shook my head. I was not born to lead. I did not know battle. Nothing could spell failure faster than this.

"Fire of my eyes."

I wasn't looking at him. I was looking away in the distance, trying not to cry, thinking of leading men into a battle where they cried and screamed and died beside me. Where I could not stop it or save them. Where I died, too, mangled and broken in the snow.

"Izolda." His tone was kind, but I would not look at him.

Why should I have to do such a thing just because a wall of heads said so? They were dead already, and past the grief of this life. I felt tears sting my eyes and I blinked them away. Besides, this was ridiculous. Putting a young woman with no experience or skill at the head of an army wasn't reasonable. It wasn't sensible. It was the opposite of useful.

"Wife." He took my face between gentle fingers as if lifting a goblet so he could drink.

This time I reluctantly met his eyes.

"As a figurehead, wife," he said gently. "You will not fight. You will be protected."

From what? I wanted to scream. But I held my mind back.

Would he protect me from watching them all die right in front of me? Because it wasn't my body that I was afraid to see ripped apart – well, there was some of that, too – but mostly it was the horror of watching it happen before me and being powerless to stop it. How could I do that? How could I ask someone to die for me and for Pensmoore? And how could

Bluebeard ask this of me?

"Would you rather see your people die for nothing because you would not sit a pretty horse and hold a rippling banner at their head?" he asked gently.

I shook my head within the hold of his fingers, but not because I agreed but because this was utterly ridiculous. Prophecies. Ha. Dead heads talking. It was my own fault for hauling Grosbeak around and increasing people's confidence in that. I wanted no part in any of this.

"I think that by their words 'Battle of the Bairn' they mean the fight against the son of the Aayaadmoore king. He will have the scrap of army on the west coast of the sea. So, you will be needed to sit your pretty horse and hold your banner there." There was teasing in his voice as if he thought he could get me to smile over this. "And I will be needed in the thick of the fighting on the east."

My eyes held his with all the intensity I felt.

"Yes, wife, I will be a slave to your efforts. I cannot watch over your shoulder, so I must trust you to do this without me."

I felt sick. This was madness.

"*What about Sparrow?*" I asked in my mind.

I felt like kicking myself, because *of course* everything was madness here and I was a fool to have expected otherwise. This was the Wittenhame, wasn't it?

"Sparrow is my right hand now, and the leader of my mortal armies. But she was not the one prophesied by the Wall of Wisdom. I will lend her to you if you wish it."

I nodded. That would certainly be more sensible, but what

would she think of being saddled to me – a mortal girl with no value but the length of her days and a weak prophecy that may be no more accurate than this prediction about the Sword and the tides of his black, black heart.

Bluebeard kissed my forehead chastely as if sealing the conversation.

"As always, the thing we lack is time. But you must rest now, wife of mine."

"*If we lack time, wouldn't it make more sense to leave now and begin our work?*" I asked with my mind, but the yawn I covered with my hand spoke to the lie. I needed my sleep.

He chuckled but his chuckle had an iron core. "You are the land now, bride of my heart. Would you see it fade and suffer because you would not rest? No. Sleep now, and rest Pensmoore with your dreams, you devilish sensibility."

And to my utter shock, he leaned in, his fingers sliding from my face to tangle in my hair, and he kissed me as if he was drinking from a stream after a long ride, deep and long and wanting. My eyes shut against too many feelings, too much emotion, and to my surprise, for the very first time, I was parting my lips to let him in and kissing him back, wondering if I could fall in love with a man so hard, so unfathomable, so utterly impractical. If my racing heart was any judge, perhaps I could.

I tangled my hands into his shirt, feeling the warmth of his skin under it and I let myself fall into his kiss, embracing him back with all the hope I had in my heart.

His lips ripped away and my eyes shot open, shocked. Had I done something wrong?

"Oh. Oh no. You're kissing me back," he said, looking like

he'd been caught stealing something. His hands fall from my hair and he leapt backward off the bed, his lower lip caught between his teeth. His eyes locked on mine and the boyishly guilty look he gave me was utterly incongruous with his slight beard and scarred body. He was breathless when he spoke and I thought maybe he was shaking a little. I certainly was. Everything inside me felt like it had been lit on fire and then the fire blown out. "Before this is over, fire of my eyes, they'll have snatched my heart, still bleeding, from withing my breast. I would not have your heart risked, too."

He swallowed and then slowly the look of aching vulnerability on his face shifted into hardness and he spun, slinking across the room like a cat sauntering into the night. The latch on the door clicked shut behind him.

I slid, confused and a little embarrassed, under the warm blankets and let myself watch tonight's view from the room – the sight of a woodland glen in moonlight, dappled with white blossoms made periwinkle by the darkness. I'd spoiled the first kiss I'd fully enjoyed. That was the problem with letting yourself go. It never ended well.

I chewed on the edge of the blanket, trying to pretend I wasn't a little hurt. And I thought about kisses and why lips seemed to crave them like the body craved water. I thought of vanishing Wittenbrand with boyish smiles. I wondered if it really was so very dangerous to risk my heart on a man I'd already married, and I thought of what it would mean to lead an army into battle. I didn't like any of the answers my mind offered to me.

Around me, the fragrant black blossoms surrounding the bed waved and within me, doubts were soon overcome with a blanket of sleep.

CHAPTER TWENTY-SEVEN

I woke to Bluebeard sprawled across the bed beside me, face down, arms and legs spread to their full extent, snoring. Of course. If I had to guess how he would sleep, this is what I would have guessed. There was nothing practical, nothing demure, or restrained, or tame in him. He was boldness and power, enthusiasm and full-commitment in everything – even sleep.

One of his out-flung arms was draped over me as if I were a drinking companion he was offering a friendly piece of advice to. My wry expression was wasted on him, and the flush on my cheeks at how nice it felt to have someone who cared about you sleeping so close was fortunately hidden. I hadn't thought before about what kind of comfort that might bring. I hadn't thought about how good it would feel to wake to the sound of someone else breathing. It was probably best that I didn't dwell on that. Not now with everything so unsettled. But I couldn't help but wonder what would come after when the game was over and the days used up. Would I have any left? And if I did, would I spend them with him? Would he sleep next to me, making that terrible sawing sound?

Would he be dead as he feared and leave me as a widow. Would he leap away and reject me as he had last night?

Thinking like that could only lead to trouble, so I took myself to the steaming black pool, drank the ever-present cup of hot tea, and then gave the gargoyle above the mirror a scathing look when it offered me a flowing velvet dress with a neckline down to my waist.

"I'm going to fight a battle, not try to cause one."

The gargoyle screwed up his face, making his eyes bulge, but I refused to be terrified.

"Not all battles are fought on battlefields," he huffed when I didn't bend.

"This one is," I said grimly.

"Fine," he said, and I could have sworn he rolled his eyes, but he spat out a pair of thick-woven leggings, tall riding boots, and a high-collared jacket embroidered with overflowing bowls of tears and – fortunately – enough room to move in. There were puffs at the top of the sleeves. There was also a small cape, and two short-sword scabbards on a belt. And every item from cape to boot was made with fabric or leather of a shade of blue ranging from the glimmer of dawn to midnight dark.

The pile of clothing was an intimidating sight but just when I was reaching for it, almost as an afterthought, he threw out a thing that might have been a silver circlet with a bit of netting behind it to catch my hair.

I dressed with care, but I lingered over the circlet and in the end, I left it on the floor beside the mirror, not sure of myself enough to throw it back, but not ready to wear it either. What was I queen of? Days, perhaps. And I had not nearly enough of them.

Bluebeard snored on, and so I took that moment to return to the Room of Wives with the little key he'd given me. I tidied it up from our stay within, straightening rugs, cleaning up chunks of mud that had dried in place, and letting my gaze trail over the women who had come before me.

Had any of them been warriors? Or better yet, strategists? Could they have led an assault down the west coast of Aayadmoore? I thought perhaps the one who had been so bent on tripping Bluebeard into her bed might have made a good warrior. She'd come at that problem from every angle before she'd been forced to stop. Idly, I picked up the journal of a girl even more wispy than I was – one with translucent skin so fair I could see the blue veins under her skin – and bright red tangled hair.

"Givanna" her nameplate read. Her book was filled with poetry, mostly. I skimmed through it. She would have been as poor at this as I, though toward the end of her book she'd written some verse for our shared husband that made me blush, and there, a few pages back she'd tried her hand at a poetic recounting of one of the ceremonies she'd heard was attended. I knew she hadn't been there herself. Bluebeard said he'd taken all the rest and kept them away from the court here.

Her verse read:

… and gossiped here to me:

"The Lords and Ladies have, I'd guess,

a pretty thing or two.

Coppertomb a silver sword,

Wittentree a marble shrew,

When asked where'pon they'd found these things,

The answers varied were.

'I found it on a rainbow swing'

'I gathered up a burr.'

But t'was Lord Towerrock's decry

that left me squint-eyed sure,

'A siren gave herself to me

and I, myself to her.'

She was a talented poet, but I had no time to read the rest of the gossip she'd accumulated. I shut the book and sighed, trying another one from a bride with silky brown skin and long black hair. Her skirt was wide and puffed out like a bell around her but there was something fierce about the way she held her chin. The plaque under her read "Tigrane."

I picked up her book, flipping through it, my eyes catching on the words "border raid."

I stopped for a moment and read.

"The Ayadmoore were raiding our borders that spring, in parties of twenty or thirty. My father allowed me to ride along to the Duke of Diasa's castle with him when he brought reinforcements to them. I found the journey educational and wish it was of some use to me now that I am stolen away as bride to this Wittenbrand prince."

There might be something to learn from this. I tucked it into my pocket. After all, I was headed into a battle. Maybe Tigrane learned something interesting that might be helpful.

I patted the lectern in front of her and said, "I'll return it undamaged," before turning to face why I'd really come. The hourglass.

I waited beside it a long moment until a single gem fell into the lower bulb.

My days. Dwindling far too quickly.

But the sight of them steeled me and gave me the courage for what would come. My husband was right. If I only had so many days to spend, I must spend each one with care.

I turned and strode from the room, leaving my sisters-in-fate behind me. If they were alive, maybe they would have wished me well. But if they were alive, then I wouldn't be here, and neither would they. I tried not to look at the empty pedestal. I didn't want to stand there frozen forever in whatever dress the gargoyle gave me. I didn't want someone to look at my empty book and wonder if there was just nothing to say.

I should write something. It had seemed a monstrosity before, but now it felt like a blasphemy not to write. Because though Bluebeard had told me I was the last, I didn't fully believe it. He had a big plan he refused to tell me about and that meant he'd need every scrap of magic he could get. My days would not be enough.

So, what should I tell my successor? What should I leave as a record? A warning? A message of hope? A note like Margaretta had left for me?

Maybe I'd think of something after this battle – if I lived to see the end of the Sword's dance with the Arrow. If I survived to see them change partners. Then, maybe, I would have something valuable to say.

It would probably be "Feed Grosbeak for me and don't talk to ravens."

Had I known then what would pass before I next entered that

room, I might have paused to leave that note. But we are none of us privileged with the full truth of what is to come. Not even men with Vaults of Fallen Enemies.

CHAPTER TWENTY-EIGHT

I returned to our room to find Bluebeard fully dressed – mostly in weapons. Two short swords were laid out beside him on the bed as well as the many knives and swords he wore strapped to his body. But he was not sharpening them or pouring over maps. Instead, he was playing an instrument that looked like a balalaika, a dark look in his eye and a scowl as if the instrument had displeased him.

Through the window, dawn lit the sky bathing him in golden light at odds with his devilish glower. It was my turn to speak again. Finally.

"What do you mean by that behaviour?" I asked my most pressing question, crossing my arms over my chest and giving him my darkest glower. "You've kissed me many times. Mostly without permission. As I am your wife, I have not objected. But the one time that I kiss you back, you run away."

His glower grew deeper to match mine, and he set the instrument aside, standing and gathering the short swords from the bed.

"And now you won't reply?" I pressed. "You, who bids me lead armies though I am but a girl with no training in military things. You, who speaks lightly of leading your own charge against the Sword. You would run after kissing me? You're not a coward, so there is something else at work here – something more than risking my heart. I would have that knowledge, Arrow."

Still, he did not look at me, but he did reply with his mind. *"I would risk all myself for you, fire of my eyes. I would risk my body in your service."*

"So I see," I said boldly, crossing the room and parting his jacket so I could look at the blood blossoming already across his fresh shirt. He submitted to my work, letting me lift his shirt and look under it to check the wound. It looked no better. It was still crusted at the edges, but the center of the wound was open and oozing blood. My stomach flip-flopped.

"I would risk my very soul in this gamble to save you."

"Save me from what, exactly?" I asked coolly, but my mind was not on his grand words, but on his wound. He spoke like a god but bled like a man. I shook my head and glanced at the mirror.

To my surprise, it spat out a long bandage with only one rude expression on the face of the gargoyle. I scooped it up and brought it to Bluebeard, gently wrapping his wound.

"This shouldn't be left to fester. Surely there is some cure for it," I scolded him gently.

"*Death cures all ills.*" His expression was maudlin. *"It will not pass me by."*

"Short of that," I said dryly, "let's at least keep this dry and bandaged."

My fingers grazed his skin as I worked to bandage his wound. It was absolutely shocking that he acted like it wasn't there. A mortal man would be dead of this by now. From the ill humors, if not the wound itself. I shivered.

"*I would risk my heart, laid at your feet,*" he said in my mind and when I looked up, I froze. His expression was no longer a glower. It was caught midway between hard determination and a soft tenderness.

A tiny gasp escaped my throat, but he held my eye as he said in my mind, "*But I did not mean to risk yours with it. Your heart is mine to guard. Mine to ward. It will not be stolen, not by me or any man.*"

"I think that's up to me to decide, don't you?" I said, trying to be gentle. He was ridiculous. "It is, after all, my heart."

His half-smile told me he didn't think that was true. A blush crept into my cheeks, hot as midsummer and I bit my lip.

"Well," I said, a little defensively. "If you're claiming my heart as your own, then it's only fair that you give me yours. After all, everyone else seems to be taking pieces of you."

His smile widened.

"Though I would prefer if you left it in your chest, running its long race at a steady beat."

I thought that perhaps he would kiss me again. Those were, after all, the most affectionate words I'd offered him. And he did step in so that my fumbling hands which had just finished tying his bandage were now pressed between us. But he shifted and the short swords that had been on the bed were jammed abruptly into the sheaths hanging empty on my belt.

"*Angstbite you know,*" he said, "*and the other is Dreadtang. Use them well. Protect my heart.*"

Perhaps this was how the Wittenbrand expressed affection. 'You melt my heart. Have a sword' or some such nonsense.

"I'm not adept in the sword," I said wryly, "but if someone comes to me bringing nonsense, they're in for a biting lecture and a strong glare of judgment."

"I suppose that will have to do. And now we must be off, wife of mine. We have a war to fight, a Sword to bring down, and a people to save."

He looked as if he might kiss me, but to my surprise – and an empty feeling that turned out to be disappointment – he did not.

Instead, he took my hand in his lovely callused one, and led me down the stairs to collect Grosbeak and his bow and quiver. I felt myself frowning when the specter returned to sit over my shoulder. I'd almost forgotten about her. I wished I could banish her the way Bluebeard did, but it seemed I was stuck with her until someone broke the "pact" from the Isle of Burning Guilt. She waved her finger in front of my face as if she suspected what I was thinking.

"There's something different about you two," Grosbeak said as I lifted his pole. His cruel snicker morphed into a yawn. I was not the only one who was tired this morning. "Are you making heirs now, by any chance?"

"I have too many who wish to inherit my lands and wealth already, traitor," Bluebeard said lightly. "I need not add to their number just yet."

He pulled a tiny knife from his pocket and made the slash of his mark on his cheek before raising an eyebrow to me and at my nod, offering me the same. We wore twin scarlet teardrops now. His sign to the world. I could only hope it would lend us victory.

But there was no time for more storms of doubt. And no time to wonder if I should have tried to kiss him again if he wasn't going to do it anymore.

Bluebeard led us to the fire where he leaned an arm against the mantle, and then his forehead against his arm as if surrendering to the exhaustion and anxiety I was still feeling even after a night of sleep.

"My fire," he sighed, his shoulders slumping slightly.

"My master," the fire replied warmly.

And then Bluebeard pulled the key from the chain around his neck, turned the key, and drew me into the flames.

I would never grow used to the madness that crashed into my soul from this kind of traveling between worlds. Never grow used to how it bored through my brain like a drill, how it left sticky trails of darkness through my thoughts and hopes.

When we emerged, it was all I could do not to vomit. I leaned over, hands on knees, coughing, gasping, trying to catch my breath.

Bluebeard did not pause to help me stand. He was already striding forward. I pulled myself together and began to follow and then froze.

We had emerged from a campfire along a bluff, looking out over miles and miles of land below. We were standing in a stone shrine built up on the cliff edge – a cut-stone floor smoothed to perfect levelness and surrounded by four pillars on each side leading up to a steepled stone roof. Green moss wreathed the pillars and edged the steps surrounding the shrine and black lichen clung to the stone everywhere I could see. If this shrine were in honor of a god or man, I did not know who it was. I stepped out from under the roof and looked back at the shrine. The only identifying feature was a weathervane set on the peak of the steepled roof, high, high above – a single arrow showing the wind was blowing due east.

“Nice place you have here. Well maintained,” Grosbeak said muzzily. A fly took off from his head, buzzing madly before being snatched from the sky by a dragonfly. “Fabulous fauna.”

A tent was pitched inside the shrine and beside it burned the indecently large fire we’d emerged from.

Sparrow rose from her vigil beside the fire, but it was not to the fire that I was looking. It was to the land. I had thought we were going to Pensmoore, but this was not the Pensmoore I knew. The land below the bluffs rose in a strange ridge as if it were made of two plates that had been jammed together by giant hands, roughening the edges of each, and leaving a long hillock of heaved rocks and earth in a scar across the land.

A scar that matched the wound on my face precisely.

I gasped and touched my cheek.

“You need to feed her more,” Sparrow said wearily by way of greeting. “And she needs to sleep. You tied her to this land. Do you think it will survive if you burn her like a candle?”

“I know my business,” Bluebeard said shortly – it seemed they would not bother with greetings. “And I bear a prophecy from the Vault of Wisdom.”

“Our pleasure at your company once again, Sparrow,” Grosbeak said as if he were a parent reminding them of their manners. His voice took on a higher pitch. “Oh no, it’s my pleasure to serve *you*, oh great prince of the Wittenhame.”

Sparrow ignored him. “Prophecies are well and good, but these are things you need to know, my prince. The harvest failed. The drought was too great. We have lost some to starvation and some to the ravages of this war, and those who remain healthy and strong fear for their children at home.”

"Pensmoore is starving?" I asked Sparrow, my voice thick. Pensmoore had never starved in the memory of my father or his father. We were a northern country, cold and with harsh winters, but there was always food to be found in our rich forests and rivers.

"Mortals," Grosbeak scoffed. "Always dying of something. It's hardly worth it to try to keep them alive."

"Shush," I told him mildly, though I did not feel placid at his words. Which mortals were dying?

My own belly grumbled, and I felt my cheeks heat. I was *not* starving, and it was embarrassing to call such attention to myself.

Sparrow cursed and stormed away into her tent. I tried to catch Bluebeard's eye, but he was distracted, admiring a songbird that had landed on his finger. Three more stood on his head and several others were clustered on his shoulders. These were rose-breasted with blunt beaks. I would have said there was no practical use to an army of songbirds at your disposal, but that would have been foolish since they had carried him to my rescue.

When Sparrow emerged she shoved bread and fruit into my hands. "Eat. Eat it all. No crumbs now."

"Oh, but I couldn't," I said, horrified. "Not when people are starving."

Sparrow took a long breath as if she were summoning patience. "I heard a report that the Arrow mixed your blood with the land, did I not?"

"Yes, he did."

"He made you and the land one. Did you not see the scar rent upon the ground here when you received that wound on your face?"

I gasped, cupping my cheek.

"Yes, that one," she said, looking older somehow as her shoulders drooped. "Every night you don't sleep, every meal you don't eat, every pain you feel and every kiss offered you," here she shot a furtive look at Bluebeard, "are felt by the land and received into it, for good or ill. So, eat, that the land might produce food and your people might not starve."

"Cute. That's not at all risky, is it?" Grosbeak said. "She's tied to the land. He's tied to her. They're all tied up in the Game of Crowns. And here I am, more tied than all of them together. It's one big rat king of a tale from beginning to end."

I ate. I ate like one on a mission, since that was what I was, and as I ate, they talked. Bluebeard laid out his plan – the two fronts, the prophecy, his hope that she would lead the second army with me as it swept down the west coast and wrenched the Sword's land from him. I wondered idly if Svetgin were fighting with Pensmoore, or if the Sword had kept him close in Aayadmoore – as bait for me.

"You spoke to Wittentree?" Bluebeard asked Sparrow.

"Almost a moon ago now," Sparrow said with a nod, and I looked back and forth between them worriedly.

"And she was in earnest?" Bluebeard pressed.

"Three moons have passed since Vireo took you from our camp," Sparrow told me helpfully before turning back to her master. Grosbeak whistled as if he was astonished, but I knew it was only drama for my benefit. He neither cared nor was surprised by this. Sparrow went on as if he hadn't spoken at all. She hadn't liked him in life and that seemed to carry over into death. "In earnest, yes. Desperate, even. I didn't like the look in her eye. Like a cornered wolf. Whatever has passed between our opponents, she has not been invited into anyone else's councils. That I am certain of. She tried to keep it from me, but it was obvious in every too-quick word and every too-generous offering."

"You did not think it deception?"

She shook her head. "If I am wrong, we will know soon enough. But I am not wrong."

"Even a star-reader can be wrong from time to time and you are no star-reader," Grosbeak reminded her. "I recall speaking to one once who told me I would one day see my heart tied to the tides, and look at me now? No heart and no tied."

"She was close," Sparrow said a little poisonously. "Your head is tied to a pole. But as for the star reader, she was speaking of sirens. You know the old song that says, '*Oft the siren sings again, tying up the hearts of men, within her silken tides.*' Perhaps you should have spent more time at the sea if you wanted that fate."

I wasn't listening to their bickering. I was too horrified by what I had heard.

Three moons. It had felt like only days. Fear flooded through me, leaving jagged pains in my bowels and belly. Where would Svetgin be now? Did he still live? What about the people we'd seen when we rode from the river to the camps of soldiers? All those villagers and townspeople. Did they still live?

"Casualties?" Bluebeard said plainly, as if seeing my expression.

"As expected. Most of the border towns are gone. We moved what citizenry we could into the inner landholdings. But not all were spared. There are places along the border where the Aayadmoore have dug in past Pensmoore's borders and places where we hold defenses past theirs. The shape of the border changes with the day. I have maps marked for you. But if you really wish to lead this offensive, you need to ride immediately. Our forces are prepared to march by nightfall. An army four thousand strong. Two hundred light cavalry. Three hundred mounted bowmen. Five hundred longbowmen. Three hundred heavy cavalry. Ten catapults and their crews. The rest are officers and pikemen." She rattled off the numbers like they were written on the inside of her eyelids. "The supply lines and defenses are rigged as you requested. There are barges for the rivers with oxen to pull them. Teams to go with each one. The men are outfitted and ready."

"And the reserve army? The one you will lead with Izolda?"

"The one *Izolda* will lead with the help of Sparrow, or are you forgetting what the head said, big man?" Grosbeak snickered rudely and made a face.

Sparrow looked uncomfortable. "Skirmishers and scouts as you requested – six hundred. And two hundred light cavalry. No pikemen. No heavy cavalry. No catapults."

"And none should be needed. Had we spared more, he certainly would have guessed our purpose," Bluebeard said firmly. "And the banner? It is ready?"

She shrugged.

"You have it with you?" His tone brooked no argument.

"Of course."

"Aren't you going to show him?" Grosbeak pressed again. I didn't shush him this time. I felt like they were leaving me out of this planning, even though they expected me to play a role. I didn't like that. I didn't like the green-eyed monster that clawed up in my throat – a close match for his sister sitting on my shoulder. But while one monster bid me silent, this monster bid me speak and prove I was just as valuable as Sparrow, just as capable and strong. My cheeks flared hot because though my jealousy might boast of my assets, I was well aware that I brought none of those things with me. Swallowing down that bitter truth was no easy matter.

"Does she have to bring that rotten head with her?" Sparrow asked, shooting a poisonous look at Grosbeak.

"Yes," I answered before Bluebeard could. And I didn't know if I was keeping him because I wanted the company and felt responsible for him or just because it irritated her and not knowing that bothered me even more. I was known for my practicality, not my spite. Vindictiveness did not suit me.

"Then you'll both leave now, too," Bluebeard said, ignoring our side conversation. "Travel the path I laid out. Do not move from it or our timing will not stay true."

He was still looking at Sparrow. He didn't even glance at me. I felt that deep in the pit of my stomach.

She nodded. "All has been done as you specified, Arrow. All of it. I'll strike camp now. I have a horse for your lady wife – the dappled grey. And yours is the roan gelding."

"Excellent work, Sparrow. Your efforts will see fruit yet," my husband said with a warm smile for her. Something in my heart went icy cold.

He turned without so much as a goodbye and strode for his horse, leaving me standing there wide-eyed and slack-jawed. At least Sparrow was too busy hurrying to obey to notice.

No goodbye? After all those words of dedication and all those kisses, he wouldn't so much as kiss me goodbye? I remembered a little late that I hadn't offered any such words in return and that my only kiss had resulted in his sudden flight. Perhaps his words and kisses had only been about demonstrating ownership of me, not about true affection. Perhaps the tiniest sign that I might feel affection for him in return had ruined that and sent him running.

Belatedly, I remembered that I didn't need him. That I was my own woman. That I hadn't married for love, and I wouldn't love him even if he wanted me to because he was a villain from a storybook who I'd only allied myself with because the alternative was so much worse.

It was good to remember those things.

"You're disappointed," Grosbeak whispered, narrowing his eyes in delight. "Everyone can see it."

I looked sharply away and came face to face with the specter on my shoulder. She nodded gravely.

Both of them could go suck horse apples for all I cared.

I felt my hands trembling and my face flushing with humiliation, but when I turned, planning to go and examine the horse meant for me, I looked up into the eyes of Bluebeard. His horse was trotting up to me – made soundless because none of its hooves touched the ground.

Our eyes met for but a moment and then he pulled the horse up. He could not speak to me here and he would not speak in my mind and possibly use up my days. He did not break his rule, but he leaned down and seized me, kissing me swift and hard – so swift that the songbirds leapt from his shoulders to the branches above, piercing the air with loud shrieks.

And then he wrenched his lips away and my hand clawed at the empty air where he had been and in the blink of an eye he really was gone, riding off into the morning sun as his brightly colored bird entourage hurried to catch up.

"Really?" I said out loud.

"Really," Grosbeak said with a bubbling laugh. "This story is just too good, and I get a front-chain seat to all of it."

CHAPTER TWENTY-NINE

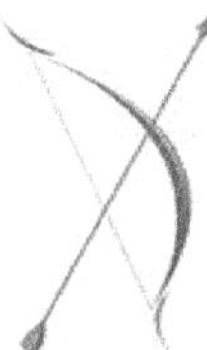

As things so often are in fairytales, the world seemed to order itself to our story, so that our pounding hooves echoed under clear, azure skies and gentle breezes tossed out horses' manes in picturesque curls and ripples. It was almost as if the dew encrusted leaves and grasses and the heady scent of wildflowers were all singing the same song. "Victory," they sang. "Victory."

And I was a fool because part of me was beguiled by their song, and I believed it. I was a fool because when Sparrow finally produced the banner in her hand, I agreed to carry it.

It was a flowing white banner of silk showing a single blue arrow buried into the ground upon its field – the arrow from the Wittenhame that had been stuck in the stone and would someday show to them all their great king. I remembered the story, and while I doubted any mortal would notice the symbol, you could not be Wittenbrand without noticing it.

"Tell me again what I must do," I'd said nervously as we approached the camped army, our horses' hooves ringing out loudly on a road that had morphed from hard-packed dirt to cobbles as it entered what had once been a small seaside town – and probably a charming one – but was now filled past overflowing with armed soldiers and their mounts.

"Keep the veil over your face," Sparrow said grimly.

At her advice, I had agreed to wear a light veil of white that covered my face from below the eyes. It hung from an odd helmet ringed at the top with groping metal branches, so it looked almost like a woodland wreath. The center of the wreath held a small citrine gem with a cloudy surface, so it only glowed yellow when the sun hit it directly. The veil was of a light enough material not to hinder breathing, but it felt odd and awkward though it was trimmed in silver and tied to hang delicately from the temples of the branch helm.

"Despite what he thinks, no one is going to trust a woman so young and unblooded as you to lead them," Sparrow had said. "Confidence is key. If you speak, speak with authority and I will go along with it, only please do not order me to do anything I have not already told you we've planned. This can go very well or very poorly, and now that you're being handed the visible reins, you can be the source of chaos that sinks us. So, be silent as much as possible. Speak with authority when you cannot. The veil will hide your age and inexperience and the expressions on your face that might give you away. You are to be a symbol – a figurehead – a reminder of why they fight. You are not to actually lead charges or swing those swords. You'll hold the banner with one hand, the pole fixed in the pocket on this saddle. You'll hold Grosbeak in the other – and fortunately for you, I had a second pocket made because it will be a long day indeed with two of these heavy poles to keep raised. Keep them high and straight, ride with a straight back and your chin up, and your very presence will inspire and add confidence to this whole proceeding."

It was a practical solution to the problem of being saddled with me, to be sure, and I approved of it for that reason. This was not my world. This was not my expertise. If I was being fair, I had no expertise. I had been raised to be an adequate wife for a nobleman of middling success – to manage money and purchasing of supplies, to keep tradespeople from cheating me, to settle small disputes, to be frugal but generous, hard-working but not ambitious. I had, on my own, learned the ways of horses, but I had no list of skills or attributes to credit me. There was nothing I was qualified to do except sit my mare as I was told.

At least I could say with confidence that Sparrow had chosen a mare who was very well matched for me in terms of size – she was strong but delicate with an arching neck and graceful feet – as well as temperament, for while I was no high-spirited lass, I appreciated high spirits, and this mare danced and pulled a little, longing to be about her work. I admired that.

I balked at the dress and cloak, though. “I’m dressed already.”

“Not like this,” she had said, holding up a filmy white dress and cloak that looked more like a living cloud than anything that might protect you from a breeze, never mind battle. It was translucent. I’d hate to wear it with the sun behind me. There’d be no hiding my shape at all.

“That’s entirely the point,” I said crisply, pursing my lips. “I am wearing as practical an outfit as can be contrived in the Wittenhame. *That* looks more like a bridal gown for a faerie queen.”

Sparrow shook it out and looked again. “Hides too much for that. Faerie queens show more skin. This is the dress of a virginal bride, a symbol of innocence and purity. It’s a dress for you.”

My eyes felt dry they were open so wide. “It’s the most impractical thing I’ve ever seen.”

“Do you want to win this battle, or do you want to argue fashion with me?” she’d said, leaning forward with a grim expression and I was reminded that while she might be my sex, she was entirely different in species and just as likely to rip out my throat if she didn't like the words coming out of it as any other Wittenbrand was.

I wore the wispy dress, rode the majestic horse, and bore the heavy branch crown with the white veil and I felt less myself than I'd ever been, even when I was stolen away for the first time by my strange Wittenbrand husband. Even when my hands were dirty with his betrayal. Even when I'd listened to my own king sell my life away. I felt like I was completely invisible.

And so, invisible and a stranger in my own skin, I found myself led to a council where the plan was laid out and the captains introduced to me. It turned out that I had become an expert in something at least – remaining silent. Sparrow spoke for me, explaining that I was the wife of their patron, the mortal woman Izolda of Savataz. This raised some eyebrows for every face gathered was of a Pensmoore set and I recognized more than one of them. And when she said I would lead the battle, their eyes narrowed, and their fists clenched. But as she spread the maps and spoke about positionings and which villages would be quickly taken and which bypassed entirely, what route would be used, where prisoners would be housed, and who would defend our flanks, they seemed to relax. As I remained silent, never interjecting, never adding my own opinion, they seemed to relax even more, occasionally catching my eye when they looked nervously in my direction but smiling nervously if they did instead of looking angry.

Very well, if my job was stoic silence, it was a thing I was at least well prepared for. I comforted myself with little peeks into Tigrane's book. It was written in an old form of the language, but with concentration I could make out what she was saying.

"This is the written account of the short life of Tigrane Hussanafe, Princess of Ptolemoore. I have written this account in the hopes that

one day my family will find it and know I did not suffer and that those who follow me might gain wisdom from my words."

Wisdom would be nice. I could use that. I'd flipped past the poem at the beginning of every book and flipped past her early childhood and found her later accounts more interesting. Her father had been preparing her to rule, and it seemed he had taken pains to teach her his business.

"*We were busy fortifying our northern border. Though we had stemmed many raids, they were continuing in waves. It was the famine that drove them – drove all of us. Desperate men do desperate things and opportunists seek to profit without working themselves."*

Like us in this raid. We were being opportunists.

"*I was assessing the arrow stores at the tower beside the Fountspring River when a band of raiders made it through the line and attacked. The Sergeant stationed with me was quick to act, gathering in his troops and furnishing the line. They were scattered, but his quick action focused them. After the tumult he told me that if a group of warriors is scattered, concentrating them again should be your first thought. Strung out, they are vulnerable. A leader doesn't leave his men vulnerable. I am sad when I think of Sergeant Quistide. I will miss his pearls of wisdom."*

I'd have to remember that.

Grosbeak was not so well prepared for silence and reading didn't interest him, but I found it easy to silence him before the council, for as they served refreshments, they laid out fruit, and just as he opened his mouth to speak – and I was sure he'd say something I would regret – I snatched up a bright orange and jammed it into his open jaw so that throughout the council he could do nothing but make muffled noises that sounded like curses. If those seated thought he was demonic or mad, I cared not at all. It only lent to my air of mystery.

I was glad when – at last – the council was over and we rode, the troops falling in behind and before.

That was three days ago. Three days of hard riding are enough to soil a white dress, though I'd done all I could to keep it clean. Enough to leave me wrung out like a rag so my stiff spine was more of a bending willow than a strong oak. Enough to make that veil feel like it was smothering me.

The first assault had been easy. We'd taken the seaside village with hardly an effort. And I'd certainly played my part. I'd ridden in at the head of the army when the defenders were slain. I looked the part of the leader of the conquerors.

Shortly after, I'd emptied my stomach along the side of the road, barely saving the veil from the mess.

The people in the little village had been close to starving. I'd never seen so many pale, drawn faces. So many too-deep sunken eyes. And then there had been the children. Those adults still left clung to them with hopeless, empty faces. And there were so few men and women left that I did not know how they would feed those little ones. Every able-bodied man and woman had fought us. And they were now nothing more than corpses on either side of the smooth road.

I wiped my palms often on my dress, feeling the stickiness of blood on them even when they were perfectly clean.

My white dress was nothing more than a mockery. My crown a disgrace.

I kept the orange shoved in Grosbeak's mouth for the entire day for I did not dare listen to what he would surely tell me – that I ought to have worn red and borne a crown of flames.

Guilt sawed through me at the next town, but at Sparrow's insistence, I rode ahead of the victors. This time I kept my eyes forward, hoping the veil hid most of my tears. I could hear the sobs and cries of the survivors on either side of the road. I thought that, perhaps, I had more in common with them than those I rode with.

Is this what my husband had in mind when he sent me on an "easy" campaign to sweep up the rear of the Sword's territory? If it was, then it changed how I saw him. I changed whether I could trust him. How could he be so gentle and kind when his hands bandaged me and yet order his troops to sweep over this land like wolves over a pack of caribou.

"It's not that bad as wars go," Sparrow had said in our tent that night. She'd not said anything else to me and since I'd been silent all day, no one was suspicious when I took my meal to my tent and did not leave it, spending my time reading Tigrane's memoirs instead of socializing with them. "Hardly any casualties. None of children or the elderly. We can't help it if they choose to fight."

"If they choose to defend their homes and livelihoods, you mean?" I asked, and even to me, my tone was more bitter than ginger root.

"You've been gone three turnings of the moon," she said carefully. "Which is why you don't know that your own homeland looks the same. The people are hungry. They lack necessities. The sooner this war is over, the sooner they can prosper again. The sooner the sick can be cared for and the hungry fed. We do them a favor by making it short and fast."

"We do them a favor by twisting them into wars there would be none without us?"

"What do you mean?" her words were cold now.

"I mean that I watched as they tossed the tiles and pulled out war. And there was no war before that. I was there as they plucked the little figurines from the molten lead. They did not have nations assigned to them before then. The Wittenbrand made this war. Without them – without you – it wouldn't have happened at all."

"Mayhap," she said, her voice still colder than the mountains of my homeland. "Or mayhap it would have happened anyway. What do you know of courts or kings? You were a minor noble of a minor house in a minor nation and at his first opportunity, your king sold your life away."

"Where is he anyway?"

"He reviled you when the Arrow brought you to his court."

"Yes," I said. "Is he with my husband on the other front or cowering in his castle?"

She barked a laugh. "Neither. Your Wittenbrand husband heard his words and took his head as the price of his ignorance. He'll brook no insult to you, bride of bloodshed. You'll never see that poxy man again."

I gasped.

"Did you think this was a simple game?" she hissed, nastily as she pinched the candle out. "Did you think it would be carved pieces on a board or cards laid out precisely with a bid? It's a game of lives. A game of nations. And if you care about your own, you'll have to be willing to sacrifice theirs. Your squeamishness will ruin the men's morale, so I thank you to keep it to yourself and trust the Arrow to know best."

"If these are his actions, then I'm not sure that I do trust him,"

I said. "I'm not sure he's worth trusting after all."

The sound she made was of utter disgust. "Don't even talk to me, wretched mortal. I have married my fate to your husband, and you won't even marry your trust to him."

I felt my face flushing, but I would not back down. Not with those children's faces etched into my heart.

"Trust is a thing earned by honor, not demanded by might."

"Says the betrayer," she'd muttered and that was the last thing she spoke to me until dawn.

I lay in the dark alone, calling in my mind to Bluebeard.

"*Husband? Are you there? If you're there, please explain yourself. Tell me why I should trust a man who sent me to slaughter my kind. Tell me why I should keep leading these men to make orphans and widows multiply and lay ruin across the earth. Tell me, if you can.*"

But whether he could not hear me, or whether he would not answer, I did not know, only that he remained as silent as the many, many graves trailing in my wake.

CHAPTER THIRTY

On the second day, I removed the orange from Grosbeak's mouth. If I was going to be miserable, I might as well have company. Besides, Tigrane's sergeant had told her to show mercy wherever she could even to the worst of men because mercy always triumphs in the end. I thought I might give it a try.

"I shall never forgive you for muzzling me," Grosbeak growled when I removed the orange. I was mounted on my pretty mare, my arms already burning from keeping both the flag and Grosbeak in place. I'd rigged them to be held entirely in the pockets when we were motionless, but if we moved, I had to hold them steady. And we always seemed to be moving. I preferred that. It distracted me from the knowledge that I was on my own in a living nightmare with no help from the distant husband who had condemned me to this role.

"It's going well," Sparrow said a little breathlessly when she rode up at the end of the second day. We had driven all the way down to the seaport of Dhayyad and found it defenseless. To my enormous relief, the port had surrendered without a fight. Unlike the dozen or so towns and villages we'd taken, the citizenry seemed to understand the penalty for defiance. After Dhayyad, the city of Gren-ayad had sent word that they accepted our rule of the region and would meet with us to discuss terms when it was convenient. A surrender without even the need to pose as conquerors. "You should be more cheerful. This is as bloodless as war gets."

And it was still too bloody for me.

We'd run into a shepherd on the road two hours ago, butchered with his sheep. I had just looked at Sparrow. Just looked and nothing more.

"You could exhort the men if you like," she said with a sigh. "You can remind them that mercy is golden. But if you do that, they will have doubts. And look what doubt is doing to you."

"I had no doubts," Grosbeak said from where he swayed on his chain. He was undisturbed by grisly news or sights. "Not even one up until the very end. Assurance is a delicious thing, worth any price."

"Misleading, in your case, I would think," I said absently. This was not his fault.

"Oh, certainly. But you can't go through life always torn up – not in days of war and trouble. You have to do the job in front of you and worry about it later."

"Killing me was the job in front of you," I said dryly.

"Exactly," he agreed happily. "And if I'd managed to get on with it without being caught, I wouldn't be here now second-guessing my choices. See? I'm not wrong. Doubts and second-guesses are best left for the dead. We have nothing else to do."

"You don't know what gift you've been given," Sparrow had told me with disgust. "It's wasted on you."

And she'd ridden off to talk to the captains and arrange the next day's excursions. Our line was thinning, stretched as it was across such a swath of land. I'd been watching that, noting how we had to leave soldiers at each important junction and with them, supplies. How we'd had to leave too few to really guard those areas so we could keep the bulk of the troop together. If we continued our streak of success, it shouldn't matter. We'd be reaching the southernmost tip of Aayadmoore before the end of another day, and from there we'd establish a head and start shipping supplies and reinforcements in. But if we saw even the slightest turnabout of success, we could find ourselves stretched out too thin and easy to gobble up.

On top of that, I sensed the captains were restless. There had been no true glory yet and, unlike me, they craved the kind of action that would fill their drinking stories and garnish boasts of prowess. They wanted to take a large target that fought back so they could earn their victory. They almost needed it, they craved it so much. The thought of that sat poorly with me.

It was these moody thoughts that were upon me when we were surprised on the plain just outside of Cataayad, the southernmost port city of Aayadmoore.

I was positioned – at Sparrow's order – on a hill looking over the plain, a forest at my back, taking a quick break as the troops passed by on the plain, row upon row upon row. She had set me up like a statue to inspire them more than once and I was used to this routine. If I was careful to disguise my book, I could read it as they passed.

Tigrane had proved a very interesting writer, full of wit, practicalities and an interesting perspective on her father's never-ending wars. I thought we could have been friends had we known each other. She had been twenty-three when Bluebeard took her – old enough that her mother despaired of her ever marrying and her father rejoiced in her ability to run his kingdom at his side. She had no siblings, no cousins, none to replace her. And I had never heard of her family line. I was frequently saddened by that. All memory of her was in this book and her lifeless body frozen in time on its pedestal. But I would remember. And I was learning much about ruling a kingdom and leading people. And with every sentence I read I watched Sparrow and the other officers and compared their actions to Tigrane's words and found myself wishing it was Tigrane leading these troops and not me. She would not have been roped into a war she wanted no part of or dressed up like a strange doll and paraded around for morale and nothing more. She would have done better than this.

Though the soldiers were traveling to battle, they seemed in good spirits and looked often toward me as they passed, their chins lifting and spines stiffening when they saw me. If I inspired them with pride, it was only because of who Sparrow had made me – the perfect, faceless figurehead. They could imagine me looking back over them with pride or with hope or with admiration or any other emotion they wanted to imagine because my face was hidden from them, my true heart buried deep within.

The last of the troops were passing by, and in a moment, Sparrow would send a rider from the front to come back and retrieve me as she always did. Her disgust at my lack of enthusiasm for bloodshed never prevented her from using me perfectly as her foil.

"Something is amiss," Grosbeak said as a cloud shifted in the sky. In the distance, to the west, the sky looked almost red, made more apparent with the rays of the sun hidden away.

The sight of it made my stomach twist.

"The battle will come in red," I whispered, putting my book away.

"So they said," Grosbeak agreed. "But in your case, I think the battle will come in moping and moaning."

"Just because you have no compassion doesn't mean I should smother mine," I argued.

"Then don't smother it, but also don't use it as an excuse to shut your eyes and stop your ears. You could have been using this time to win over the captains of Pensmoore's army and endear yourself to the troops."

"Sparrow wants me to be a distant figurehead."

"And is that what the Arrow demanded when he left you here? No. He told you to lead. But instead, you're sulking like a nineteen-year-old girl."

"I *am* a nineteen-year-old girl, in case you haven't noticed."

"Ah, but there lies the trick of it, for you've been one now for nigh on thirty years and you should know better."

"I know the names of the captains," I objected. Was that red I saw on the field now, too, and coming down that nearby hill? Or was I imagining things? "And I know what they want – glory and honor and bloodshed. And what they'll do to get it – anything. And I've decided I want no part of my people. I want no part of their war. I just want to live a quiet life."

"Oh, isn't that so nice," Grosbeak said nastily. "And then someone else can go fight and die so you can have your nice life of peace. And he can get his hands bloody, and his conscience stained, while you sit in your superior white dress."

"I didn't choose this dress," I said sharply.

"But you chose that attitude and isn't it an unflattering thing. Everything worth having has a price. And the price of peace is sometimes war. What do you think the Sword will do to this place if he's left alone for a hundred years to do as he likes? What was he willing to do to you?"

I flinched from his words.

"You aren't a passive, useless person, Izolda. You are not a decoration to act as a living statue. Why do you think Bluebeard sent you to this battle?"

"Because of a prophecy," I said grimly. "And because I was bound on – "

The specter wrapped a hand around my mouth, and I rolled my eyes. Grosbeak had been there. Who was she protecting my words from?

"I think he sent you because you have skills that Sparrow doesn't have. Look."

And as he said that, a tide of red rolled over the hill and into our troops. It was like watching an arrow fly through the air and puncture plate armor. Like watching a mist lion leap and bear a deer down to the ground. Our line flinched and then shuddered as the impact of red-coated bodies slammed into them.

Stunned, I watched as a second group poured out of the city walls ahead, blocking off that way of escape for our lead-most troops. That left only the ocean and the way back, but the line was crumpling where the hammer of their forces had hit us, buckling and bending, and then – in the space of heartbeat – we were two groups cut off from one another.

Retreat. We had to retreat. And *I* had to sound the retreat.

I spun my horse to see if anyone was behind me. There were only the last few lines of soldiers who hadn't marched past me yet, but they weren't running forward to help their fellows, they were forming a line, pulling in cooks and porters and the others that usually made up the rear of the line and forcing them into position as a third wave of red rolled in from the rear.

I realized without having to be told that these weren't local forces. I'd looked at the maps and heard the captains as their spies reported and then they discussed what they would do. I'd listened as Sparrow rattled off estimates of manpower and horses and how far off lords and their house guards were located. These were none of those groups. This was the Sword and his army – those I had thought my husband went to fight in the east. They had laid a clever trap and we'd fallen into it like a duckling into the jaws of a shark.

It only took a heartbeat to realize this. One more to watch as Sparrow tried to form up her group on the other side of that red river to join us. A third to know what I had to do.

I lifted the banner, rode to the line trying to form beside me, and roared in my best imitation of my father, "Up Pensmoore, up! To me!"

Ready or not, this battle had come for me.

CHAPTER THIRTY-ONE

"This is not the front seat that I paid for!" Grosbeak protested choppily as his head swung back and forth on the end of the chain. My very pretty horse was capable of fancy footwork – a boon in our present situation. I danced her to the center of the men forming and grabbed the flag from the pocket, lifting it to wave it back and forth. "They should have left you with a guard!"

"They dressed me in white, Grosbeak. Clearly, I was meant to be the sacrificial lamb."

Behind us, screams mingled in the air with the clash of steel, a hymn to death and fury, a song to melting ambitions. I clenched my teeth against it, trying to stop my ears to individual cries lest I ache for each voice. My belly felt like water and my legs trembled where they gripped the dappled mare.

The soldiers needed a rallying point. With forces on every side pressing in and cut off from the front of the formation, they needed some shared goal. That's what flags were for. That's what *I* was for.

I tried to focus on that and what I could remember from Tigrane's beloved Sergeant, instead of on the clash of steel and the cries of fear and panic. These were men of Pensmoore, and while I'd spent the last three days furious with them, appalled by their success, aching at the misery of even an easy war, they were still my people, of my homeland, raised on my land.

The battle wasn't here yet, but it was quickly forming up. It seemed almost incongruous with the soft breeze and dappled sunlight in this wildflower field, but we were preparing to wash it in blood.

Three rows of fighters formed up in front of me. They would not be enough against our enemy. Those who had come up from behind us were running down the road in an effort to meet us here – our cooks and farriers with their weapons clenched in trembling hands and determination etched in every face.

But they weren't the only threat. In the center of what had been our formation, more ambushers slammed into our men on the forest side, gaining ground.

Our defenses there were little knots of men – threes or four here, a dozen there – trying to fight from horseback as they faced an equal number of light cavalry riding from the forest and rushing along the side of our formation – if you could call this ragged grouping that – in a sweeping maneuver meant to drive us back.

A sudden memory of my childhood overtook me. Svetgin setting up his rows of toy soldiers. Rolgrin laughing as he made horse noises and pretended to draw two of his horses along the side of the neat soldier ranks.

"You can't do that! There's only two of them!" Svetgin had protested.

"It's a sweep. It's meant to keep them in place until my heavy forces pin them down."

They'd learned that in the strategy classes my father's arms man taught them. I was suddenly wishing I'd been included, too.

Tigrane's recorded memories were not enough to teach me battle.

"You should get down off the horse, lady," a man wearing a sergeant's baldric suggested as he trotted past me. "You make a pretty figurehead on a hillside but you're a target for archers now."

He didn't stop to watch if I obeyed. He and his group of ten reached the line drawing up at what had been our rear and was about to become the front of our fight. The sight of them arriving put a new strength in the faces of the bluff workers around me. I could almost hear them thinking, "ah, real soldiers."

I wasn't so optimistic. We were armed haphazardly, caught out unprepared. Meanwhile, the group surging up the road we'd just traveled were heavily armored and carried heavy maces. The armor made them slower, explaining the need for the light cavalry to pin us.

Cold sweat broke out across my brow. I could see it all from where I sat, the sergeant and others like him hastily setting up the line, the groups of our own light cavalry being forced back where they were stretched out in small groups between here and at what had been the center of our line but was now a river of death. We were spread out too thin. And that line at what was now our backs had crumpled. It was only the chaos of fighting individuals and the distance between us and them that gave us even a breath of safety from that bulge that cut our rear contingent off from the front of the army.

Worse, the front army had the captains and Sparrow in it. How had we not planned for this? How had *I* not noticed it? I, whose only skill was noticing things other people missed. I'd been too emotionally tumultuous to pay attention to the details, too torn up by the horror of war. And I wouldn't apologize for that, though now I might reap the whirlwind consequence.

In a flash of insight, I realized another truth, Sparrow and her captains had positioned themselves all in the front to stay as far away from me as possible. The men who died now died because I had been so miserable that my attitude had pushed the officers away. I felt a flash of cold, harsh guilt, harsher than any specter sitting on my shoulder. In mourning lost lives, I may have doomed more.

Biting my lip, I peered at the faraway group of officers and their part of the army, trying to judge if they were holding. They were locked into a smaller space than we were – not spread out but balled up in a churning huddle as they fought attackers on every side, weapons flashing as they moved with lightning speed.

Grosbeak cursed and I tasted blood as my tooth went right through the flesh of my lip as I finally saw a detail no one else was noticing.

"Trust mortals to botch a perfect battle," he muttered. "At least they have the colors right, red versus blue."

I urged my horse forward to where the sergeant who had warned me off was dressing the line.

"Sergeant," I called.

"Not now, lady. We are preparing to meet the attack coming down the road."

"Sergeant," I tried again. "You're forming up in the wrong place."

"Lady, you form where you stand, or you fall. And I told you to get off that horse."

I looked up, judged the distance between the heavy infantry marching toward us, judged the forming line, looked back over my shoulder at the harried cavalry drawing inward toward the sea, at the crumpled line, at the knot of trapped officers.

And the words of Tigrane's journal came to mind.

"My tutors tell me that if you find yourself facing foes in multiple sides, reduce the number of sides which you must defend."

Right, then.

I'd been sent to lead. If I was going to die, then I would die leading.

I wrenched the veil off my face with one hand and threw it to the ground.

"Form your line, Sergeant," I ordered, energized by the feeling of air on my sheltered face, "and then we will retreat, slowly, backing up to join our spread-out forces and increase our numbers."

"You don't know war, lady," he said, still moving down the line, working as he spoke. My horse followed, dodging rushing men as they worked. The wagons had been cut loose from the supply horses. Carts had been overturned across the road. They were making quick work, but by my estimate, we had minutes until the tide of men hit us.

"She doesn't know defeat, either," Grosbeak said flippantly.

There was a roar from behind us. The last of our men fighting on foot in the middle space had been overwhelmed.

The tide from behind was roaring forward. We would find ourselves in the middle between them both. We needed one less side to defend.

"We'll gather up what cavalry we can as we retreat and try to sweep to position our backs to the ocean."

"A losing proposition. Do you not know that tides change?" the sergeant replied.

"Do they change in an hour?" I asked. "I'm asking you to hold just that long."

That made him pause. "Just an hour? Ha! Do you know how long an hour is on a battlefield?"

"Every hour of my life is weighed and measured," I said through gritted teeth. I could see this in my mind. It was the right solution. "Every day of mine is being spent. I can count them as they pass, and I know their futility. I know also what I ask of you. Now, form the line, set a steady retreat, and sweep to the ocean while I round up the light cavalry scattered from here to the enemy."

"While you what?" he asked, aghast. Pausing for the first time to actually look at me. "While you *what*?"

I didn't answer, taking my inspiration from my taciturn husband who never answered those kinds of questions from me. Instead, I turned my horse and kicked her up to a trot. The sergeant knew his orders. I could only hope he'd follow them.

"Look at you, ordering military men around like you think you know what you're doing," Grosbeak snickered.

"I can see more because I'm on horseback," I said shortly. I had to hold both the banner and his head pole to keep them steady as I rode.

"Maybe this slaughter agrees with you after all."

"I assure you, it does not."

"And yet your orders were exactly what I would have given when I was one of Bluebeard's war leaders."

I'd forgotten that he was ever more than a talking head.

"It was the practical suggestion," I deflected.

He laughed again, this time with seeming enjoyment. "Oh, war is a practical thing, mistress. It's all about cold calculations and weighing what cost you'll pay for what return. Like a cart merchant with a barrel of apples to sell, but the apples you're selling are men's lives."

"They're giving them no matter what," I said tightly. "I'm just trying to increase the cost to the buyer."

"And if you'd thought that way from the start, maybe we wouldn't be selling so many apples," he said.

His insight cut to the quick. I could see the truth of it, and I hated myself for it. Hated that my very compassion had tripped me up and made me useless.

"You were never meant to be ornamental, Izolda. You've not the face for it, nor the temperament."

He was right about that, too.

I reached the first group of riders as they were ending a bloody skirmish. Their attackers had ridden on, leaving them broken and splintered. Three horses were down, kicking in their own blood as one of the riders stumbled from one to the next, ending their misery with his blade. His coat was torn and bloody, his face streaked with sweat and dirt. I found my stomach flipping at the sight.

"Pensmoore," I said in greeting as the survivors turned their exhausted eyes to me. I straightened, trying to look confident. "Have you mounts for the wounded?"

The man who had been killing the horses looked around him,

devastation on his face. He was counting.

"Aye, lady," he said after a moment. "I'm sergeant here."

"Take your men and join the foot. They're retreating to make a stand with the ocean against their backs. You can meet them halfway if you hurry,"
I ordered him.

He looked helplessly at the trees. "Orders are to hold in line if attacked. This is my spot in line."

"I'm changing those orders," I said grimly.

"No offense lady, but pretty crown or no, this isn't your field. This isn't your army." He sounded tired. Too tired to argue, though he was making a try of it.

"Ooooh. Big sergeant," Grosbeak hooted.

I wrenched off the crown of branches and threw it at him, pitching my voice to make it loud enough for his men to hear, too. He caught it, astonished, as I spoke.

"I don't care about crowns. I don't care about captains. But I care about Pensmoore. It's why I carry her banner. It's why I lead this army, whether you believe it or not. And it's why I'm going to get as many of your tattered hides home to your wives and sweethearts as I can, even if I have to hang a dozen more heads from my lantern pole to accomplish it.

A lone soldier gave a half-hearted cheer before a friend hushed him.

The sergeant was motionless for a full breath, staring at me, his own chest heaving as he tried to catch his breath, but whatever he saw in his face was what he needed to say because when he did speak, he nodded, dropping the glittering crown to the ground, fluttering veil and all.

"Hashek, Roirden, ride with the lady to enforce her will. You'll be gathering the whole line, lady?"

"Yes."

He nodded again. "Aye then, we'll take our wounded where you've sent them, and god send our foot are still there when we arrive."

I glanced over my shoulder and clenched my jaw in time to see the first of the enemy slam into the lines I'd left with the sergeant. I could only hope he really would lead them to where they could get the ocean behind their backs before they were flanked.

"Hurry," I said, but there was no time for more, so I rode.

The two men he'd called off fell in behind me.

I gathered up two more knots of men – these without any surviving officers – and sent them to assist the foot without any more argument. Maybe it was the men at my back. Maybe it was the lack of veil and crown. With it gone, all eyes looked to my banner and every now and then, one of the men would touch his cheek as if in honor of my husband's sign. Their patron saint. The one who had sent his wife to fight this battle.

And fight this battle, I would, though he'd be hearing about it from me later.

It was at the fourth knot that we encountered the enemy. There were little unpredictable dips in these plains, and the fourth knot of men and wounded horses were situated right beside one of those. I pulled up beside them just as the enemy charged out of that dip, howling and waving their swords as if their sheer noise might slay us where we stood. I checked that the flag was secure and grabbed Grosbeak's pole.

"I am not a weapon. I am not a weapon. I am not a weapon," he chanted, but he need hardly have bothered. I didn't get a single swipe in. Hashek and Roirden cut the enemy down before they could touch me or the four surviving men. They had only two horses between them, but they didn't hesitate to mount up and ride in the direction I pointed.

"You need to get back to the foot," Grosbeak said from where he swung on the chain. "Look."

I did look, cursing when I saw what he had.

Our foot had obeyed my orders, angling so their backs were to the ocean, but the reinforcements I was sending were not enough.

The enemy army who had attacked our line in the center were rushing toward the men I'd gathered, abandoning their search of the wounded and dying. One glance showed their red-coated masses splitting us so far from the front of what had once been our line that the thought of rejoining again seemed nearly impossible.

I swallowed down a knot of fear. There was no time for that now.

I scanned everything, assessing it quickly. There were a few more scattered groups out here, but the time it would take to gather them was too valuable. I looked to them and then back to the foot.

"I'll ride to them," Roirden offered, and at my nod, he whipped his horse into a gallop.

It was the best we could do.

We spun and turned back to the lines of foot I'd left to fight, riding hard to meet them. My hair was loose from its braid and streaming behind me like a second flag and with it, my fears and hopes streamed out, too. It was ridiculous that I was here at all, ridiculous that I was trying to lead where I should have just held my tongue and left this to those who were responsible to act. But how could I have remained silent when I could *see* what was coming?

I tried one more time to call my husband. *Please,* I said with my mental voice. *Please listen to me. Please come to me. I will not rage or yell if only you will come to me. I will not throw recriminations at you, if only you will save me.*

He did not come. He did not answer.

I clenched my teeth and rode towards the men I had positioned to fight a final battle. The first wave of attack had been quelled, but our enemy was drawing together and preparing for another thrust. I would live or die with these men I'd gathered. They could not escape the enemy now that they were pinned on one side, soon to be savaged on the other, with their only guarded side held by the sea. It was an impossible situation. And one I'd thrust them into.

I scanned their eyes and faces as we drew closer. I noted the determination swirling with fear and fury. And I saw how their eyes lifted to me, painful hope flashing there.

"If you'd ordered them to the trees, they'd be slaughtered one at a time. Like carrots in a row ready to be picked," Grosbeak reminded me. "It was better this way."

Even so, I couldn't be so confident. And it was on my word that they'd amassed there. I needed a plan to save them, and I needed it now. I tried to see what was obvious that I might be missing. I tried to think about what Tigrane had written.

But nothing came to me, not even when we reached the edge of the line, trampling fallen bodies in the mud under my horse's feet – remains of the last wave of fighting. I held tightly to my churning belly and tried not to think of the horror of their desecration and how damned my soul must be at the indifference of my action.

The moment we joined our diminished army, Hashek spun to join the defense. I touched him lightly on the arm in thanks and to my surprise, he saluted.

"Whenever you call, lady, I shall listen."

I felt my eyebrows raising but I couldn't seem to straighten them as his words were echoed down the line.

"Whenever you call!" the men said.

A little shudder went through me. I'd better figure out how to call. And fast.

I rode to the back of the line, my dapple's hooves splashing in the tide.

There were just under fifty or sixty defenders here. Someone cried out. The enemy reforming on the road side of us was moving again, ready to come in a second wave. I quickly assessed what we had to fight.

Rallying the spread-out light cavalry had added maybe another thirty men on horse trying to harry the flanks, but with the second force closing in things were grim. Would it be enough?

I reached the sergeant as he was passing orders about the care of the wounded at the back of the line.

"We're here, banner lady," he said, looking up from his work. His tone was wry with disbelief. "I hope there's a second half to this plan of yours."

There wasn't.

I closed my eyes and hoped.

CHAPTER THIRTY-TWO

A rallying cry from the enemy sounded. They must have seen the second force waiting to join them. My heart pounded in the cage of my ribs. I felt like I couldn't take a breath.

"Breathe, Izolda," Grosbeak said. "Think. What do you have that no one else has? What can you use?"

I had common sense. A bodiless friend. A specter that shut my mouth for me if I mentioned certain things. A missing husband who had dropped me right into this mess. A room of secrets that opened with a key. Nothing that would help. Even the room could only provide temporary relief and delay the inevitable – and that was assuming my army would fit in it.

My teeth set on edge. My head was ringing as the next wave of attack crashed into our fighters. The sounds of fighting ripped through my concentration. Shouts and battle cries and the clash of steel and screams of death blocked out everything else.

We were pushed back until my dappled mare's feet were half-sunk in foaming seawater. It licked green against her grey legs.

There had to be something I hadn't thought of yet.

I clenched my palms tightly closed and felt one sting just a little – a stinging feeling I had gotten so used to that I'd forgotten it had existed at all. It was the sting from the cut on my palm when Bluebeard bound me to the earth. That might have proved useful had we been in Pensmoore. It might have led to some kind of magical connection to the land that could save us all. But we were not in Pensmoore and this land was not tied to me.

A soldier fell beside me, and I leaned down to grab his arm and haul him to his feet. Our eyes met, locked in desperate fear. A blade slid into his chest and blood bubbled up to his lips. I gasped, letting his arm go as my dapple danced to the side.

Another man took his place, pushing the enemy back while I was still staring at the man I'd tried to help, but we were losing ground. Someone was yelling that we couldn't bring the injured into the water. I hadn't even noticed that my dapple was knee-deep. When had we given so much ground?

I rubbed a hand over my weary face, flinching at the pull in my wounded shoulder. No time for that, Izolda. No time for pain or "could-have-beens." There was only me and these brothers of my blood, stranded out here in a strange land where we should never have come. We'd be buried far from home on foreign shores. Maybe even this beach. But we weren't part of this place. We were part of one far distant, one that filled my lungs with sweet air and my heart with gladness when I thought of it. Pensmoore. The land itself – the hills and trees and brooks in spring, the snow in early winter, drifting down like a gift, and later winter, driving like the angry hand of a vengeful god.

My last thoughts would be of home. Maybe theirs would be, too.

A clash beside me distracted me again and I lashed out with Grosbeak's pole, shoving an enemy in the back as he battled a soldier I recognized. Hashek. He plunged his sword through the man and twisted to drive a second enemy backward, their red coats disguising the mortal wounds he dealt.

I swallowed, scanning the line. Everywhere I looked men fell and bled and died. We were losing ground too quickly, being swallowed by the sea, and yet still my army fought.

I let my eyes cling to them for a moment, an acknowledgment that they were fighting and dying just because we'd asked them to, and I wondered if Bluebeard's story were true about the god who made the world in his chest so that the very tides were his breathing. I reached out with my mind as if I could feel it, too, and as I reached, I felt the earth beneath me shake – though that must be my imagination – at the strength of my love for another place far from here.

I could almost feel it on my palms, taste the snow, hear the whinny of horses, see the dawn staining the snow pink. I closed my eyes just for a moment – maybe my last moment – and breathed it in.

I wouldn't think of regrets or of what a terrible idea this had been. I would think only of love. May my last breaths be laden with it.

"I told you I had a front-chain seat," Grosbeak said. "Look."

I opened my eyes.

A gasp caught in my throat. I'd done something after all.

The men of Pensmoore glowed slightly.

They pushed up from the sea like the tide reaching for the earth, made faster somehow, larger, stronger. When they dodged, blows seemed to slow. When they moved, they sped so fast they blurred before my eyes. When they struck, their blows had the force of thunderclaps. They drove our enemy back, their ragged defense turning suddenly into a forceful counterattack.

White froth churned up as we pressed from sea to sand and

then sand to rocky shore.

"Toward your fellows, Pensmoore," I called, realizing they were pushing out in every direction. If we lost focus, we'd be separated and slaughtered, even with this mystical strength and speed. "Fight for your home."

I lifted the banner from its pocket and raised it as high as it would go, kicking the dapple forward to lead the charge. My people joined me, their eyes bright, hope in their faces and power in their hands, their strikes fast and sure.

"I love a good charge," Grosbeak shrieked as we rode, and I couldn't tell if he was serious or mocking us all. "Forward! For honor! For glory! Forward!"

It was like some unbelievable ballad. The story of seventy beaten down, huddled on the beach, almost lost to the waves and the foe and then rising up against hundreds – and winning. A girl on a dappled horse leading, her banner filled with the wind.

I caught the eye of a nearby soldier and at our shared glance he roared, a smile tingeing his face. The next gaze I caught was the same and the next. We rode on a wave of renewed hope and we rode together.

I could barely contain my giddy relief.

We pressed toward the other half of our people, pushing hard. My mouth fell open in wonder as the enemy parted before us, slain or scattered, and turning around in confused circles as if they, too, could not believe what was happening.

"To me, to me!" I called, riding at the forward edge of our rising wave, watching as the enemies before me were pulled down at the last moment before they could impede the dapple or me. It was like I was the hull of a ship parting the water. It was as if I was the figurehead on her bow, leading the charge.

I didn't fight it. I leaned into it hard, letting it carry me along.

An enemy blade struck toward me. I swiped him aside with Grosbeak's pole. It shouldn't have been possible. He was too large and experienced, I too small and too green. And yet, he was swept aside as if by forces great than me.

And I realized that when my husband bound me to the land, he'd bound me to every person who had grown up upon it, fed by its bounty, loved by its kindness, nourished by its rain. We were one in this. One with each other, one with our forebears, and one with the land.

I threw a man from my path with a single snap of Grosbeak's pole. I was more than a slim girl riding a horse. I was Pensmoore.

"If you're going to keep using me as a weapon you could at least let me carry a dagger in my teeth!" Grosbeak protested.

We burst through our enemy, emerging suddenly in the ranks of the other half of our army, all of us heaving and gasping with the force of that charge. Behind us, a trail of shattered bodies, clad in red, lay ruined on the beach. We ringed our compatriots eagerly, looking for familiar faces.

I'd expected someone to seize my authority back the moment we joined them. I'd expected a harsh demand to know what I was doing. What I saw instead were white faces and trembling hands. In the center, a group of pale-faced soldiers was a ring of dead and the only one of the captains not in that ring was cradling Sparrow on his lap, his face like that of a ghost. And I would know since I had one who was ever with me. I glanced at the specter and she raised an eyebrow at me.

Sparrow had a dozen arrows in her chest. I swallowed at the

sight of them and then searched her face for life.

Her eyes met mine, rolling slightly as they moved.

"Orders, lady?" the sergeant asked me, running up to the side of the dapple. He gave Sparrow a single glance before turning his full attention to me. "They're turning. I think they're running. Should we pursue?"

"Hold fast!" I called out so everyone could hear. We couldn't afford to be scattered again. "Gather in our wounded and shore up the line," I told the sergeant in a quieter voice, and then I leapt from the horse, bringing Grosbeak with me.

I hurried to Sparrow's side, my face set in a grim cast.

She coughed, spitting blood.

"Day," she gasped.

"What's that?" I asked, almost choking on the words. My throat was rough from shouting. My hands were trembling. I thought Wittenbrand didn't die easily. But she looked like a pincushion. Who would even waste that many arrows on one person? My mouth felt stuffed with wool at the sight of it.

"They're running," the captain said, his eyes burning with intensity. "Now is the time to pursue. Get some of our own back."

"Just one day," Sparrow begged, her voice so faint I could barely hear it. "Get it for me and I will live."

I looked from the captain to her and back and the key tingled around my neck. What should I do?

"She's delusional with pain," the captain said firmly. "Pursue our enemies or we may find ourselves mired here a second time."

I bit my lip.

"Last time you took a day he overreacted," Grosbeak reminded me. "Took it very personally. Is Sparrow worth that? Is she worth a single day of your life?"

"If we don't move now, they can rally. Pin us here. We need to pursue or retreat," the captain said again.

"If you want my opinion," Grosbeak said, "you'll leave them all and ride as hard as you can for the border of Pensmoore."

"No one is asking you," I said sharply as I sucked in a deep breath and drew the key from around my neck, and turned it in the air. The room opened with an audible gasp from the onlookers. "Hold this position," I ordered them. "I'm going to get the war leader her day."

CHAPTER THIRTY-THREE

"You should redecorate in here," Grosbeak said as we entered the room I was beginning to think of as the Room of Wives. He was peering back and forth, swaying on his chain as I ran up the aisle of other women. "Tell them who is wife now. You know, put your personal touch on things – something somber in black and forest green with just a hint of red for all the blood you make the Arrow shed."

"If these other women are any judge, I won't be wife for long," I huffed dryly, skidding as I reached the hourglass and its falling garnets. Good thing I'd lost that helm and veil, or I wouldn't be able to run like this.

"Oh, I don't know. You just survived your first campaign, that has to count for something."

"So did Tigrane. That didn't keep her from losing all her days."

"Ah, but he married her and these others in the mortal way, not the Wittenbrand way. It's not the same."

"So, everyone keeps saying," I muttered, seizing a gem from the garnets gathered in the top bulb. It was just a day, right? Just one day that might be full of sunshine and walking through waist-high fields of grass under a blue sky with my horse nickering beside me. I blinked back sharp tears.

Grosbeak seemed to realize what was going on in my head. "It could be the kind of day when you have the ague and you spend the whole day out of your mind shivering in your bed and moaning incoherently."

"Thank you," I said, patting him on the head. "That was shockingly kind coming from you."

I spun before he could answer, garnet clutched in my hand, shoulder on fire, and sprinted back down the aisle of wives.

"Everyone keeps bringing it up your marriage because no one does that," Grosbeak rambled as I ran. "No Wittenbrand would marry a mortal in that way. We seldom marry *each other* in that way. Did you hear how binding it is? 'As long as rivers run and moon shines, as long as the earth has bones and death has claws, as long as the ages pass and fail, so long shall I be husband to you.' That kind of vow is like magic. It's insane to do it. Madness. It's got all the force of reversing a siren cry."

"I don't even know what that is," I said breathlessly. Why was this room so long?

"Oh well, you know, if a siren catches you in her net, you're stuck for life even if you wiggle free, but the pull can be reversed if you can match the note. It will shift your binding to whoever played that note. Luckily, they're not regular notes or a person could end up a marionette dancing at the end of the strings of one master after another – but who am I to talk, right? I'm the king of marionettes."

He was very chatty for a bodiless head.

I reached the far side of the room, panting from my sprint. A stitch was forming in my side. I should have ridden instead of run. Why didn't I think of that?

"But I digress," Grosbeak said, clearly enjoying himself. "It's the curse at the end that makes the Wittenbrand vow so strong. 'If ever it be otherwise, may I waste away with sickness and may famine eat my strength…"

I turned the key in the lock and ran through the door while it was still opening, hardly listening as Grosbeak kept speaking the marriage vow.

"… may my enemies overtake me."

I burst out into the mortal world and drew up short.

"Done," a voice drawled out, answering Grosbeak's words. "I so like granting wishes. It makes me feel like a jhinn."

I looked up. And further up. Icy cold filled me, rushing down my legs and pulling my nerve with it.

The Sword's naked blade was inches from my throat, and he peered down at me in haughty delight from the back of a magnificent white charger – white, not grey, for nothing could be as white as this mount was, not even snow. The charger bore a sword of bone on its forehead as a diadem, much like the skeleton of a fish I saw on the wall of a tavern that time my father took me on the ill-advised trip by boat upon the heaving sea. The fish had been called a swordfish.

"A sword horse," I said dazedly.

The Sword laughed. "I shall immediately begin calling them that. It's a very fitting name. It's a shame you didn't consent to be my wife, mortal girl. You could have entertained me with little charms like that one."

But I wasn't listening. The Sword never had anything to say that was worth listening to. Instead, I was trying to edge around his sword horse – despite the wicked gleam in its rolling eye. Red coats surrounded the Sword and what had been the doorway to the room. And through the little gaps between them, I managed to catch just a glimpse of my own people. They looked down at their feet, shame their shared emotion.

"How long," I gasped.

"How long were you in your little closet?" the Sword asked dryly. "Maybe ten minutes. Not long. It could have been days. You mortals always seem to forget that any passage into our world risks the loss of what you're seeking to the ravages of time. But this little adventure cost you just enough of it to spring a tidy trap and snatch up your tender army. I do love playing War. It's my favorite of the games. It satisfies on an almost spiritual level, don't you think?"

I tried to lean around the sword horse.

"Sparrow?" I barely kept my voice from trembling.

The sword horse stepped forward, blocking my view again.

"Uh uh uh, my lady," the Sword warned me, preening his golden hair. "They're my hostages now. If you want them safe and returned to your lands, then you'll need to do as I ask."

"Where did you come from?" I asked tightly. "How were you hidden here? We'd won."

He laughed. "Well, of course you did. But you didn't think I wouldn't be watching, did you? You didn't think the Arrow was the only one who could weave pretty little doorways when he needed them? I always keep one eye on what's mine."

I swallowed at that. The way he was looking at me could suggest that he meant that he was watching his lands or that he was watching *me* and the thought of that tasted like a mouth full of maggots.

I tried to edge around the horse again and it leaned forward and bit at Grosbeak like an apple.

"Hey! No! Bad horse!" he yelled. And then his yell turned into an ear-piercing scream.

All my anger unfurled at once. I cuffed the horse in the nose – a thing I'd never do to such a magnificent animal under normal circumstances – and strode past it, chin held high.

I reached within, feeling the power of my land. I needed to give it back to my people so they could fight. I needed – I rounded the horse to see them penned by a ring of red, weaponless and defeated. A look of betrayal hunkered low and growling in every eye I saw. I swallowed.

They looked away, refusing to meet my eyes, and the power I'd felt in my blood – the power I could give to them – fizzled out like a flame in a harsh rain. I couldn't give them what they wouldn't accept.

In the center of their group, the captain still held a gasping Sparrow, blood trickling from her mouth.

"I offer you a bargain," the Sword drawled from behind me. "Their lives for yours. But no, I'm being dramatic. I don't plan to kill you. Let me be more precise. Their *freedom* for yours. Agree, and I'll weave them a little gate and send them off with all the fanfare of a conquering army. Refuse, and I'll kill them all. And either way, I get you."

"I need to speak to Sparrow," I said tightly. I needed to get her the day. Just one day to heal herself as she'd promised, and then she could lead them, and they could fight their way out.

"The bargain comes first," the Sword said, leaning down and out from his horse like a trick rider. The fearsome creature barely shifted to accommodate his weight. Impressive. "Accept, and they go free. Decline, and they die, but either way, I take you."

I shook my head. "There's no bargain there."

He smirked. "There is if you're one of *them*."

"She's barely holding on, lady," the captain called out, his voice raspy with something. Pain? Fear? "We might not be able to move her."

Grosbeak was oddly silent, his breath rasping as if he was trying to hold back a panic attack.

"Would you like to watch her die here?" the Sword asked, and he sounded more curious than threatening. "If they go free, she could be seen by a mortal wise woman or what have you, but perhaps this is not what you want. Perhaps she is your rival? I could imagine that. She has been close to the Arrow all these years. And now she is his right hand. Interesting, don't you think? He chose *her* for that and not you."

"I just need to speak to her," I said tightly. I had to get her the gem. I had done all this to give her my day and if I didn't do it now, then it had all been for nothing.

He sneered. "They tried to tell me you'd give yourself for them. Isn't that adorable. But I knew it would not be enough."

He snapped his fingers. and a horse was led forward from the back ranks of his people.

I gasped.

"But I remembered you had a weakness. A brother."

Svetgin was tied to the horse. On his shoulder perched a wraith identical to mine. She wrapped both her hands around his mouth while another wraith held him fast, like a squirrel gripping a tree – both arms and legs grasping his arms tightly to his sides. His eyes met mine. Hopeless. Despairing.

"He's not part of the bargain, of course, but if you don't bargain for all of the others to go free, I'll kill him with them," the Sword said. "And I'll enjoy it as I always do. We call that 'upping the ante.'"

"Release them," I said roughly. I knew he was needling me, knew he was manipulating me, and yet I couldn't help myself. The stakes had risen to be too high for me. "My freedom for theirs."

The Sword laughed, but he flicked a hand elegantly and said, "It is agreed."

And then, before I could gasp, the Sword reached out a hand and the men of Pensmoore began to flicker, winds whipping all around us so hard that Grosbeak's head suddenly flew out, pulled parallel against the chain.

"Captain!" I called and I threw the garnet – my single day – at him as hard as I could. It might not make it. It might fall short. The wind might catch it and pull it away. I'd never had much of an arm for throwing which was why I hadn't tried before. But Sparrow needed my day. It all had to be for a *reason,* right?

Something – something that looked like the ocean reaching up like a long curving arm, rose up beside us. No time to look.

The captain caught my garnet, his mouth opening with shock as he looked from me to the rising wave, and then – like magic, because that was what it was – the men of Pensmoore and Sparrow with them, disappeared.

I gasped, caught between relief that he had the day and panic that I didn't know what had happened to them.

And then something icy seized me in its grasp – something that smelled of brine and despair and the drowning of all hope.

CHAPTER THIRTY-FOUR

The day after my father took me to the sea, I woke in the night screaming. I had dreamed that the sea itself had risen and swallowed me up and I was drawn into a place where I could neither see nor hear and when I opened my mouth to scream, fish swam in and choked me.

My mother, sweet soul that she was, had sat up with me and made me honeyed tea and petted my hair and coaxed me back to my bed and down into the depths of sleep again, but for many moons after that, the act of falling asleep – of sinking unconscious into the darkness – had felt too much like that nightmare and I found myself up in the night, reading by candlelight until my eyelids could no longer stay open rather than surrendering to that heavy grip willingly.

And now, once again, the sea had a hold of me, and once again it bound me in its embrace and drew me down to its heart, filling my ears with the roar of its fathomless churnings.

I was tumbled and battered and beaten by the roar of the tide. It sucked me under and no fighting, no gasping, so surrender could free me. I clung to Grosbeak's lantern pole, hugging it to my chest like the last loaf of bread in a starving village, my eyes squeezed shut to keep my stomach from churning more than it already was.

By all rights, I ought to have drowned. And yet, somehow, I was breathing, and my lungs were not even aching, though I knew I was breathing water and that water, in turn, was chilling me inside like ice water sipped slowly on a teeth-achingly cold day.

Hours, or perhaps days passed before I bounced gently against something, bobbing up and bouncing again. I opened my eyes with reluctance fighting panic down as it clawed at my throat – as desperate as I was.

When my eyes opened, the world around me wavered unsteadily as if it was just as inebriated with misfortune as I was. My panic left jagged black lines across my eyes.

Breathe, Izolda, I told myself and then nearly laughed hysterically at the thought. I was underwater. I was telling myself to breathe. I was insane.

"I am not fond of the sea," Grosbeak said, wobbling bubbles coming out with his undulating voice.

And then hands were tangling in my hair and when I tried to spin to look, they shook me roughly and dragged me through the water by my hair, towing me behind. The world twisted and elongated, and I heard someone screaming just out of reach and I knew without needing to be told that I'd been dragged from the mortal sea to a sea in the Wittenbrand.

These moments of madness were getting worse and as I tilted along a line of dark thoughts it took everything inside me to pull me back from the brink and tell me to open my eyes – to keep living, keep fighting. Not to give in to the howling without and within.

When it finally abated, I found my feet, coughed and to my surprise, I could hear Grosbeak speak.

"There's just no creativity in the ocean. It's water and fish and a few sodden plants and then more water." His voice was slightly blurred as if the water masked some of the sound of it, but it was clear enough despite the wobbling bubbles that rippled up from his mouth.

We were surrounded by what I took to be waving grass. But as I peered at it, I realized there was not a plant in sight. I clenched my jaw as hard as I could to keep from screaming as the Sword let go of my hair enough that I could turn and see him. I kept my eyes locked on my enemy because I didn't want to look at *them* rippling where they stood at the bottom of the sea.

"I take it back, Izolda," Grosbeak said. "You shouldn't redecorate. There are much worse ways to store those who have run out of days."

And he was right, because we were surrounded by what must have once been living souls. Now, they looked a lot like the specter that guarded me – tall and wispy, pale and hollow-eyed. Their hair swirled upward in the water and their arms were above their heads, waving softly in the water as if they were hanging upside down instead of standing on the ground.

I refused to look. Refused to acknowledge that all their faces had turned to us.

"I am beneath the sea," I said calmly, trying to remind myself that in this utterly impractical world I was still sensible. My voice was just as warbling as Grosbeak's. It sounded as if another girl was speaking my words. "With my best friend who is a talking head, and my brother who is wrapped up in specters like sea kelpie, around us there is a thick lawn of dead souls and my worst enemy."

"Right, right, right, wrong and wrong," the Sword said with a laugh and there was a fey look to his eyes that made them more alive than I'd ever seen them. They shone with shivery delight and every breath of seawater he drew in was drawn in with shuddering ecstasy. "Those souls are not dead though they are not precisely living, and I, dear Izolda, am not your worst enemy. Not at all."

I gave him my most skeptical look. "Then prove it. Release my brother."

He laughed. "You're nothing if not predictable, mortal girl. But I need you compliant for this next part. And for that, we need your dear brother as your surety. Come, now. Time is something that you – of all people – should not want to waste."

He snapped his fingers and to my surprise, a half-clamshell lifted like a coracle bobbing to the surface of a river. A moment later, shapes lifted from the swaying souls ahead, shapes that were harnessed and tethered with cords of seaweed and gold, their reins studded with diamonds the size of my fists. Such heavy reins for such delicate creatures. They were the size of three carriages and soft as down pillows, but they ballooned out like pillowcases, their blush-pink sides swelling as they opened up. Tiny streamers flowed behind them like too many forgotten tails. I was surprised to realize that I found them beautiful. Incongruous, utterly odd, ethereal, and yet lovely.

There were a half dozen of them and as they rippled upward, coming alive like a gladiola blooming in a row of blossoms. And as each joined the others they began to sing, a wreath of subtle, barely-heard, twisting melodies and harmonies that built and deepened with each addition made.

The coracle lifted, and the Sword tossed my brother onto it unceremoniously. He yanked me by the arm until I was settled in the front of the clamshell with him, and my brother tucked in beside me.

I tried to meet Svetgin's eyes but his were blank, staring off into the distance as if in a trance.

"Oh, you'll pay to use these, Sword," Grosbeak chortled. "The magic you're expending! I could animate an army of dolls with it!"

"And do what? Replace the legs you'll never have again?" the Sword sneered as our coracle rose and bobbed into the rolling depths of the frothy sea. "Replace the poor judgment that led you first into my pay and then into the power of the Arrow?"

"I need neither now," Grosbeak said glibly, "for my new mistress takes me places you could only dream of, Sword, and the tales I see – sweet sleep of death, they are good. Every twist a gem, every new character a ripe plum of juiciness. In fairness, I should thank you and offer you the same, though I fear I cannot wield a blade to lop your head off."

"Peace, beheaded one. Had I need of gossip I would have married for truth," the Sword said, but his heart hardly seemed in it.

A peace had come over him since we'd reached the sea that was so odd it tickled something in the back of my head. I tried to think. Did it have to do with the song of the strange empty creatures?

"Why are we here, Sword?" I asked carefully. "Are you here to sing for your sovereign?"

He laughed. "Hardly. I shall replace him."

"Replace him?" Grosbeak asked, shocked. But I was not shocked. I had figured out the riddle, too.

"I am the culmination of desire, the fruit of death. I am the summit of loss, the passing of weight. What am I?" I said. "It's the Bramble King's riddle."

I glanced over at Svetgin, to see if he was listening, but his eyes were still glazed over, either in pain or exhaustion. He neither moved, nor watched, nor struggled. I clenched my jaw, worried for him, but there was nothing I could do yet. I needed to focus and find a weakness. There was always a weakness if you knew where to look. I knew that before and Tigrane's book had reminded me of it. Her father had lectured her often on "chinks in the armor." "There's always one," he'd told her, and she'd written it down. "And it's usually where you don't expect you'll find it. It's usually at the strongest point."

"Inheritance," the Sword said, and there was hunger in his eyes that overwhelmed the peace that had been there before. "This year – this Game – is different. Whoever wins this one, wins everything. The whole world."

"What would you do with the whole world?" Grosbeak sneered. "You can't eat it."

"It's not about eating it," the Sword said, baring his teeth to my friend. "It's not about consuming or reforming or controlling. It's about mastering. I've always wanted to be the best. The very best." He looked at me then, his eyes so hungry that I shivered. Not hungry? He was the hungriest man I'd ever seen. "I want it so much I can taste it when I wake. It coats the back of my throat as I try to sleep, it taints every bite of food, every drop of drink, every stolen kiss. It works its way under my skin, itching, itching, itching until it's all I ever think about. I want it like the moon wants the tide. I want it like the plant wants the sun. I want it with all the heart I have left."

"Sorry, I think I drifted off," Grosbeak said. "What was it you wanted?"

I rolled my eyes.

The Sword's breath was almost like panting as he answered. "I want to be the best and I want everyone to know it. I want it to be undeniable." His voice calmed a little and he spoke now in a voice different than I'd ever heard from him. "When I was a young man, I had everything I could ever want. Affection, respect, my needs and wants met. I lacked for nothing. And I thought I would find happiness in it, but it was nothing but ashes in my mouth. I remember my mother gave me a pony made of sunbeams and sweetgrass and it was beautiful beyond compare and I rode it every day until one day I rode past a mirror being delivered to the house and I saw myself atop that golden pony and was struck so powerfully by the sight that I fell from his back and lay so still that they tucked me into my bed and nursed me for weeks until I could speak again. They thought me touched by some ill magic, but it was only the magic of understanding, for in that moment I saw that all around me was fair and good and noteworthy, but I was not. There was nothing intrinsic in me that gave me the same value. Do you understand that, mortal girl? Surely you must. You, alone in the Wittenhame, are plain and serviceable and utterly unremarkable. There is nothing of note in you from hat to shoe. Surely, you must understand what it is to see nothing in your reflection. To know you are born to nothing and will return to nothing and that nothing will be your bread and sup all your days.

"I rose up," he said, "and I said 'enough' and enough is what it will be, for I will *win* at this game. I do not care how or why, only give me the best opponents, the brightest, the cruelest, that I may make for myself a crown of their bones and show the world I am no longer that empty boy on an undeserved pony."

I glanced up to the crown he still wore – the one with my husband's rib woven into it – and my stomach flipped within me like a struggling fish.

"And how will you do that, Sword?" I asked.

"Oh easily," he said as he flicked the reins. "I'm taking you to the Vow Breaker who lives beneath the sea, and she will sever your ties to the Arrow, and leave him flapping like the end of a rope in a high wind and then I shall strike his heel and he shall tumble to the ground where he belongs. And when the Arrow is gone, there will be none to challenge me."

"And me?" I asked. "And my brother?"

He waved a hand. "You may go. You matter not to me. What are you anyways but empty shells beside a golden pony?"

I bit my lip, thinking furiously. He had to have a weakness. A chink in the armor. But what was it? What? Something practical that the impractical Sword wouldn't think to protect? Something so impractical that I'd never think of it?

We traveled for a very long time. So long that the bones of my seat began to ache. So long that my mouth became parched. So long that I eventually took Tigrane's journal out to read, unsurprised that it was not marred by the sea, for the Wittenbrand sea did not behave as I thought a sea ought.

I tried to read it, but it was hard to see anything that could help me figure out what to do when an insane man kidnaps you, drags you beneath the sea, and claims he will break your vows. The only thing written about vows was to avoid them and simply honor your word. Wise, practical advice. I would have liked Tigrane's father, I thought. There was also a comment she wrote about Bluebeard that seemed to be of note, though it would not help in this situation.

"He seems to always be waiting for something," she wrote. *"As if it might appear around the next corner at any time. He takes no joy from sup or drink or company but he spends what time he has to command, that which is not taken up with the troubles of his Wittenbrand affairs, in writing poetry. Sometimes I read it, and it seems to be for someone who is not me, though I've witnessed no lovers and if he has a lover, that one abuses him terribly by never giving him any time at all. I think sometimes that he is a man out of time with the world – even this odd world – as if he was born too soon and living only on time purchased or loaned, swindled or thieved from others."*

Incredibly insightful, but it had nothing to do with the Sword. I wished Bluebeard had introduced her to his rival so she could write a note about him, too, but then perhaps it would be her whisked away in an under-the-sea chariot and what good would that do.

I put the book back in my pocket and waited as the hours drifted away and my eyelids grew so heavy that they began to drift despite the danger I was in.

"Izolda?" Grosbeak hissed, waking me. "Izolda!"

"Mm?" I blinked awake, wondering if I'd missed something.

"You'll want to see this."

I looked up, rubbing my eyes to clear them, and gasped.

Our strange chariot had taken us to a cloud of creatures just like the ones pulling us and as they parted before us, we sailed out over what could be thought of as an ocean plain. Moonlight trickled down, filtered by silver and black brackish waves, and with every ripple and wave of the sea, I had a sensation that something was watching me.

And then, that sensation winked.

And I realized what I was looking at.

I had thought the Bramble King was impressive. I had thought he was huge and so much a part of the land as to hardly be man at all anymore. This woman was more so. She *was* the sea. I felt her flowing through my veins as the water of her person called to the water in mine. I felt the sharp pain of her coldness go up my spine as deep called to deep. I could only make her out in the occasional swell of water on water. She was of the sea and in the sea and she was the sea and she held us and surrounded us and breathed her current over us – her one winking eye the size of the Sword's whole palace.

And I felt like my throat had frozen closed when a single word fell from her lips and reverberated through the water like the boom of the ice when it swells over a lake.

"Well?" she asked.

"I am not well," Grosbeak muttered. "And I may never be again."

CHAPTER THIRTY-FIVE

"Bondbreaker, Lady of Sea," the Sword said, addressing her with reverence, "Queen of Depths and Ruler of the Dark Below . . ."

He went on, but I was not listening to her many titles. I was watching the ripples of the water that suggested the shape of a woman in these depths. I felt her – somehow – prodding at me, the ripples of her water lapping at my skin, and something deeper, something more insidious connecting with the water within my own body – with the blood that beat in my heart and pulsed through my arteries, with the water that cushioned my brain. And she was in that water somehow, measuring, reading, knowing me in ways I did not want to be known.

I shook my head. Ridiculous. She could see nothing of me that was not plain to all, and what was plain was not what mattered. I gathered myself inward and held on tight to my soul.

The Sword leapt down from his shell chariot as he was still speaking, pulling both me and Svetgin after him and as our feet cleared the chariot, the water ahead of us rippled and revealed a strange stone circle half-sunk into the sand. It leaned drunkenly to one side, the pillars ringing it reaching up like skeleton ribs from the wreck of a ship. From each one dangled a barnacle-encrusted cage large enough for a pair of eagles.

What was I going to do? If I tried to flee, the Sword would kill Svetgin – or do something worse like plant him among the grass of souls. If I tried to attack the Sword or hurt him, both Svetgin and I would die, for it was the Sword's magic that kept us safely breathing underwater and we were far too deep to swim up to the surface.

And if I did nothing at all, he claimed this ancient, goddess-like being could sever my marriage to Bluebeard. Of the three, one would think that would be the easiest outcome – the loss of a marriage I had not asked for and had not consummated – whatever could be the problem with that? And yet, I found the thought left me hollow and twisting with anxiety.

If the Sword succeeded and my vows to Bluebeard were severed, what then? Would I never see him return to me clothed in songbirds? Would I never again see that flash of understanding in his cat's eyes or watch him leap into action faster than I could take a breath? Would I go back to living a quiet life as a mortal girl, carefully managing a household, perhaps, or working as a servant in one now that my family was no more – using all the practical skills I possessed so well. I'd be incredibly useful and valuable to those around me as more than a hostage. Perhaps I'd even find a similarly useful husband and raise healthy children. I'd have everything I claimed I wanted.

I realized – with utter horror – horror that gripped my heart and twisted it until I felt sweat on my brow despite the cold of the sea and felt my stomach heave and gasp and reel – that I did not want my mortal life back – I didn't even want a better mortal life back.

I swallowed, terrified of what I was finding as I looked within. I was bound to Bluebeard – oh yes, but with more than vows of marriage and more than common purpose. For under it all, when

I looked in my own mirror as the Sword had, what I saw was not a desperate desire for mastery. What I saw – what made me so ill that I dry heaved on it – were thick ties of loyalty and the first quickening of what could only be considered love. Perhaps, some other woman stronger than I might have welcomed these things in her heart. Perhaps, Tigrane would have. Perhaps, in her great courage, she would have embraced them with joy. But I stared them full in the face with the chill of understanding knowing that my doom was upon me.

The words of the little song that Sparrow had quoted bubbled up in my mind. *Oft the siren sings again, tying up the hearts of men, within her silken tides.* My siren husband had stolen my heart, it seemed, without me ever realizing it. Not in passion or infatuation, but by slowly, step by step, purchasing my loyalty with his blood.

And I was sick with the knowing of it.

Made sicker still by the thought that this great sea could swallow up my ties and break them apart and I would find myself suddenly bereft before I'd even realized what I had.

"Lady Vow Breaker," the Sword was saying, finally done his acknowledgments and salutations, "I beg of you aid. This woman was taken against her will, forced into a marriage neither asked for nor wanted. Break her bonds to the man who took her and set her free."

He wanted to break me free of Bluebeard but leave him with his eternal Wittenbrand vows so that he could not access my magic but could not take for himself another wife. Clever.

And if I had been the Izolda from just a half a moon ago, I might have said, "yes," but instead I whispered "no" and my whisper reverberated through the sea.

The sea's reply was deafening. It felt as if it originated within my own mind – but loud, far too loud, so that I clutched my head in my hands trying to protect it from something I couldn't keep out. "*The blood is yours, the red wide sea, but the tide is mine and the endless deep.*"

"Yes, Queen of Tides," the Sword agreed.

"*Only sacrifice of the empty shell, the heartless husk, or the endless well,*" she whispered, and the whisper made us stumble it was so powerful.

"Is it just me or is the rhyming getting old?" Grosbeak murmured in a cloud of bubbles. I was too frozen with worry to reply. "It's tacky, is all I'm saying. Sure, there's power in rhymes but you wouldn't catch me dead talking like that."

The Sword swayed but gathered himself. "An offering, I have already."

"*Then let us weigh this offering and come to know if you grasp the heart of what lies below,*" she whispered and the voice echoed through the sea once more, and I felt it in the blood of my veins and the water of my brain and I was sick with the intimacy of her words. Sicker still when she moved and for just a moment I caught a glimpse – almost a vision of a ship sinking beneath the waves, its occupants fighting and thrashing as they were dragged into the depths.

The Sword snapped his fingers – a hard thing to do under the sea – and the specters dragged my brother to the nearest cage, and though he twisted and kicked, they dumped him neatly inside it. There was a crunching sound as he tried to find his feet. The specters wrapped around his face and torso made that difficult. I peered into the other cages, squinting, and my heart sped up a pace when I realized that every cage was lined with bleached bones. Other offerings. That explained the crunch.

"Leave him alone," I whispered feebly, but I had no way to stop this, no way to know how to prevent it now that it had begun.

"The offering is made," the Sword said, and I lunged, wielding Grosbeak's pole like a spear. What cared I if I killed him and drowned for it? He was going to kill Svetgin anyway. At least if we got him first, we could try to swim for it.

"*One half is here and one apart, two halves must be close before we start,*" the Vow Breaker whispered but this time I didn't flinch. This time I struck out with the pole.

Grosbeak's chortling scream was mostly bubbles. It cut off when the sword caught his pole and wrenched it from my hands, tossing it into the nearest cage. I felt my face go pale.

"I don't count as an offering," Grosbeak protested. "I'm already dead. Suffering is for the living!"

"Let's test that theory, shall we?" the Sword said, flinging the cage door shut.

He drew his sword effortlessly despite the heaviness of the sea and how it hampered movement.

"And now we call your husband, mortal girl," the Sword said, stalking around me on the seafloor, his every footstep kicking up a cloud of sand and fleeing fish.

I stumbled backward, my pale skirts tangling my legs and my hair swirling around me in blinding ribbons.

"He can't hear me," I said, fighting to keep my voice steady. Even if he could hear me, mind to mind, I would not call him. I'd betrayed him once and twice – both by accident. I would not betray him a third time.

"This, he will hear," the Sword said. His blade jabbed through the ocean and though I could see it coming, though the water hindered it a little, it did not stop the thrust and I was not fast enough to dance aside.

The blade plunged into my side, and I gasped, crumpling over the blade, grasping at it, trying to keep it from going further, going deeper. My palms shredded and my side leaked red clouds into the seawater. I gasped, and choked, and gasped again. Pain shuttered across my mind, driving thought and reason away. The agony doubled as the Sword drew his blade slowly back out again.

I fell to my knees, pressing my shredded hands to my shredded side, my legs splayed out beside me.

"Izolda! Girl! Can you hear me!" Grosbeak's frantic voice, cloaked in bubbles, rippled through the sea to me. I clung to it with my mind. Someone was watching. I was not alone in this pain. He was cursing as he watched me look down at my ruined body. "What have you done, Sword? You terrible fool. What have you done?"

"You should be proud, Grosbeak," the Sword said calmly. "I finished what you started."

My eyes opened a crack – long enough to see his blade in the sea, my blood swirling around its length in a slender sheath-like cloud.

I gasped and my eyes shuttered closed again.

"I'll rip out your tongue," Grosbeak cursed. "I'll give your eyes to the bats and your hands to the dogs, and you don't even want to know where I'll put your feet."

"But spare my ears," the Sword said flippantly. "They've already suffered enough from having to look at you."

I heard a sound like the beat of a heart. Faint. But there.

I let my eyes drift open again, afraid to even breathe when every breath was pain. I'd fallen over into the sand. Everything was sideways.

And then there he was, stalking over the sand, short hair swirling in the water, sharp eyes glimmering, violence in every line of his face.

I was dreaming. And it was the best dream I'd ever had. I tingled all over with it, melting even though I was ice cold.

He came in cautiously, carefully, like he expected a trap. He shouldn't come at all. He should run and run and run. I opened my mouth to say that, but the words wouldn't come, and all I tasted was blood.

"Ah," the Sword said from somewhere above me and there was so much satisfaction in his voice. Satisfaction morphed to triumph. "You have found me, oh my enemy."

And then pain burst through me simultaneously with the sound of a stick breaking in half. I choked on a scream and my lungs protested with a feeling like something popping inside my chest. I drifted in a sea of pain.

"Do you like the bait with which I set my trap, little fish?" the Sword asked. He reached up, touching the rib slotted into his crown and seeming to twist it. "Does it lure you in? It's so hard to tell. Some fish like what's bright and shiny but some … well, you have to chum the water with dead and dying things to get their interest."

A growl – muffled by bubbles – rolled out from where the

heartbeat was, and my own heart leapt in response.

And then I was lifted up and for a moment, I thought that perhaps my husband was saving me, like he'd saved me so many times before, but when I was flung through the water, crashing into the bars of Grosbeak's cage and landing on the floor of it, I knew it was not he who had lifted me. I lay in a crumpled heap, fighting to lift my head enough to see and when I finally did see, I almost wished I could not.

Bluebeard's eyes met mine through the shifting water and the look of distinct agony in his eyes seared me to the core.

My wife, he said in my mind and my heart was chanting back, *my husband, my husband, my husband.*

CHAPTER THIRTY-SIX

"I'm here for what is mine," Bluebeard said, stalking toward me and with his mind, he said, *"And I am chilled to the core at what my tardiness has wrought, wife. Have you not heard me calling for you these past days? Why did you not answer my pleading? Why did you not bid me come?"*

"Heard. Nothing," I gasped, tasting blood in my mouth.

My husband's face was a stone, and I did not know if that was rage or pain in those eyes.

The Sword slipped between us, blocking his view, sword held out. "But I have taken up matters with the Sea and asked her to unbind what was bound, to unravel what has been woven. He is here, Lady Unweaver, Queen of the Ocean, Maiden of the Sea. The second one in the bond that I wish to see broken is here. And you can break that bond now, as you promised."

And to my surprise, the sea replied in prose instead of poetry.

"I sentence you thus, men of Wittenhame. Fight to the death. Throwing knives will be your weapon. Each of you will have one hand pinned to a pillar, your enemy pinned to the opposite pillar. You shall drive in the pin yourself. Dance all you want, dodge all you want, throw as you must, and may the fated winner win."

"And *if* I win?" the Sword was quick to ask. "What shall be my reward?"

"Then you take your prize – the girl, unbound from the Arrow."

"And if the Arrow wins?" he pressed. "What shall be my penalty?"

"Then he keeps her bound to himself."

"And if she dies before we do?" Bluebeard asked, his voice like a tiger in a parchment cage.

"She will not," the Sea said, and I felt more than saw her shift. "It is said the Sea has no mercy. It is said the Sea is heartless, the breaker of all ties, the unmoorer of all hopes, the queen of despair. And these are all true, but never let it be said that the Sea lies. By my word, so am I bound."

I closed my eyes – only for a moment. Just to breathe for a moment. Blackness shuttered over them.

I woke to eyes right in front of mine and a horrible nightmare of a face. A fish was sucking along the forehead, as if cleaning it of debris.

"Oh good, you're awake again. You didn't miss much. Roll me over a bit so we can both see," Grosbeak said and with effort, I moved my hand, slowly, slowly, and shifted him from in front of my face, turning him so we could both see out the closed door of the cage.

Thinking hurt. Everything hurt. Trying to hold onto thoughts was like grasping at my blood tainting the sea. But I had to think. I had to think. I couldn't just watch Bluebeard fight for my life. I had been around the Sword a lot. Surely, I must have noticed some kind of weakness.

While I'd been passed out, the pair of them had taken their places. They stood with one hand spiked to a stone pillar by a throwing knife stuck through the palm. I swallowed down bile at the sight of the knife in Bluebeard's hand. Red stained the water around the wound, just as red stained the water around his side, reminding me of his everbleeding wound.

"They're pinned with Wittenbrand blades," Grosbeak told me helpfully.

That meant the palm wound in Bluebeard's left hand was another wound inflicted by Wittenbrand steel. Another wound that would not heal. Another scar to bear forever just to save me, protect me, keep me from the siren call of death.

Sirens. There was something about that which tickled my mind but the thought wouldn't swim close enough to be grasped.

"Sing me the song, Grosbeak," I murmured. "The song."

We were in a swinging cage hanging from a pillar, equidistant between the competitors. Svetgin opposite us, was caged and bound in ropes of specter. He would watch me die here. Probably. Each breath certainly felt like death.

"Which song? I know many. One about victory, maybe? Or a cheerful ditty about a girl who was stabbed in the side and then cut off her attacker's head and kicked it around a field for fun?"

"Not that one," I gasped. Grosbeak and I had very different ideas about what was cheerful. "It sounds terrible. The one about the sirens."

I didn't hear his next objection, because my eyes met Bluebeard's and his look was a caress.

I tried to call to him with my mind, but I couldn't make it work, couldn't force the thoughts to come. I tried again.

"*You don't need to do this,*" I told him with my mind. *"Don't do it."*

His mental voice was sharp and clear as ever. "*I find you more beautiful and precious than all the jewels beneath the earth and sea.*"

And then, as if that was all there was to say, he tore his eyes from mine and nodded to the Sword and the Sword nodded back and to my shock, the water around me pressed down, hard, hard, hard.

It took a minute before I realized it was not just me struggling to breathe that made the water feel so heavy. We were rising. And as we rose, the pillars righted themselves, and the platform drew level, and our cages swung to hang perpendicular, as everything slowly rose upward from the ocean floor.

Beside me, Grosbeak sang – his voice marred by bubbles, but clear enough to hear. "Oft the siren sings again, tying up the hearts of men, within her silken tides."

It was something about that song. Something about tying up hearts of men. Something about being bound. And then, as the water began to grow lighter – blue now, rather than black – I realized what was bugging me so much. It was the comb. That mother-of-pearl comb that the Sword had used when he took me to his Petal Ball. He'd treated it with care and reverence like a treasured possession. The one with the emerald set into it.

And it could mean nothing. It could just be the way he treated all his personal items. Or it could be that he really did love it, but for other reasons – reasons I didn't know about like I hadn't known the story about the horse and the mirror. And yet. There was something about that – something that my practical side was screaming to me was important.

"Did it help?" Grosbeak asked when he was done.

"It didn't hurt," I gasped, the words wracking me with pain. "I fear I am fading, dear Grosbeak."

"Hold on," he said grimly. "You won't want to miss this however it plays out. I must say, I've never seen anyone mad enough to bargain with the sea. You can't win with her, you know. There was that king once who tried to flog her and you saw what happened to him."

"I did not," I gasped.

"Well, I mean you *could* see what happened if you like watching someone chained to the bottom of the ocean and eaten by fishes only to be reborn and live through it all again the next day. After the first few days, it gets boring. By then you've seen it all the different ways there is and there's no point watching again."

Sometimes I forgot how bloodthirsty my pet was.

"I don't want anyone to resurrect me when I die," I managed between gritted teeth.

"You say that now, but we'll see how you feel when it's over," Grosbeak said. "Try to hold onto that sweet innocence in the afterlife. It suits you."

"I can only do what's practical and possible," I murmured.

He laughed nastily. "In that case, I doubt you'll keep it for long."

The platform emerged from the frothing sea into the warm air. I gasped in my first breath of air after breathing sea and it tingled through my lungs and down to every nerve ending so that I did not know if I was grateful for it, or dying because of it.

Brackish water poured off the platform in a rush that soon

turned to thick runnels and then to tinkling trickles until everything was completely above the surface of the water and under the Wittenbrand sky.

It was dawn above the surface, and we rose into it among rose-and-gold-tinted clouds of fluffy white. They were layered, cloud upon cloud, up and up, into a sky of the softest lavender. Soft golden rays branched and divided around the graceful pillars of this strange platform and were I not in so much agony, I might have been curious as to whether it had been put to similar purpose before and whether that time had also seen a morning more fit to a wedding than a slaughter.

In my mind, my husband's voice was clear as a sounding bell, "*Hold on, fire of my eyes. Do not fade from this world before I can tend to your wounds again.*"

And as if his words in my mind had rung a bell somewhere or blown a trumpet, the clouds parted, and tiny white petals began to rain down with a single note of angelic song. It sustained, wavering in the air like a butterfly not sure if it wanted to land – and then the voices split and wove into a canticle.

As if it were planned – and maybe it was, what did I know? Perhaps all of this was a fever dream, and I was drowning to death below merciless seas – the clouds parted again and this time they were edged with spectators looking down – Wittenbrand, one and all. They lounged on the fluffy clouds sipping steaming drinks or dipping pastries into them as if milk tea and blood sport were how they started every morning.

Glazed by waters still retreating, the stone platform reflected the audience back on themselves and in the center of the anticipation were the barnacle-encrusted cages and the two competitors – both of whom were still grand despite their soaking, still looking as if they'd stepped from oil paint works of themselves.

"My husband," I managed with my mind, the rest of the thought stuttering and fading. But, like a hand placed over mine, I heard his mental words, strong and sure.

"Hold fast, my heart."

Bluebeard bit his lower lip, the throwing blade perched between two fingers and that hand held up so that his smallest finger met his jaw as he considered his opponent. His eyes were not on mine any longer, even if his thoughts were.

I closed my eyes for a moment, gathering my strength and what shreds of hope I had left.

"Keep your eyes open," Grosbeak complained. "We're just getting to the good part."

I forced my eyes open again.

The Sword swept a grand bow to the crowd, dancing his first knife over the backs of his knuckles and then flipping it in the air only to snatch it back with perfect precision.

But it was the Sea who spoke, her words stark and pitiless, reaching into the depths of each of us where her waters thrummed and roared. I could not see her face anymore, and yet we were all cushioned on her breast like a sleeping infant.

"We play to the death. Begin."

CHAPTER THIRTY-SEVEN

The singing morphed at her words, and this time, the spectators joined in, as if this were a folk festival, as if these two were not squaring off for a throwing knife fight to the death.

"Fly with the Arrow,

Dance with the Sword,

Give your heart to the barrow,

Die with your Lord."

I forced my eyes open and looked up at the singing crowd. The pillars surrounding our platform had changed – subtly. They were topped with rippling banners and strings of bunting hung from one pillar to the next. The banners and bunting fluttered in the wind, and I gasped as I realized they were specters tied by spectral hands and feet so that their bodies rippled merrily in the wind.

"They say you can judge a society by how they treat their dead," I whispered as my eyes flickered from one ghastly face to the next. The expressions of the translucent dead flickered from agony to horror to terror and something inside me flickered with them.

"And how do you judge?" Grosbeak asked.

"I find the Wittenbrand wanting," I said as firmly as I could with my breath sawing so painfully inside my lungs.

"And how shall we bury your dear husband when he falls? Should he be a flag for the next duel?"

"He won't fall," I gasped.

"So much faith," he said, laughing nastily. Mist rose off his head in a cloud of soft pink as the dawn burnt the last drops of water from his hair and face. If not for that laugh – if not for being Grosbeak – he might almost look angelic.

"*Are you dying, fire of my eyes?*" Bluebeard's voice in my mind was sharp and focused.

I thought for a moment and decided on answering with the truth. *"I am not dead yet."*

"This battle is one I must fight. Hold yourself together a few more minutes and I will bring you to safety." His words in my mind were tense, coiled, like a snake waiting to strike. *"I found Sparrow. She told me of your battle. If pride had a name today, that name would be Riverbarrow."*

Sometimes, I forgot that was his name. I wanted to think of something meaningful to say. Something practical.

"He's blinded by ambition. If you rile him, you'll have an advantage," I said.

His half-smile twinkled as he caught my eye, as if he could grant me assurance and strength in a single look.

"*Sing for your sovereign,*

Bow to your Dream,

Make haste for the fallen,

Rise in esteem"

The choir was still singing when the first knife flew out from the Sword's hand. The singing cut off sharply.

Bluebeard shifted his weight in a manner that looked lazy, but the knife missed striking his shoulder by the tiniest hair's breadth, and I thought that perhaps the dodge had not been as easy as it had seemed. His return throw was immediate. While he was still shifting to dodge, he flicked his wrist like he was snapping a fan open, but rather than a fan, a dagger flicked from his fingers, gleaming as it spun through the air.

"Speak to my riddle, Sword. Who moved like a snake and like a fish? Who tried to rob wives from me before and paid the price? Whose head did I take with you watching on? Who stands as a warning of what is to come?" Bluebeard asked.

The Sword danced out of the way, graceful as a swan on a crystal lake. The soft petals raining down around him almost tricked my eye into thinking we were back at his Petal Ball.

"You want to speak of women you've killed, Arrow? You want to speak of breaking my heart and claiming the head of my lover for your collection? Then let us speak of what I will do to your current wife when this is done, and let us speak of your other wives, collected in a closet. There are things I can do to them, even now that their time is up. Things that would make you squirm. You, who thinks himself lily-white while he is drenched in scarlet."

The Sword whirled and spun into a kneel, graceful and smooth despite one hand pinned in place. His knife flew from his hand like a bird released from a cage.

Bluebeard didn't move this time and my heart seized in my chest. What was he thinking? He was going to –

He snatched the blade from the air, a look of concentration on his face, and then flung it back, but not before I saw the glimmer of sweat across his brow. His pinned hand was still leaking blood and his jacket had been pulled back as he moved, revealing the patch of red in his white shirt from his wounded side. He would weaken from all that loss of blood, wouldn't he? And then he'd be pinned here, an easy target. I chewed on my lip and tried to hold back my own pain enough to think.

"From a man's mouth comes the treasures of his heart, even as in his vaults his heart is seen," Bluebeard said as if he were quoting something. "What do you keep in your vaults, Sword? Is there anything within your empty heart?"

"I have no need to hide what matters to me, Arrow," the Sword said, waving a hand before him, palm up, as if demonstrating his innocence. "I am transparent to all, open to see and be seen. I wear your rib upon my brow and your wife upon my arm. What need have I or vaults or treasures?"

And I thought I detected a spark of fury in Bluebeard's next throw. It narrowly missed the Sword's face, leaving a streak of blood along his cheek where he'd narrowly dodged it.

Clapping from the audience masked any banter they might be throwing out with the knives.

"I did the right thing, trying to kill you," Grosbeak said happily to me. "Look what it has achieved for me? I'm seeing the world – two worlds – and all the best events of the season."

"Well," I said through teeth clenched in pain. "The head wall did say to keep my token close."

He laughed. "And what? I'm your token now? Yes, do keep me close, Izolda."

He was still laughing as he sang the chorus to the folk song in his terrible, off-key voice. It was made even worse by enthusiasm.

"And if ever you be broken

And gasp on the ground,

Hold up your fine token

And join with the sound."

If he really was my token, I'd been holding him up this entire time on that lantern pole. I'd done that much at least. I clenched my teeth against a moan. I was feeling nauseated as the bleeding in my side made my head light. I should pack the wound. I just didn't seem to have the strength.

"Speak to my riddle, wife of mine. What knits broken flesh, what salves all wounds, what will I give to you when all this is done?"

"*Time,*" I answered, though there was little comfort in it since my days were numbered.

"*Wrong,*" he said in my mind, silky and smooth. "*Kisses. And I shall rain them on you like the tears of a spring sky.*"

The Sword danced away from another thrown knife, and this time I saw his strain as his hand pulled against the knife pinning it. Blood flowed down the pillar. How were these knives driven into stone pillars anyways? Pain flashed across his face and as if that pain had inspired him, his next three knives shot out one after another in a steady rain.

Without pausing to dodge, Bluebeard tossed his out, too. I couldn't keep track of how many had been thrown now. They were a blur of knives and dodges, dancing, dancing, ever closer to being struck.

A knife found its mark, blooming in Bluebeard's throwing shoulder. But his knife struck the Sword's thigh almost as quickly. The Sword wrenched the knife free with a wild look in his eye, sending it spinning back to my husband.

"If you like riddles so much," the Sword taunted, "then maybe you'd like to know what the Bramble King's riddle means. Maybe you'd like to know that this is my grand move that will cement my victory."

"What's not a riddle, Sword?" Bluebeard asked in a bored voice, pausing just long enough to wink at me. "What's so plain that it's not hidden at all?"

"Then you know I'll take his place when this is done. This whole Wittenhame will be mine to do with as I please. And I please a lot of things. With you gone, none of the others can stop me. It's a bold move, but I'm a bold man. What do you think our home will look like when it's made in my image?"

And then they were back to being a blur of movement. They both moved so fast that I couldn't keep up with every spin and dodge and throw.

I fought the pain wrapping its tight claws around me. It was getting worse. Not just the throbbing in my leg but the aching agony in my side that broke me with each shuddering breath. Was this what my husband felt all the time since giving his rib to me?

I could only squeeze my fists and clench my jaws and hope, hope, hope.

A voice in my mind broke through the pain. "*As long as rivers run and moon shines.*"

My eyes fluttered back open in time to see a second dagger

strike Bluebeard – this time in his leg. I felt like I could feel the hit, too.

I trembled with the shock of it as the crowd cheered, little snatches of song lacing their cheers as if this was a beautiful event, a wedding or a name day, and not a sickening death sentence. I swallowed down a moan of despair.

Bluebeard shuddered at the wound and his voice in my mind was shakier. "*As long as the earth has bones and death has claws.*"

My eyes squeezed shut again.

I could feel those claws trying to close around me. I hated this helplessness. Hated that there was nothing I could do. I was the one lying broken on the ground just like the song said. I was the one who had kept her token close. If only I had the strength to lift it and wave it and then the song would come true and we would all be saved, wouldn't we?

Or maybe I was having fever dreams.

"*As long as the ages pass and fail – that long shall I be husband to you.*"

He was saying our Wittenbrand wedding vows again. He was making promises even as he fought for me. Promises that our bond would not be broken. Promises that he would find a way forward. And what had I to give to him in return?

I could promise something back, but the best promise was an action and I was beyond action.

"Yes!" Grosbeak crowed from beside me. "Such a good strike."

I lifted my heavy eyelids. One of Bluebeard's knives had hit the Sword directly in the chest. And then another. He stumbled slightly, his crown shifting to lean drunkenly to one side,

Bluebeard's rib within it gleaming softly in the sunlit dawn.

The crowd roared again. They loved blood – whose seemed not to matter.

"*Flesh of my flesh and bone of my bone you will be.*"

Bluebeard's eyes met mine, pain and promise, agony and desperate determination. And the warmth in those eyes broke me.

"How can either of them survive?" I moaned feeling as if I would be ripped in two by the sweetness of my husband's silent vow and the agony of watching him bleeding and fighting for his life. "They'll never recover from so many wounds."

My breath sawed through my lungs. I clung to the look on Bluebeard's face, the calm certainty in his eyes as he spoke the next words, as if there were no one else here but him and me, as if he wasn't fighting at all.

"*Spirit of my spirit.*"

And I found I wanted that. For the first time, I couldn't help but wonder if we could be married, married. One in spirit. One in more than purpose. Living together, eating together, playing card games with those odd folk of his.

He bit his lip so hard that blood came when his eyes bored into mine.

"*Heart of my own heart.*"

But he *shouldn't* be looking at me and making sweet vows. He should be focused on his fight. It was almost as if he expected something from me – something that would help him somehow. But what? What could I give?

"Oh, it's not Wittenbrand steel they're throwing, so they'll likely recover from the knife wounds," Grosbeak gabbled, not realizing that in front of him the greatest drama of all was playing out silently between an ancient Wittenbrand and the broken mortal he had taken as a bride. "Just copper and silver. It's only Wittenbrand steel in the dagger pinning their palms. Dining out will be grisly after this, but then it always is, and at least it will make dinner party conversation interesting."

And then I realized what I could give. I could give my vow in return. And my heart soared as I forced myself up on my elbows and said in my mind as clearly as I could through the fog of pain and fear.

"*Fall what may, we shall be one,*" I said in my mind.

And his eyes shuttered closed for just a beat, a tiny smile of absolute satisfaction on his face and when he breathed out, I felt almost as if he were right here, as if I could feel that very breath on my face.

He turned back to the Sword, steel in his eyes, his chin jutting out, flinty and unmoving, and when he leaned forward onto the balls of his feet for his next throw my heart seemed to stutter to life like it never had before.

"Izolda?" Grosbeak pressed.

"I don't care," I said with a shuddering gasp, "about dinner parties."

"Good. Tell yourself that. Tell yourself you're only focused on winning, like the Sword does. Though how he got so wound up about it, I don't know. It's almost like the power of a siren song with him."

Knives were flying again, fast and sharp, and I could hardly see them through my glassy tear-filled eyes. What I'd said – the vow I'd just made – it had shifted something in me that I didn't know was there to be shifted. If I were the sea, all my tides would be in time with Bluebeard's breathing like the earth in the story about the world and the god who had made it.

"Grosbeak," I said, panting as I heard the dull thunk, thunk, of more knives striking flesh. I could hardly breathe. "You're remarkably obsessed with sirens."

I was grateful for his rambling. I needed to clear my head before I was utterly swallowed up by this new thing – this overwhelming, alive thing inside me.

"I was hoping to fall in love with one while we were here. It seemed like convenient timing. After all, I can hardly chase her until I die when I have no feet, and I've always wondered what that kind of obsession would feel like. You know, the kind that keeps you going when all the odds are against you? The magic kind."

"It looks like *that*," I said, pointing vaguely to where the Sword tossed a knife from an arm that already had three blades sticking out of it. His blade struck true, and I flinched at the sight of another knife stuck onto my husband's shoulder. He swayed slightly and I bit my lip, blinked back the tears spilling onto my cheeks. This had to stop.

"If she sang courage into me, or charm, or anything else, it would never leave," Grosbeak went on, sounding like he was in a daydream. "Not even if she died. Did you know that? It would fill me up. It would make me whole without a body. Nothing could stop it."

I did know. It was how I felt right now.

I coughed, tasting blood, fighting for that practicality I prided myself for. "Except for the wrong note, right? Didn't you say before that you could change a siren song by matching the exact right note?"

"Of course. But who could ever do that?"

A chill came over me, tingling up my arms and down my legs until I shivered. My thoughts were stuttering, racing over each other in their hurry to drag me over the finish line and reach the conclusion they could see in the distance. A siren, filling you up with something that wouldn't change even after death. A head on my husband's wall. A matching mother-of-pearl comb. It was all suddenly so clear.

The Sword had been enchanted by a siren at some point. I would bet everything I had on it. A dead siren whose head my husband had taken and placed in his Vault. And that meant that the Sword could be weakened, or maybe even conquered, if someone, somewhere, sang precisely the right note. But there had been singing all around and in the Wittenbrand there always was, so surely, surely someone would stumble onto it, wouldn't they?

No, it couldn't be so easy.

The roar of the crowd was so loud now that I could barely hear Grosbeak though he was still speaking. They chanted both names, crowing with delight at every hit. If I knew the Wittenbrand, they were probably betting on the result.

"Sword!" someone called from the crowd, and it was Lady Tanglecott, dressed in a long, flowing white dress edged in pink by the rising sun. Her perfect blonde curls framed a face that would have inspired song in any mortal world.

She held in her hand a gleaming throwing knife that looked to be entirely of gold. She strode forward, flanked by her pair of four-winged striped lions, their bright cat's eyes – so like my husband's – searching the crowd and their pink tongues licking hungrily at their chops. When their eyes landed on me, I flinched. I was wounded prey. They knew it and I knew it. But her hold on them was flawless and they stayed close as she tossed the golden knife.

The Sword caught the underhand toss easily, his eyes gleaming with pleasure when he examined the blade. His breath gusted out in magenta-tinged clouds and sweat matted his golden curls. He was panting and worn just as my husband was, the jagged hole in his pinned hand stood out bright against the angry flesh around it as every dodge, every dance, every escape from death opened the wound further.

There was a gasp of delight from the crowd as Lady Tanglecott said, "I think I owe you a Wittenbrand steel throwing knife with a golden handle, don't I Sword? I'd hate to have you die without seeing my debt repaid."

Laughter rang out from the crowd, but my eyes narrowed because I knew this was no little jab at my husband. None of these regular blades could kill him easily – but any mark this blade made would last -and any mortal wound with *this* blade would surely kill him.

I held my breath as the Sword took careful aim.

My husband spread his hands apart, waiting, his body relaxed, mouth quirked in a mocking smile, but in his mind, he spoke to me.

"My body, I dedicate to none other."

The Sword took aim and tossed and like the expert swordsman he was, my husband danced forward and caught the blade with his palm just seconds before it pierced his heart. It stuck through his hand, and I gasped. He would have matching wounds now, one on either palm.

He leaned down and plucked it free with his teeth but as he was drawing it out, Lady Tanglecott cried out again.

"I was mistaken, Sword! I believe, I owed you, two." And quick as a hummingbird, she tossed a second knife, twin to the first and the Sword snatched it from the air.

The breath gusted from my lungs. I could see it all unfolding before me as if time had slowed to a crawl.

My husband, one hand pinned, the other stuck through with a knife he was trying to pull free with his teeth, his eyes widening as he realized he was trapped.

The crowd, laughing, swaying together, and singing that damnable chorus again.

"And if ever you be broken

And gasp on the ground,

Hold up your fine token

And join with the sound."

Me, lying broken on the ground.

Broken.

On the ground.

And suddenly I remembered the grass egg I'd ripped open. The one that had sung that same chorus to me. And with my heart in my throat, I reached up into my hair and pulled out the little golden bell ornament I had fastened there, and lifting up my token, I rang the bell.

CHAPTER THIRTY-EIGHT

The bell was so quiet compared to the cheers and singing that I thought no one would hear it, but the Sword staggered, his head whipping around to look directly at the bell dangling from my fingers.

For a moment, confusion lit his face, and then he sagged like a bridge with too many horses in the middle. His hand lowered for a moment and the look of desolation in his eyes gutted me. I didn't even like him and it cored me out and left me empty. No one should look like that. No one should look like they were watching their hope thrashing in its own blood.

He gasped. And then he rallied, his shoulders straightening, his chin rising again.

All the compassion I'd felt a moment ago fled and fear seared through me. It hadn't worked. It had barely slowed him.

The gold-handled knife rose in his precise grip, and I saw Lady Tanglecott rise up on her toes in anticipation, her mouth forming a delighted "oh".

The crowd quieted, every breath held fast.

And my glorious husband raised his chin in defiance of fear and death, his cat's eyes narrowing to a slit and his jaw clenched against the blade sure to strike and leave a lasting mark.

"My days shall be yours and your happiness my own." My mental voice was desperate. I couldn't help it. Why did he not seize my days? Why did he not spend each one to fight this?

"*The bounty of my wealth is yours,*" he said like a vow and then his eyes opened and met mine. And I fell into them, deep, deep, deep not bothering to catch my heart as it fell for there was no point guarding it now that we were both at the end.

How funny to come to the end of your life and find in that moment that you are already mortally wounded and this with the dart of love? I'd been married now for half a moon, but it felt like I'd just been married here and now as I spoke these words and meant them as a vow this time and not just a ward to stay alive.

And then someone screamed.

And the scream reverberated through the audience.

Our gazes wrenched apart, and I looked over to see the Sword jamming the Wittenbrand steel knife into his own throat and ripping it out with a brutal tearing motion. His head began to roll to the side before his hand stopped its grisly work.

"I love my afterlife," Grosbeak breathed reverently. "It's so much better than my before life."

This time, I did vomit, spilling what little was in my stomach all over the floor of the cage. The movement pulled at the wound in my side and made me vomit all over again. Darkness flooded over my vision. It was all I could do not to pass out. Only the reminder that I'd tumble into my own sick kept me together. That, and Grosbeak's cursing.

"Mortal hands and mortal bellies that's gross!" Grosbeak moaned, brought low from his moment of ecstatic revelry by a sensible reaction to what was going on. "Gods of rivers and thorns save me from mortals with vile constitutions."

He made a dramatic vomiting sound, spitting and choking as if he was going to die. It shook me from my own stupor, and I pressed myself up palms splayed across the barnacle-encrusted cage floor, watching in doleful fascination the thread of blood that poured from my side as I found my hands and knees and then forced myself to twist into a seated crouch.

When I finally pulled myself together enough to look up, I saw the spectators drawing back, the bunting and banners falling limp and morose. Even the rose and gold of the clouds had faded to a somber grey.

"*The moment this pin is removed, and my magic is restored to me, I will come to you, and I will repair every wound and bind every slash and heal you with kisses sweeter than honey. Only have faith in me, my wife,*" Bluebeard told me with his mind and this time when I met his eyes, the light of victory was in them. We'd won. We'd survived.

Tears of relief flooded my eyes, and I drew in a long, shuddering breath.

I drew it in too soon. I relaxed too soon.

My fate was like a girl in a tale, for always, I forgot that there were no happy endings for me, no moments of quiet after the monster was slain and the lady rescued. No cheer from the onlookers and a large banquet laid out and peace in the land that lasts for a thousand years. Oh no, not for me.

From that grey backdrop of life-drained clouds, a face emerged, and then a head, and then a throne, and the Bramble King opened his eyes and looked down on his shrieking, scrambling subjects. He paused for a moment, as if taking in the pandemonium below him, the broken corpse of the Sword, the pinned figure of the Arrow, the exultant Lady Tangledcott with her head thrown back and arms spread wide as if receiving a blessing – three of his players emerging from a deadly game. He blinked and then without a flicker of change to his features, he said in a voice of finality, "The death of the Second Move is upon us. And with it, the Third Move is born. His glory fades."

And then he sank back into the grey clouds, the rumble of thunder his herald, and the flash of lightning his trumpet, and we all held our breaths, frozen for a moment in our places as if we were afraid he might return and announce our punishments for being petty, squabbling children in a game that was meant to pull him down and plant another on his throne.

And it was there, into that frozen tableau that Lord Coppertomb emerged, walking to the center of the platform with a kind of casual disinterest as if nothing here met his standards. He paused to look Lady Tangledcott over and something I could not read passed between them, and then as he moved past her, she turned and swept her hands forward and her mist lions leapt into the clouds and her with them and they vanished as one.

And I did not know why, but their disappearance made my heart speed up because it knew what I could not – that this was a handing over of the reins, a changing of the guard. And my heart knew the face of treachery and shrank from it.

There was a sound like something shifting, and then something in my belly seemed to drop. The platform was lowering.

"The bargain, lady," Bluebeard said steadily and I realized he was speaking to the sea. And then his voice sounded a little less sure as he reached with his knife-crossed hand and tried to wrench the knife from his pinned hand to no avail. This time his voice was a growl, but I heard the desperation in it. "The bargain,

Queen of Seas."

The sudden silence made me look up and my heart stuttered to a stop. The observers were gone. I watched as the last of them vanished into the clouds. Somewhere above, a single gull cried into the darkening sky – a cry of loss and desolation.

"Ohhhh!" Grosbeak said as if he'd just understood something. "It was a fight to *everyone's* death. I get it now. That makes so much more sense."

"It does?" I asked, breathlessly. I realized I didn't even know if the cage I was in was locked. I hadn't had the strength to even find my feet and try it.

"Of course! The sea has no mercy. It never made sense that she was going to let one of them live."

"A point to the reanimated head," Coppertomb said coolly. "And for your observation, a reward. I will not kill you today, Grosbeak."

Grosbeak smiled, but I could tell by the way his eyes were hooded that it was not a nice smile, though he was wise enough to keep his thoughts within.

Coppertomb turned to my husband as a sudden wind ripped the banners and bunting away so that they swirled for a moment in the air, and then were gone. Coppertomb's tidy, monochrome clothing swirled around him with that wind, but he did not seem to notice. Not even when the edge of the platform furthest from Bluebeard tipped and began to sink under the hungry waves.

Coppertomb stepped over delicately and snatched the Sword's crown from his brow before the waves could take it and to my shock – though how did anything shock me, now? – he pulled a penknife from a pocket and with a deft hand, extracted one of the Sword's molars and slotted it into the crown. How many bones would fit within its swirls and gaps?

He rose and faced my husband again.

"I see you've been investigating the four mysteries, Arrow. You should have stuck to the ship on the sea or the snake on the rock."

"I already know the way of the eagle," Bluebeard said, drawing himself up. There was no pleading in his voice, and he did not address the sea again. But I saw the burning in his eyes, the anger leashed only by the strongest of self-control, and whatever he was saying on the outside, he was saying something different to me with his mind.

"*If ever it be otherwise,*" he said with his mind and the vow felt like a caress.

"*Husband,*" I said with my own mind, and he shuddered at my word, his eyes half-closing in pleasure for just a moment.

Coppertomb, unaware of the love story playing out in our silences merely raised an eyebrow and said dryly, "May we all take such joy from small things."

"So, you were behind this somehow," Bluebeard said. The look of barely suppressed violence in his eyes was at odds with his knife-quilled figure. He did not slump or bow under the weight of the blades, not even the Wittenbrand ones stuck through his palms. "And here I thought it was Lady Tanglecott."

"*It's b –* " I tried to tell him it was both of them, but my specter reached her hand around to clamp my mouth, shaking her other finger under my nose. Not even now, not even with us sinking below the waves, would I be allowed to say anything.

The water rose as the platform tilted, dark bottle-green sea swirling with red blood and the Sword's viscera. It swallowed his corpse, dragging it below the waves unnaturally as Coppertomb opened Svetgin's cage and drew him out. My brother stumbled forward, empty-eyed, still bound by wraiths.

"What good is a trap if your prey sees it?" Coppertomb asked. "And who would suspect a first-time player of setting his opponents against each other. But fear not, Arrow. I am well aware it was a strange year. That had it been any other, you would have had no weakness to exploit." He was halfway to my cage, now. "I had to take the opportunity while I could, don't you think? What other time would you play into my hand so single-mindedly?"

"And now what? You let the sea serve you and take me to the depths?" Bluebeard challenged, but in his mind, he was still speaking the rest of his vows to me. "*If ever it be otherwise, may I waste away with sickness and may famine take my strength.*"

"My will alone, I solely enact," the sea's voice boomed out and I flinched as the platform shuddered. *"None binds it thus except by pact."*

"I'll make your pact, Vowbreaker," Coppertomb said quietly. He pulled a flat circle attached to a chain from his pocket and considered it before looking up again. "I'm no fool to come to the sea empty-handed. Take this enemy of mine and bury him deep and in exchange I give you the lives of fifteen Pensmoore ships in the North Sea. My agents await with orders to scuttle it on my signal."

"Agreed," the sea replied.

Coppertomb snapped his fingers.

I felt suddenly lightheaded and as if I was seeing a vision, I saw sudden snatches of ships tumbling down into the sea, in one a man held an axe, scuttling the ship under him. In another, a man snuck furtively into the hold, lighting a fire when he arrived. The rest were just glimpses of desperate men wailing as their ships were dragged under and they were trapped like flies in amber beneath the hungry waves.

"Don't faint," Grosbeak hissed. "You can't save them, and you'll fall on top of me and then I won't be able to see what comes next."

Which was a very sensible thing to say. I fought to control my horror.

"*May my enemies overtake me,*" Bluebeard's voice rang in my mind, and it was heavy with sadness, thick with regrets unspoken and deeper than this angry sea in its fullness of commitment.

In my mind, I joined him as he finished our vow. "*And siphon from me the blood of my life.*"

I put my hand to my side, and I held it up to him and our eyes met as he held out his wounded hand to show me, too.

"*Done,*" the sea said, and it echoed through our bones. "*Your price is for one living Wittenbrand, and one I accept, the rest will leave and not be kept.*"

The door of my cage squealed as it opened, torn by the wind. I knew Coppertomb was striding toward me, but I didn't look, my eyes were locked in goodbye with Bluebeard's and there was something about the farewell in his expression that was sweeter than honey, more comforting than a warm fire, and safer than my bed in the midst of a storm.

I clung to it as Coppertomb pulled me roughly from the cage. I could not stand on my own. I crumpled around the wound in my side, my crushed leg unable to bear my weight. Coppertomb supported that weight as he snatched up Grosbeak.

Still, I clung to Bluebeard's gaze as the Wittenbrand threw my bodiless friend at my husband's feet and then reached into my bodice, snatched away my golden key, and tossed it there, too. Clung to it even as Coppertomb held me up like a broken chair, wobbling unstably on one leg.

"Whoa! Wait! I wasn't a part of the deal," Grosbeak sounded panicked. "I stay with Izolda."

His head landed barely out of the water as the platform dipped wildly into the sea, leaving only the pillar where Bluebeard stood unsubmerged. Water swirled around my knees, dragging at my sacrificial white skirts. But it was not me being given as a sacrifice.

"I think not," Coppertomb said smoothly and though he turned to me, I did not look at him.

I was drinking in the last look of my husband, his short hair still slick with the sea's water, clinging to the curves of his head and curling slightly around his ears, his beard, a little longer than he usually kept it – enough that the blue of it was distinct – his bright eyes almost white they were such a light blue, and his crooked smile promising secrets revealed and knowledge unveiled. I would never know all those secrets now.

"I am not a wasteful man," Coppertomb said as he shoved me toward my brother and to my surprise, Svetgin caught me awkwardly as I moaned in pain. The specters were gone from his mouth and arms as if they had never been there – I saw them missing in the corners of my eyes, but I would not wrench my gaze away from Bluebeard's steady regard. Not when this was my last look, my last chance to fill myself with all that steadfast sureness. "I do not misplace tools. You've been very useful, my little tool, and now I will put you back where you belong, a surety against the day when I have need of you again."

The water climbed now to my waist and Grosbeak's protests were lost in bubbles as he dipped beneath the water.

Bluebeard watched me steadily as Coppertomb moved, putting a hand on my shoulder and one on Svetgin's.

"My husband," I gasped, desperately, feeling panicked. My heart was beating so loud, my breath sawing in my lungs so strongly that I almost missed the echo of his voice in my mind.

"*My wife.*"

My last glimpse was of his cat's eye winking at me and then everything was gone.

I blinked my eyes and there was no Coppertomb, there was no Wittenhame. We were on a mortal beach somewhere – a place where the colors had leached out of the land and the sky was an indifferent blue. And in between waves of pain so thick now that I couldn't keep conscious, I heard my brother sobbing those deep sobs that men try to hide when they are overwhelmed by them, and he was murmuring between their tempests, "Hold on, sister, I will find help. I'm sorry. I'm so, so sorry."

And then that, too, was gone.

Read more of Izolda & Bluebeard's story in "**Give Your Heart to the Barrow**", Book Three of Four in the Bluebeard's Secret series.

BEHIND THE SCENES:

USA Today bestselling author, Sarah K. L. Wilson loves spinning a yarn and if it paints a magical new world, twists something old into something reborn, or makes your heart pound with excitement ... all the better. Sarah hails from the rocky Canadian Shield in Northern Ontario – learning patience and tenacity from the long months of icy cold – where she lives with her husband and two small boys. You might find her building fires in her woodstove and wishing she had a dragon handy to light them for her

Sarah would like to thank **Barbara, Melissa, and Eugenia** for their incredible work in beta reading and proofreading this book. Without their big hearts and passion for stories, this book would not be the same.

Sarah has the deepest regard for the talent of her phenomenal artist Luciano Fleitas who created the gorgeous cover art that accompanies this book. Without his work, it would be so much harder to show off this story the way it deserves. She also wants to thank her editor, Melissa, who tried her best to make this book better. Any errors remaining are all Sarah's.

Thanks also to my beloved husband, Cale and sons Neville and Leif who are endlessly patient as I talk to them about bookish passions.

Visit my website for more information:

www.sarahklwilson.com

Reviews are always welcome! If you liked this book, please tell someone!

www.ingramcontent.com/pod-product-compliance
Lightning Source LLC
Chambersburg PA
CBHW070536310726
48982CB00010B/1394/J

* 9 7 8 1 7 7 7 2 6 4 5 9 8 *